As they approached the "Want to skate?"

"I don't know how."

"I'll show you."

Skate with Ted? "Why?"

He rolled his eyes. "It's fun."

Fun. With Ted. Her internal dialogue sounded like a children's primary reader. "Okay."

Ted ushered her over to the skate rental and paid for them both. Finding an empty bench, he handed her the skates. "Don't lace them too tight, but don't let them gap, either."

She'd never be able to balance, much less skate on them. And skating with her boss was not going to lessen her attraction. Not sure why she agreed to this, she slipped her feet in the boots and laced them, covering the laces with the Velcro straps. Her leaden feet fell to the side when she stuck her legs out in front of her.

"Let's go." Ted stood.

Let's go? How the heck did you stand on these things? He held both hands out, lips only slightly quivering, and waited for her to place her hands in his. When she touched him, warmth spread through them, up her forearms. His grasp was firm, and he tugged her to her feet without incident. They walked to the ice.

Now what?

"Ready?"

His voice was low, his breath warm, and somehow intimate, though they were in such a public place. He took her hand and led her into the rink.

I'm gonna fall, I'm gonna fall, I'm gonna fall.

Unlock My Heart

by

Jennifer Wilck

Scarred Hearts, Book 2

This is a work of fiction. Names, characters, places, and incidents are either the product of the author's imagination or are used fictitiously, and any resemblance to actual persons living or dead, business establishments, events, or locales, is entirely coincidental.

Unlock My Heart

COPYRIGHT © 2022 by Jennifer Wilck

Cover Art by *Jennifer Greeff*

The Wild Rose Press, Inc.
PO Box 708
Adams Basin, NY 14410-0708
Visit us at www.thewildrosepress.com

Publishing History
First Edition, 2022
Trade Paperback ISBN 978-1-5092-3964-1
Digital ISBN 978-1-5092-3965-8

Scarred Hearts, Book 2
Published in the United States of America

Dedication

This one is for Jennifer Sellers Edmondson,
high school friend and techno geek extraordinaire.
I couldn't have done this without your help.
Anything I got right is thanks to you;
any mistakes are 100 percent my own.

Chapter One

Lip reading was exhausting.

Ted Endicott walked out of the staff meeting and rubbed his eyes for what seemed like the thousandth time today. More than anything, he wanted to go home to his quiet house outside San Francisco, relax in front of the fire with a glass of scotch, and unwind. His computer security firm wasn't large—two analysts and systems engineers, three new product and service developers, three sales reps, plus HR and admins—but with his laid-back style and office culture, there was significant background noise, despite the carpet and noise-absorbing ceiling tiles he'd insisted on. Even with hearing aids, it was difficult to understand what people said when there was background music, chatter, computer noises, or phones. Unlike corrective lenses, hearing aids amplified all sound, not just those he wanted—or needed—to hear. Unfortunately, it was only two in the afternoon. And CEO though he might be, he was always the last one out the door.

He shut his office door behind him and breathed a sigh of relief at the welcome quiet. His own office, designed with noise-dampening materials specifically for someone who was hard of hearing, was his sanctuary. He grabbed a laptop, sank onto his black leather couch, and proceeded to work as he slogged his way through emails. The lights flickered. He looked up and motioned his new assistant, Sherry, into his office. She waited for him to direct his full attention to her.

"Sorry to bother you, Ted, but the new programmer candidate, Abby Marlow, is here for her final interview. Do you want me to put her in the conference room?"

"No, have her come in here."

He rose and tried not to stare as Abby walked in, which was harder than one might think when you needed to focus on someone's lips to understand what they said. Granted, at six foot three, he was tall, but she was tiny. Maybe, if she stretched on tiptoe, she was five two? Straight ebony hair flowed past her shoulders, a black pantsuit accentuated a tiny waist, and gray eyes flicked from his face to his ears and back again. He rarely noticed people's eyes. Wonderful.

Shaken out of the fantasy intruding into his thoughts, he clenched his jaw, spitting out the words. "They're hearing aids. They won't go away no matter how long you stare at them."

Her flawless creamy skin turned a deep rose, and he stifled the strange urge to comfort her. He took a deep breath and smelled…strawberries.

"I'm sorry, that was rude of me," she said. "Probably a good thing they won't disappear, though, since you need them."

His gaze widened at her boldness, and he considered adjusting the volume on his aids on the off chance he'd misheard her. But her eyes sparkled with a silver fire, and he had to admit she'd handled the misstep with aplomb. He directed her to the chair in front of him, where he could watch her speak. Despite using hearing aids since he was a teenager, he still read people's lips as a backup. He sat behind his desk and leaned forward.

"You'd guess right. So you're here for the coding position? Why do you want to work at my firm?"

"Because your firm is the best."

Was she honest, or pandering to his ego? His gaze swept from her mouth to her eyes. He never noticed people's eyes—lip reading was too important. But hers? They were striking—thick lashes surrounded flinty gray and silver-toned irises. With a start, he returned his focus to her mouth and their conversation. "Why do you say that?"

"If you contact the top ten companies in any industry category and ask them who they'd look to for cybersecurity protection, they all answer Endicott Security."

"And you want to work for the best?"

"I want to learn from the best."

She was good. And she'd stopped staring at his ears. He looked at her résumé and cover letter. "Your skills are impressive. You have a lot of work experience in the field. You're reputed to be a hard worker." His secretary checked her references prior to her interview, and her former boss raved about her skill and dedication.

"Thank you. I worked my way through college, and I've been drawn to computers since, I don't know, I was a kid." She waved her arm in an off-hand manner, like a cross between a sexy woman and a mischievous child. He pulled up short. He couldn't think a potential employee was sexy.

He folded his arms across his chest. "You weren't into dolls or Lego or soccer?" Throughout his childhood, he had tinkered with things, taking them apart to see how they worked. His father never understood why and assumed he was too dumb to know what to do with them.

"Only if they had a computerized motor I could hack."

A kindred soul. He laughed in silence, and for the first time, Abby broke into a smile. This time, Ted couldn't breathe. He couldn't describe how beautiful she was when she smiled. Stunning. It was the best he could do. And it was a poor approximation.

It was also a terrible idea to think about her beauty.

Blinking, he realized he should respond. "Your parents must have been proud."

It was as if a mask dropped into place, and her features froze, reminding him of a blank canvas. She remained silent. Okay then.

Returning his focus to her résumé, he noted her high GPA, her tech industry awards, and her previous experience. His company was in desperate need of another coder, and she was the perfect candidate. He asked her about her recent experience, let her go on about her former employer's latest project, while he watched her lips move, and finally, he cleared his throat and asked, "Have you any questions for me?" It was what he was supposed to do, but he couldn't focus on the words. He was too busy drowning in her silvery-gray eyes, which changed with her every thought. He was a grown man. He should be more respectful of her and her talents.

"How does your office culture work?"

He frowned, and she repeated her question. Dammit. With a deep breath, he refocused on her lips. They were rosy and plump. Get a grip, Ted. He swallowed and looked past her left ear in order to concentrate. "It's my company, but I can't succeed without a great team. I guess you could call it a collegial atmosphere. Everyone is responsible for completing his or her work, but I'm laid back when it comes to how. Providing of course no one breaks any federal laws, stretches the moral code, or misses any deadlines." He smiled and hoped she'd return it.

She did.

God, she was gorgeous. *I am in deep trouble.*

"What kinds of projects would I be given?"

"To start, we'd want to see what you could do. You'll assist the team with their current projects. Overall, we're responsible for Black Box testing of our clients' full spectrum of applications. We use all methods necessary to investigate our clients' landscapes, find vulnerabilities in their networks and applications, and attempt to exploit them. Then we help them take steps to protect their own environment."

"How about presentations to clients?" She leaned forward and gripped the armrests.

"Maybe farther down the line, but it depends upon your performance and talents." He rose. He had a ton of work to accomplish and needed to continue with his day.

She followed him to the door. "Thank you so much for your time," she said.

"You're welcome." He accompanied her to Sherry's desk, returned to his office, and stared off into space. Abby was the most qualified candidate yet. She'd fit in well with his other employees. She was eager to learn. His company was desperate for another coder. If he were smart, he'd hire her before she got away. But he couldn't look at her without drooling, a fact which made him look like a chauvinistic ass, not to mention was probably in violation of her right to work in a safe environment. As a wealthy and powerful CEO, he'd been around beautiful women. Hiring Abby should be no big deal. But it was.

****

The following Monday, Abby arrived at her new job at Endicott Security Company, psyched to be at one of the world's premier cybersecurity companies. As long as she performed well and worked hard, she'd never end up like her mother. It took all her restraint not to bounce in the elevator. She spent her morning filling out paperwork, meeting her coworkers, and learning about the company benefits. Her pulse raced. Greg Stanton, the lead programmer, was her guide.

"One last thing," he said. "About Ted's hearing issues..."

The walls of her stomach tightened. Her screw up. She didn't mean to stare. It just...happened. First, his gorgeous looks stunned her. Blond hair, piercing blue eyes, maybe a foot taller than she was. She'd looked at him and seen the thin wires wrapped around his ears. Unfortunately, before she could recover, he'd caught her.

"If you're smart, you won't make a big deal about it. He's got all the tech he needs to accommodate him. People who pussyfoot around him or treat him differently don't last long here."

"Good to know. Thanks."

She was about to grab some lunch when Ted walked onto the main floor. The five programmers, well, six including her, were spread around the room.

Ted stopped to talk to each of them. When she caught his attention, he nodded and turned to Greg.

"Can I talk to you a minute?" He pulled Greg aside.

Abby swallowed the anxiety that slithered up her spine. Ted had stopped to talk to everyone but her. Was there a reason? She looked over at him as he talked to Greg. His back was to her, but his shoulders were bunched, and his hands were fisted at his sides. When they finished, he stilled, clenched his jaw, and left the room. Red-faced, Greg returned to his cubicle.

What kind of a company was this? And with a CEO as touchy as Ted Endicott, how long would she be able to keep her job?

****

How the hell will I manage this? Ted wondered and closed his office door. He wanted privacy. Even in his own office, his physical awareness of Abby was off the charts. What the hell was wrong with him, and how could he fix it? If he couldn't be on the same floor as her without noticing her beauty, how in the world was he supposed to work with her? This was his goddamned company. He was the flippin' CEO. He either needed to control his own reactions or figure out a way to get rid of her.

And that would be awful. Abby was fantastic. Supremely qualified and talented. He couldn't refuse to hire her because she was beautiful. That was his problem, not hers. Unfortunately, his hormones hadn't yet received the message, and Ted couldn't think straight when she was around. Even considering a personal relationship, supposing she'd want one, would violate his company policy—policy he'd created. He stormed to the computer, opened his texting app, and texted Human Resources. Five minutes later, the light over his door flashed, and he yelled, "Come in!"

James Ross, the head of HR, entered. "What's up, Ted?"

"How can we rescind our offer to Abby?"

"Abby Marlow? The new programmer? It's her first day. What happened?"

"Nothing."

James folded his body into the chair across from Ted's desk. "Uh, you can't fire someone without cause."

"I'm about to violate my own damn policy," Ted said. Maybe he could hide in his office for the next six months. That should be enough time to learn to behave like a normal human.

"Which one would that be?"

Ted clamped his mouth shut, and after a minute, James frowned. "She's gorgeous, isn't she?"

Ted glared, taking no comfort in the fact that James also noticed Abby.

"You can't fire her because she's beautiful."

Ted snorted. "Why the hell not?"

"She'll sue your ass, win, and own you and your company."

James was an idiot. "What the hell good are you?"

"You know I'm right." How James could sit there while Ted's emotions raged was the reason he'd hired him in the first place.

"It doesn't mean I have to like it." Even though James was right. Dammit.

"Nope, but it does mean you can't fire her. Not without cause, and you don't have any."

"Yet," Ted said.

"I'd advise you not to hint to me or anyone else you're out to get her, since it won't go well for you, either."

"Leave." Ted pointed to the door.

James smirked before he left the office.

What the hell was wrong with him, and how could he fix it? Ted ran his hand through his hair and groaned. He needed a haircut. And he needed to avoid his new programmer at all costs.

Chapter Two

Ted sat in the upholstered velvet chair, his gaze on the lips of the beautiful woman who sipped her Prosecco across the table from him in the most expensive restaurant in town. He tried to loosen his neck muscles. At least when Carol drank, she couldn't speak. Candlelight, though romantic, played havoc on his lip-reading abilities, and the background music added an extra layer of noise that his aids magnified. He stretched his mouth into what he hoped was a smile, although he knew full well it was fake.

Here they were in the most romantic—and expensive—restaurant in Silicon Valley. If anyone else were in this predicament, he'd laugh. His company had completed a major IT security project for Carol's firm, and at the celebratory party six weeks ago, she draped herself over him and had yet to show signs of straightening her spine and walking away. At first, his hearing aids intrigued her, but she grew tired of the need to repeat herself or to make sure to look at him when she spoke. She was clearly only interested in him for his money. And for sex.

The sex part suited him fine at first. Now, he wanted more out of a relationship, just not with her.

A movement out of the corner of his eye caught his attention, and Ted flagged the waiter.

"Can I get you anything else?" The waiter glanced

at Ted.

"Check, please?"

With a nod, the waiter walked away.

Carol licked her bright red lips and eyed him seductively. "Ready for a nightcap?"

For once, no part of him stirred. He'd be worried if he weren't so relieved. It was time for this relationship, such as it was, to end. He handed his Black Card to the waiter and turned to Carol. "Not tonight."

She frowned. "You know I meant sex, right?" She'd raised her voice, as if she thought volume would change his mind, and he wanted to laugh. Especially when others turned toward them.

He signed the bill, rose, and pulled out Carol's chair. She turned into his arms, and he stepped away.

"Yes, I know what you meant," he said in a low voice. He was pretty sure his voice was low at least, and he was positive he'd understood her. Although at this point, who cared? He ushered her out the door, gave the valet his ticket, and waited for his Porsche.

"What's wrong with you tonight? You barely said three words."

"Sorry." He climbed in, waited for her to fasten her seatbelt, and roared away. The silence of the car was heaven, and when she reached for the radio, he stifled a groan. He wanted nothing more than to remove his aids and bask in the fuzziness of muted sound. But he never took them out around the women he dated. He never cared about them enough to emphasize what he couldn't do. He nodded along to her conversation and replied in monosyllables when necessary.

When he turned into her apartment complex, she jerked. "I thought we were going to your place?"

He stopped in front of her building and turned. "I told you, Carol, not tonight. In fact, I think it might be time to let this relationship end. It was a lot of fun, but I don't think we're right for each other."

She wrinkled her nose, and he thought of a Shar-Pei. Despite the cost and exclusivity of the breed, she wouldn't be amused.

"We're right for each other, Ted. You just don't see it yet. In fact, I think maybe you need some sleep tonight—alone. You'll be in a much better mood after you get some rest." She patted his leg and left his car.

Sleeping alone was the best idea she'd suggested yet, and he sighed as he put his car into drive. Too many women who held little interest to him. He was tired of playing the field, of the meaningless sex, and the concern about money and power. He needed something more and wanted to settle down with someone. An image of Abby flashed in his mind, and he shook his head as his car hugged the curves in the road. She might be different from the typical wealthy socialites and high-powered executives he dated, but she wasn't for him. She couldn't be.

****

Abby couldn't sleep. After lying in bed for hours, she threw back the covers and glanced at the clock. The neon blue three on the clock's face mocked her and reminded her of how tired she would be later in the morning. Rubbing her face, she threw on a pair of black jeans and a sweater, slipped her feet into her favorite pink flats, and left her apartment, her brand-new keycard in her pocket. *Might as well be productive if I can't sleep.*

A half hour later, she strode into the office. As

expected, the bullpen was deserted. With a sigh, she sank into her ergonomic chair, fired up her computer, and wrote scripts for her team. After a little while, the silence stifled her. She turned on her MP3 player, plugged in her earbuds, and nodded in time to the rap music as her fingers flew across the keyboard.

By five o'clock, she'd made some progress and was ready for coffee, preferably the kind she could deliver through an intravenous drip. Not finding a caffeinated drip in the break room, she filled the pot with water and waited while the coffee brewed. She groaned with delight at the nutty aroma. As soon as it was ready, she poured a cup.

She exited the break room, turned the corner, and plowed into a large, hard body. She shrieked, as much from the shock of another person as from the pain of hot liquid on her hand. Ted loomed over her. She raced to the break room and ran cold water on her hand, as she struggled for breath from the sharp sting.

"Ow, ow, ow!" The water swirled in the stainless sink, and she focused on the pattern to try to forget about the agony.

"I'm sorry."

She jumped again at the sound of Ted's voice and this time, she glared. She wanted to scream at him for not looking where he went, but she was guilty of the same thing. Besides, he was her boss. Swallowing the epithets on the tip of her tongue, she turned away, her hand under water as she blinked away tears. It hurt like hell, but she couldn't curse in front of the man.

"Let me see your hand," he said.

"It's fine." She kept it under water. Her skin turned pink, but at least there were no blisters. Yet.

She flinched at the pressure on her shoulder.

"Let me see your hand, please."

"I said it's fine." Or it would be if he'd let her keep it under the water.

"I won't hurt you." His gravelly voice was low, as if he spoke to a skittish animal. She wasn't skittish, she was in pain.

Staring at her hand beneath the faucet, she sighed. "I know, but I don't want to take it out from the water yet."

He ignored her, turned off the water, and pulled her hand toward him. If he were anyone other than her boss, she would have admired the feel of his skin against hers, the gentle touch of his long fingers on her wrist, his spicy scent. But her hand hurt, and she objected to how he took charge of the situation without consulting her. She frowned at her reddening skin.

"It doesn't look too bad," he said.

"Easy for you to say. You're not the one in pain." She winced as he turned her hand over, as much from her rude words as from the pain. It appeared her tact wasn't awake yet. Or it ran for cover when she'd screamed.

He let go of her hand. "I'm sure it hurts worse than it looks." Reaching above her head, he pulled a First Aid kit from the cabinet and removed burn ointment.

"I'll handle it."

Once again, he ignored her and smoothed the ointment onto her hand. The gentle stroke of his fingers was hypnotic. "I didn't expect you to be in this early."

"You shouldn't be here this early," he said.

Did he blame her for the accident? Shouldn't he look where he went? No matter how alluring his touch, his bossiness was more than she could bear. She seethed as she pulled her hand away.

"Thank you for your help." Without waiting for a reply, she stalked out of the break room to her desk.

****

Not only did he allow his human resources department to hire a beautiful woman whose looks made his common sense disappear, but he also found an early bird. It wouldn't be a problem under normal circumstances, but today was not normal.

Unable to sleep after his date with Carol, he'd come into work, intending to get through a backlog of filing and emails. He was productive, until he smelled coffee. If his brain was firing correctly, he would have put in the hearing aids he removed in his office—the silence was a blessed relief after last night's noise, and he missed the light from her cubicle. He was confident no one else was around.

He was wrong.

He suspected in addition to burning Abby, he offended her as well. It was bound to happen when you couldn't hear everything the other person said. He heard noise—the water running and the timbre of her voice, but the actual words? One or two, here or there, since she wasn't facing him.

From the harsh set of her mouth and the pink splotches on her cheeks, he was pretty confident he owed her an apology for something more than banging into her.

After he cleaned the coffee she left on the floor, he retrieved his aids and walked to her desk in the bullpen, but it was empty. With a sigh, he returned to his office and, once again, almost plowed right into her. He gripped her upper arms to keep her upright and swore under his breath.

Her gray eyes flashed silver, like the mercury in a thermometer—shiny, alive, and fluid.

"...a habit with you," she said. "Are you like this with everyone or only short people?"

He flared his nostrils. "You seem to be the lucky one. I want to apologize. For before and for now."

Silver softened to rainy-day gray, and she tipped her head. Her hair fell forward and hid her face. "No, I'm...the...needs...apologize."

As loathe as he was to admit a problem, he needed to put a stop to this now. His chest tightened. "It's easier for me to understand you when you look at me."

She met his gaze, and her face reddened.

Why was she embarrassed? He was the one who'd admitted he'd been rude and careless, as well as confessed to his inability to hear her.

Meeting his gaze, she spoke. "I forgot. What I said was I'm the one who needs to apologize. I was rude to you, and it was unwarranted. You're my boss, but I was in pain and..."

His lips twitched. He couldn't help it. She was babbling and standing up to him and risking her job and was utterly adorable. He considered admitting he hadn't heard a word she'd said in the break room. She'd never once looked at him. But he couldn't admit it to her. While he'd accepted his hearing loss, it often left him at a disadvantage, and it wasn't something he talked about with others, especially employees. His father's reaction throughout his childhood ensured that.

"Relax. Consider it a free pass. I'm sure I more than deserved it. I made you spill coffee all over your hand."

The briefest of frowns creased her forehead. She examined her hand, turned toward him, and spoke. "I think it'll be okay. Thank you for understanding."

He nodded. "You're here early."

"I couldn't sleep."

"Well, if you need to go home and crash later, go ahead. In the future, if you're here at odd hours, make sure to leave the desk light on so people know you're here." He hid behind "people," but it was the best he could do. He often worked odd hours and took out his hearing aids, and if he couldn't hear her walk around, he needed a way to know she was here.

James told him he couldn't get rid of her. He had no clue, though, how he was supposed to get used to her.

Chapter Three

Three days later, Ted returned to San Francisco from Gull's Point, Maine, where he and the rest of his CAST associates helped Simon, a renowned landscape architect, protect open land from a developer who wanted it for commercial use. CAST, the partnership he and three college friends had formed to invest their money and use their wealth to help others, helped the town turn it into a therapy garden and public park. Ted and the rest of the partners had attended the town hall meeting to lend their support to the project.

Ted yawned as he unpacked his Coach leather bags and stretched out on his king-sized bed. Simon was one lucky bastard. His girlfriend, Meg, was everything Ted looked for in a woman. She'd fallen for Simon despite his facial scars and without any apparent interest in his money. The two of them together made his heart hurt, and when he'd talked to Meg, he enjoyed their conversation more than he had in a long time with any female. Meg was Simon's. It was as clear as if Simon spray-painted "Mine" across her forehead. She was a lovely woman and treated him well, as she treated Simon well. And all the while he spoke to her, he wondered if Abby would have behaved in a similar fashion, enjoyed everyone's company, wanted to check out the waves at the beach. With him.

He jumped. Where the hell did that thought come

from? His conversations with Abby weren't anything like those with Meg. He barely knew Abby. He misunderstood half of what she said. With a scowl, he put the rest of his clothes in the laundry for the housekeeper tomorrow. But he'd enjoyed the play of emotions across Abby's face. She'd been angry. He'd sympathized with her pain, but admired her grit. Abby wasn't interested in him, and he couldn't be interested in her.

The next day at work, he sifted through the three days' worth of mail organized into piles on his zebrawood desk. One envelope—he groaned. The formal schedule for next week's cybersecurity conference in New York—the biggest of the year.

Everyone who was anyone in the industry would be there. Not attending never crossed his mind. Besides, he was a keynote speaker, a panelist at three discussions, and the subject of multiple media interviews. That was in addition to his desire to walk the trade show floor. It was a professional wet dream. But his difficulty hearing would turn it into a nightmare—large crowds, poor lighting, background noise. For God's sake, he was an industry expert. Anything he missed, even the smallest detail, might cost him his reputation and his company millions of dollars in damage.

In previous years, he'd taken Marge, affectionately known as his bulldog. Anyone who wanted him went through her first. She used her position and knowledge to give him the help he needed—seamlessly and surreptitiously. But she'd retired two months ago, and Sherry, his current admin, wasn't available. Sweat popped on his brow. What the hell was he supposed to do? He hated pointing out how difficult these situations were for him to anyone else at the company. Even Greg, his friend since grad school and his first hire when he started this company. He managed in a controlled environment, such as the office, where he'd designed the space to accommodate his needs and used extra technological aids. At a trade show? A different beast altogether. He'd worked hard to overcome his father's assumptions of him, and he'd never again let anyone else think he was stupid. He'd have to arrange his own accommodations.

He sighed, grabbed his tablet, and walked into the conference room for the staff meeting. He swallowed as someone's too-strong aftershave smacked him in the face. Fluorescent bulbs lit the room. A large table sat in the center, its surface a smart board. Each person there was either an analyst, systems engineer, or sales rep, and there was a computer tablet in front of each chair, with the meeting's agenda, a list of the current clients, and what each client needed from whom. One by one, each person updated the team about their progress on their individual projects, what problems they faced, and what they needed from the group. Afterward, they looked at Ted, who provided additional direction. Finally, it was his turn.

"The cybersecurity conference is next week." He ran through his schedule and previewed what he'd present. As he spoke, he took notes—client meetings in quiet conference rooms instead of on the trade show floor when possible, no Q & As with audience members since they'd be too far away for him to read lips; one-on-one meetings instead of large groups; transcripts for all workshops. He let everyone around the table discuss the conference for a few moments, but his gaze was drawn to Abby. He focused on her lips and read her, saying how much she'd always wanted to go to this conference.

Greg raised his hand, catching Ted's eye, and Ted nodded. "Who's going with you?"

Ted rubbed the nape of his neck. "You, Cory, and Tom."

Greg raised an eyebrow. "What about an assistant?"

His colleagues turned toward him. Ted gripped the edge of the table. Greg was an amazing programmer, but he wasn't discreet. His stomach sank, even as he glared at his friend.

"I'll make do. Thanks."

Across the table, Abby stared. He swore to God, if she continued to stare at his ears and his hearing aids, he would fire her. He scowled at her, and she spoke. "If you need an assistant, I'm happy to go. I've always wanted to check out the conference."

Right. "No thanks, I'm good. We need you, along with Paul and Bill and Angie, to assist our clients here."

She bit her lip and remained silent. At least she knew when to stop.

Unlike Greg.

"I'll look into speech transcripts," Greg said.

"Greg." If the meeting weren't paperless, Ted would wad some up and throw it. An entire ream of it. He ran his hands around the edge of his tablet and, for a brief moment, considered it. But it was expensive. Besides, that kind of behavior was childish, and he wasn't a bully.

"And Cory can check out available assistive

technology at the conference," Greg said.

"Greg."

Ted reconsidered his desire not to destroy the tablet as the room around him went silent. He noticed two things. First, it was easy to tell when a room full of people went silent. The air around him thickened, like when he removed his aids. Second, for someone who should have known not to push him about his hearing, Greg missed all the clues, which was unlike him, and resulted in everyone else's silence and discomfort.

"Maybe Abby…"

"Greg!"

Everyone around the table jumped, and Ted couldn't deny the small sense of satisfaction in knowing he'd raised his voice loud enough to make the others react. What the hell? Why single out Abby when he'd already said no?

Abby turned red, and for a moment, Ted admired the flush as it swept across her face and neck. He refocused and sympathized with her embarrassment. He looked at her and nodded once.

"Give Greg and me the room, please," he said. Everyone left. When the door closed behind the last person, he turned to Greg. "What the hell is going on with you? Why did you discuss my need to have an assistant at the conference in front of everyone?"

"It isn't a secret. I mentioned the typical arrangements we make any time we go to conferences. In the past, Marge handled everything. Since she's gone, why not Abby?"

Ted raised an eyebrow.

"Abby is the only one who is free to go."

"I don't need a babysitter."

"Of course not. You need an assistant. She's perfect, and I suggest you take advantage of her desire to come."

Ted swallowed as images entered his mind, images Greg suggested.

"Please tell me you didn't mean what it sounded like you mean," he said.

"What? No." Now it was Greg's turn to flush. "Although, she's hot, single, and brilliant. But you don't need the HR nightmare."

Movement outside the conference room caught Ted's eye. Abby passed. Ted frowned. There was no way she could have heard them, could she?

****

Oh my God, it was too embarrassing for words. Abby tapped her foot as she waited for the elevator to arrive.

She never intended to eavesdrop. But she'd turned in her seat and seen Greg and Ted's discussion in the conference room. They were discussing her. She'd seen Greg say Abby, and she'd seen Ted shake his head. He wanted her gone. She'd spoken when she should have remained silent and offered to be his assistant when she was a brand-new programmer. What business was it of hers? Between her rudeness last week and Ted's apparent dislike of her, she was about to be fired.

Maybe Ted would change his mind. She needed to get away. If only this elevator wasn't the slowest on the planet. She was about to take the stairs when Ted reached her. He'd yell at her, like he'd yelled at Greg in the meeting. Public humiliation and termination. Her stomach sank.

Except he stood next to her, said nothing, and

stuffed his hands in his pockets. His breath was quiet, not like someone who tried to restrain his anger. He was still and composed—no tapping foot, no angry glare. Maybe he planned to watch her leave. Finally, the elevator doors opened, and she stepped inside, only to have him follow her. But still he remained aloof. She pressed the button for the lobby. She needed to get away from Ted as fast as possible.

As the elevator descended, Ted leaned over and pressed a button. The elevator lurched to a stop. She grabbed the bar on the wall and squeaked.

"We need to talk," he said.

It wasn't like she had much of a choice. CEOs didn't fire employees in elevators, right? Remembering to look directly at him, she raised her head. "Sure."

"Did something happen out there to upset you, or did you happen to hear what Greg and I discussed?"

Lie, lie, lie. "I didn't hear it per se..." Her stomach tightened.

He frowned and folded his arms across his chest. Did he have any idea how attractive his chest and arm muscles were when he flexed?

"What do you mean, 'per se?' "

"Well, even a hearing person recognizes their name on someone's lips."

His mouth tightened.

"I saw Greg say my name, and you shook your head no, and I figured you discussed me. After how rude I was to you last week, and how you made it obvious I wasn't your ideal choice for the conference, I assumed..." She squeezed her hands together and inhaled.

He held up a hand, and she stopped midsentence.

"Don't assume. And don't give up this programming job. You're a terrible lip reader." His nostrils flared. "I was angry at Greg, not you," he said. "Greg told me how brilliant you are, which is true. You're right, though. I don't want you with me at the conference."

He'd paid her a backhanded compliment, at least, she thought so. "So you're not firing me?"

"Firing you? You're too talented for me to fire. No. I need you to work on your assignment here, which is why I don't want you at the conference."

She nodded, not sure what to say. Her mouth dried, and her legs weakened. Thank God she still held onto the bar in the elevator.

"And stop jumping to conclusions, as they relate to me or to my opinions of you."

She nodded again.

He pressed another button, and the elevator jerked and resumed its descent. "Were you going somewhere in particular or fleeing?"

This time, it was she who smiled. "I'll go upstairs as soon as we reach the lobby."

"Good."

He wasn't firing her. He didn't want her at the conference, but he wanted her to work for him. And her handsome boss had smiled at her.

Chapter Four

Abby propped one foot on the park bench and lunged, stretching her glutes, and caught her breath. Sweat trickled down the nape of her neck. Birds chirped in the brush, and the clove-scented stock bloomed along the edge of the trail as she waited for her pulse to return to normal. She switched legs, stretched again, and began to walk. Following the trail in the park, with the Golden Gate Bridge in the distance, she exited onto the street. With a quick glance at her watch, she walked to the sporting goods store a few blocks away. She needed more running clothes, and the store had a sale.

Pulling her hair tie out and shaking her hair loose, she entered the store and walked to the runner's section in the rear. The indoor temperature was perfect, and she'd cooled off enough to flip through the merchandise without fear of sweating all over everything. However, when she turned around after grabbing a pair of running shorts and a matching tank top in pink, she gulped.

Her boss strode toward her, his blond hair gleaming beneath the overhead fluorescent lights. She thought of hiding—she was sweaty, her hair was a mess, and she bet she smelled. But he made eye contact with her, his face brightened as he got closer, and she was stuck. She sucked in her stomach as she realized what she wore—knee-length leggings and a sports bra. She thrust back her shoulders, despite her discomfort at revealing her body. It was Saturday. She was off the clock. This was a sports store. He'd have to deal.

"Funny seeing you here." He stopped in front of her.

Her face heated, but she made sure to look at him. "I literally ran past this place. Are you a runner?" Her gaze lowered to his clothes—jeans and a T-shirt. Stupid question.

"No, but I cycle." He pointed toward the adjoining section. "I need another bike repair kit, and I read they had a sale today. I've waited all week to check out their racing bikes."

She raised an eyebrow.

"What? I can't like a bargain?" he asked.

"I assumed a powerful CEO…" She swallowed.

"You seem to assume a lot."

Her face heated more than it already was, but his eyes twinkled, and other parts of her body heated as well. Flustered, she looked away. He chuckled under his breath. The deep thrum made her stomach quiver. She looked at him again.

"Do you live nearby?" he asked.

Her breath hitched. "About two miles away." Why did he care where she lived?

"How far do you run?" He folded his arms across his chest.

Once again, she admired his muscles, emphasized in short sleeves. "Daily? About five to ten miles. It depends on my stress levels."

He paused. "And today?"

An additional ten if you don't stop flexing your biceps. "It'll be five by the time I get home."

"I'm going to look at the bikes. Join me?" He

walked toward the cycling section, and she followed. Ted strode toward one of the bikes. Abby knew nothing about bikes, except they had two wheels. And cyclists wore outfits that showed off…everything. Did Ted wear them? Well, now her thoughts were off in unnecessary directions. She shook her head to clear it as a saleswoman approached. Ted knelt next to the bike he was interested in, and the saleswoman spoke.

"Hello, may I help…" She paused, staring at the back of him. Abby followed her gaze. His hearing aids were obvious from this angle. The woman turned toward Abby.

"Would he like some help?"

Abby's mouth fell open. Ted rose, drawing her attention away from the salesperson.

"Um, I don't know."

Ted said, "Can you tell me—"

The saleswoman ignored Ted, turning away from him midsentence. "You know, someone who's deaf might want to reconsider riding these," the saleswoman said. "It could be dangerous."

Abby laughed before she caught herself at the unexpected comment. *Why can't someone with hearing issues ride a bike?* The saleswoman misinterpreted Abby's laugh and joined her. But Abby wasn't amused. In a flurry of movement, Ted spun around and left the cycling department.

"You know nothing about him," Abby said, "or you'd never suggest something so stupid. Guess you lost a sale. Or two." She dropped the clothes at the woman's feet and followed him out of the store.

On the sidewalk, she scanned the area. Ted's broad back retreated from her, and she jogged to catch up.

"Ted!"

He didn't respond, and she assumed he couldn't hear her. When she reached him, she pulled on his arm. "Ted, wait."

The old "scary boss" Ted made his appearance—hard, cold, distant. "What?"

****

She pulled back, eyes wide with alarm. He waited for a slice of satisfaction to run through him, before he paused. Why did he care what she thought? She'd laughed. Big deal. It shouldn't bother him.

His ears might not work, but his brain was perfectly functional. As were his legs. And right now, he would use them to get as far away from Abby as possible.

But she grabbed his arm and wouldn't let go. He glanced at her hand, which dug into his bicep. Her bubblegum-pink nails held his attention longer than he meant for them to, and he hurried to focus again on her mouth.

"Ted, wait."

His chest constricted like he'd run a marathon. This…woman who worked for him was rude and obnoxious. And sexy.

"I have things to do." He curled his hands into fists.

Her expression was filled with concern, something he neither wanted nor needed.

"Why are you running away from me?"

Was she serious? "You're joking, right?" Since he couldn't always hear the tone, he sometimes missed sarcasm. This must be one of those times.

"No, I'm not. I get why you left the idiot

saleswoman, but why are you running away from me?"

She'd called the saleswoman an idiot. His harsh breaths eased. He swallowed. Not him, the saleswoman. Squinting, he tried to figure out what happened.

"I don't understand." His neck heated in shame.

Abby looked around and pointed. "Let's go to the park and talk. Please?"

Something about the way she said "please" made him relent. Without another word, they crossed the street and entered the park. The street was a decent size and filled with background noise, loud enough he could hear it, but here in the park, sounds were muffled, and he stretched his neck to relieve the tension. They walked toward a bench, and he sat at one end, as far from her as possible. She faced him. She'd gotten the hang of that necessity right away; therefore, her response in the store confused him. It shouldn't hurt, but he couldn't deny the tightness in his chest.

He hated when people thought he was stupid.

"Tell me why you ran from me," she said.

"Why did you laugh?"

Her mouth opened, her eyebrows arched, and she rubbed her hands on her thighs.

"Oh my gosh, you thought…I meant…" She took a deep breath and enunciated each word. "I was not laughing at you." She waited a moment, as if she waited for him to process what she'd said. "I couldn't believe she said those things, and I reacted out of shock. But it was directed at her stupidity, not yours. You're brilliant."

His chest expanded, and relief swept over him, which was odd. He wasn't sure why he cared. The scent of strawberries—her scent—wafted toward him.

"You left, and I told her off," she added. "And dumped the clothing I planned to buy at her feet."

This tiny thing came to his defense? "Thank you," he said.

She nodded. "The bike sale wasn't worth it."

"No, it wasn't." His cheeks burned at the thought of it.

"Are people rude to you often?"

He shrugged. "People often confuse difficulty hearing with stupidity. I used to keep my hair long enough to cover my ears. But I decided 'F' them." He couldn't believe he confessed that to her, his employee.

"Good for you."

Greg's suggestion—to take Abby to the conference as his assistant—and her volunteering—popped into his mind and, all of a sudden, it wasn't as bad as he thought. Sure, there was work here, but the thought of spending more time with her, this woman who was full of surprises, appealed. Warmth coursed through his body. He leaned against the bench and stretched his legs in front of him. "So do you want to go to the tech conference next week?"

"Why the sudden about-face?"

"I might have been wrong—not about your talent." He held up a hand. "I could…" He paused. Was he ready to show her how much he needed her help? Crap, he hated this part. "…use an assistant. I'll give you time to explore on your own and work too. I don't need a babysitter." He swallowed the bitter bile in his throat.

"Good. I'm not a fan of screaming children."

Her teasing tone surprised him. Her way with words never failed to put him at ease. "You never babysat as a child?"

Her smile dimmed, and she seemed to force it into place. He'd have to remember she was touchy about her childhood. Not waiting for an answer, he continued. "So you'll come to the conference?"

She nodded. "I'd love to."

"Excellent. Sherry will make the arrangements."

He waved goodbye and watched her jog away. He wasn't sure how she'd compare performance-wise with Marge, but watching Abby's ass as she ran, she sure was prettier. He'd have to be careful.

****

The next morning, Abby put the final touches on the platter of muffins and carried them into the living room where her best friend, Eden, sat with their coffees.

"Gosh, I've missed this." Abby sank onto the overstuffed green sofa.

"Your new job and my travel keep us busy," Eden said.

"Speaking of traveling, guess where I'm going?"

Abby told her about the tech conference in New York, and her friend beamed.

"Awesome. You've wanted to go to that conference for years."

"I know. I could never afford the trip on my own." Her stomach ached with the phantom hunger pains from her childhood and, like a reflex, she grabbed a muffin. Years of hunger, used clothes, and uncertainty over how long she and her mom would be able to stay in their latest hovel took their toll, even now. She'd never risk her savings, even for something she coveted. Now it wasn't necessary. Ted had taken care of it.

"How long will you be there?"

Abby folded her legs beneath her. "Well, the

conference is four days, and I'm going as my boss's assistant. I'd assume the entire time. His secretary made the travel arrangements. I'll know more later."

"What's he like, the new boss?"

Her insides warmed as she thought about him. She'd already told Eden the basics, but she'd left out he was hard of hearing. For some reason she couldn't pinpoint, it felt like an invasion of his privacy.

"He's brilliant and proud, but kind."

"It's an odd way to describe a guy you work for. Is he single? Are you interested in him?"

Abby pulled up short. She hadn't considered whether or not he was single. She'd assumed he was, but he could have a girlfriend. Or several.

"I can't be interested in my boss, Ede. It's the surest way to get fired, and I won't lose my job over a man." Although she pictured the intensity in his blue eyes when he stared.

"I love your focus." Eden stuffed a piece of blueberry muffin smothered in butter into her mouth. "Want to go out Friday? There's karaoke at the bar down the street."

The sound of her buzzer prevented further conversation. With a frown, Abby answered.

"Delivery for you, Miss. May I bring it up?"

"Sure, Fred, thanks."

She opened the door and took the package from Fred. The Fed Ex box indicated it was from her office. "Weird. I wasn't expecting anything, certainly not on a Sunday."

Eden came over as she pulled open the box. Inside was a wrapped package and a card. Eden read it aloud. "Thanks again for your help. Since it's my fault you couldn't purchase what you went in for, I've taken care of it. Plus, a little something extra I thought you'd like.

—Ted."

Abby slipped her finger beneath the folds of the paper and ripped it away. Inside was a gift card to a different sports store for two hundred dollars.

"Um, you might want to rethink your whole 'I don't get involved with guys I work with' plan, Abs." Eden's lips twitched.

Abby snorted. "Oh, please. It's a gift card." An expensive one, though.

Something dropped, and Eden picked it up. "Not just a gift card."

Abby reached for the item and almost dropped it once again.

He'd bought her a fitness tracker, an expensive one. It wasn't on her purchase list yesterday—it was on her wish list, but he couldn't know.

"Still think it's not a big deal?"

Chapter Five

Abby strode into Ted's office first thing the next morning. He jumped, and a flush crossed his face. A sliver of guilt snuck in, but she squashed it. She'd spent all day and all night yesterday thinking about his gift, and she was ticked.

Dropping the package onto the credenza, she gripped her hands in front of her and faced him. "Thank you for the gifts, but I can't accept them."

He rose and folded his arms across his chest. She hated when he stood like a gym coach. The position emphasized his muscular chest and arms—today displayed in a blue Henley that also emphasized his piercing blue eyes—and she forced her gaze away. Based on the flash of parentheses bracketing his mouth, he noticed her distraction.

She didn't care.

"Is it not enough?"

"What? No."

"You dislike that store? I won't go back to the one we were at"—he shuddered—"but if there's somewhere else you'd prefer to shop, I'll take care of it." He raked his gaze over her body, and heat followed his gaze, like a flame burning along the wick of a stick of dynamite. It was only a matter of time before she exploded from desire, and that would be too embarrassing and too dangerous to allow. She frowned.

"The store is irrelevant. I can't accept the money or the fitness tracker you included."

He strolled around to the front of his desk and leaned against it. Although only shortening the distance between them by four feet, her breath caught in her throat. Was this a panic attack? She couldn't breathe. This is ridiculous. She'd been closer to him yesterday at the store and afterward in the park. Why does it feel like there's a tether between us, and he cinches it tighter with each second that goes by?

"Why not? I thought since you're a runner, you'd like it, and I haven't seen you wear one. You don't have one, right?"

"No, I've wanted one for a long time."

"I don't see a problem."

He'd crossed his office until he stood near the credenza, a few feet between them. His large hand rested on the package she'd put there, and he fiddled with the paper wrapping.

He was as dense as early morning fog over the bay.

"You're my boss, and I can't accept such an expensive gift from you."

"You defended me yesterday, which prevented you from buying what you'd been intending to purchase. I made up for it. It's not like I bought you lingerie."

She closed her eyes, hoping for—something— anything to explain her position. Lingerie might have been better. It would have crossed a line she could point to.

"You're my boss. Bosses don't buy gifts for employees."

"I do. All the time. Ask any of them. I bought Greg baseball tickets when he couldn't get them. I bought someone else opera tickets." He raised his hand and pointed in the general direction of the bullpen, where the other programmers tapped away at their computers.

She was still annoyed. Most of those employees were male. And the female ones? They expressed no interest in Ted. Not like the interest Abby tried to bury. There was no way to explain it to him. Her earlier irritation disappeared, replaced with a weariness that seeped through her.

"Abby? What's wrong?"

She covered her face until he touched her wrist. There was so little space between them, Abby noticed a small patch of whiskers Ted missed during his morning shave. The desire to touch it, to feel it beneath the pad of her fingertip, overwhelmed her, and she clenched her fist at her side.

"I can't read your lips behind your hands," he said.

"You mean you don't have X-ray vision?"

He dropped her wrist. The imprint of his fingers remained, and goose bumps pebbled her arm, long after he'd let go.

"Still working on it." Ted ran a hand through his hair and scratched his head.

She wondered if it felt as silky as it looked.

"I'm sorry I made you uncomfortable. If you don't want to accept the gifts, I won't insist."

She wanted to. More than anything. She'd spent hours last night drooling over the website for the fitness tracker he'd purchased. It was top-of-the-line, better than anything she'd ever be able to afford, with more features than she'd be able to use. And the gift card would enable her to buy more than one pair of running shorts and a top, as she'd planned.

Her mother always said to take what you could get from guys. But she wasn't her mother, and she knew better. Mixing work with pleasure was the surest way for her to lose her job. He was the CEO of his own company. It wasn't as if he could dismiss himself. No, he'd dismiss her, or make her life uncomfortable. She'd have to leave. Word would get out she'd slept with the boss. It would destroy her reputation. Finding a new job would be impossible. She needed the money and the job security. Never again would she live like she did as a child. No matter how attractive Ted might be, no matter how thoughtful the gift was, no matter how much she might want to accept it, she wouldn't.

"I'm sorry," she said. "It was a nice gesture."

She left his office without allowing him to respond. But his stare burned a hole in her back as she retreated to the safety of her desk. And somehow, doing the smart thing was cold comfort.

****

Ted's hands hovered above the iPad in his meeting with Greg. Abby reminded him of a cactus, an orchid cactus, to be specific. He read about them in a book once and admired their beauty. Vibrant red and fuchsia petals and leaf-like fronds, they stuck you if you were careless enough to touch them. With her gray eyes and long, straight black hair, she lulled you into thinking she was like every other beautiful woman. She wasn't.

She possessed morals she stuck to, something he admired. Although if he were honest, he wouldn't mind a little mixing.

A movement out of the corner of his eye caught his attention, and he turned.

"Earth to Ted," Greg said.

Dammit, he'd drifted away and missed everything Greg said. "Sorry, I was daydreaming. Can you repeat that?"

An unreadable look passed across Greg's face. "Sure. We're almost ready to perform a Black Box test of Sentec. Should be finished by next week. Then we can have them take a look." He pulled up files on his tablet and shared them.

He focused all his effort on Greg's project, and after several minutes, Ted tapped the screen and nodded. "Looks good. Let me know when we're ready to present."

Greg rose and paused at the door. "It's got to be something important to distract you this way. I hope she's worth it." He winked and left.

Dammit, he'd lost his edge. He had too much to accomplish before the tech conference. Not to mention how much focus he'd need when she was with him. She'd be an asset, but with his attraction to her, leaving things as is wouldn't work. He was her boss. He needed to be extra careful not to act in a way that could be considered inappropriate. She intrigued him. Unfortunately, the type of relationship he hoped to find wasn't possible with an employee.

He stared out the window to the street below. Ever since he'd gone to Gull's Point and seen Simon's and Meg's relationship, he knew something was missing in his own life. Maybe it was time to act.

But Abby? She'd made it clear she wasn't interested in a relationship with her boss. He couldn't ask her out. However...Friday night was a business dinner with Sentec. John Allan, the company's CEO, wanted to discuss other business opportunities, and Ted had no doubt Carol, in her capacity as VP of technology, would be there as well. Abby would provide a buffer against Carol's advances, would show John their commitment to hiring women programmers, and would give him a chance to see how much help Abby could be in social situations. The additional time with her would be a welcome bonus.

All that remained was to convince Abby. How difficult could it be?

****

Abby sat in front of her computer working on a new security protocol when her message dinged.

—Are you available Friday for dinner with a client?—

Abby squinted at Ted's text and glanced toward his office. From his position at his desk, he gave no indication he was aware of her.

"Hey, Greg." He sat in the cubicle behind her. "Have you heard anything about a client dinner on Friday?"

"Yeah, It's with Sentec. Why?"

"He asked me if I was available."

Greg swung around in his chair. "He asked you?"

"Yes. Should I say no?"

Greg gripped the table in front of him. "No. You should go. It'll be good experience for you. The tech VP is a woman."

She frowned. "So?"

Greg's face was a blank. "So I thought you'd want to make contacts with other women in the business."

Swallowing her automatic retort, she looked at things from Greg's perspective. He didn't know she hated her gender discussed in business conversations. In fact, he might have a point.

"Okay, thanks."

Pulling open her calendar, she double-checked her availability.

—Yes, I'm free. Where and what time?—

He responded right away.

—Cioffi's. 7:15.—

She'd walked past the place. It was dim and expensive and…romantic. She reread his original text. "Client dinner." Greg confirmed it.

This was a client dinner. Nothing to worry about.

—Also, wear something nice.—

She looked at her black skinny jeans and purple bejeweled T-shirt.

—Nice? You mean I can't show up Goth?—

A part of her wished she could retract her snarky response. Another part objected to his assumption she needed guidance with her clothing.

—Funny.—

—It's a business dinner. I've got it. It IS a business dinner, right?—

—Why wouldn't it be?—

—Cioffi's is kind of…unbusinesslike.—

Crap. She shouldn't have said anything.

—The client, Carol Timmons, picked it.—

There was nothing left for her to say. She closed out of the message program and refocused once again on work. Except her gaze strayed toward Ted's office. Her message program dinged again.

—Come into my office please.—

Her heart thundered in her chest. She always overstepped when it came to him.

She peeked around his door. "You wanted to see

me?"

Ted pointed to a chair on the other side of his desk. "Is there a problem with dinner?"

She fiddled with the jewels on the hem of her T-shirt. How much should she tell him? "No. Greg acted like he thought it was odd, though."

"Don't worry about Greg. Think of this dinner as practice before the conference." She rose, but he raised an eyebrow and pointed to the chair.

She sat again.

"I may be hard of hearing, but I'm excellent at body language. You are the poster child for discomfort. Spill."

She bit her lip.

"Please." He pinned her with his probing stare.

When she could no longer remain silent, she sighed. "I don't know why I'm uncomfortable, but the restaurant…"

He leaned back and rubbed the nape of his neck. "Would you feel better if I told you I'm uncomfortable too?"

"Why?"

"Dim lighting makes it hard to lip read."

"Why are we going?"

"Carol is…well, you'll see when you meet her. She's difficult to say no to, and sometimes it's easier to go along with what she wants. I pick my battles, and frankly, dinner location isn't on the battle map. Not right now, anyway."

Somehow, his confession made her feel better.

"Are you sure you wouldn't prefer to have Greg go with you? I wouldn't want him to think I took his place or anything…"

"No, I want you. I'll pick you up at six forty-five."

"I can meet you there."

"I'll pick you up so we're sure to arrive at the same time."

"Like good soldiers?"

His face split into a grin. "Exactly."

She looked at her watch. "I've got to finish my work."

He nodded, and she left his office. An hour later, she met Eden at the bar for their weekly girls' night out. Music from the sound system offered a heavy bass thump in the background.

"I was beginning to think you weren't coming," Eden said, her voice raised.

"And miss this? Of course not. I ran late at work." Around them, twenty- and thirty-somethings raised their voices to be heard, and the bartenders clinked glasses as they prepared beverages.

The bartender slid her mojito toward her.

"Did you order this for me?" she asked Eden.

The bartender pointed to the other end of the bar. Abby craned her neck. Two guys in their late twenties, if she had to guess, stood together, watching her. They raised their glasses, and a frisson of excitement shot up her spine. Here we go. She raised hers and took a long sip, licking the moisture off her lips.

"This will be fun," Eden said.

The guys shouldered their way through the crowd and approached them. "Hey, ladies, enjoy the drinks?"

Abby nodded along with Eden. She sipped her mojito and enjoyed the tart, minty taste. The lime flavor and sweet aftertaste of rum made it her favorite drink.

The ginger approached her, and her heart

quickened—she'd always had a thing for gingers.

"I'm Taye." He held out a freckled hand with a light dusting of pale red hair.

"Abby." She tried not to wince at his extra-firm grasp.

"Do you come here often?"

Good Lord, she hoped he was a better conversationalist than this. "My friends and I come here most weekends. I've never seen you around, though."

"I'm from out of town. Visiting Paul." He pointed to his friend who chatted with Eden. She looked like she was having a good time. Abby refocused on Taye.

"How long are you here?"

"Leaving Sunday." Her pulse increased. This was the kind of guy she liked—no strings, no possibility of commitment, nothing messy.

"So what do you do?" he asked.

"I'm a computer programmer." Out of habit, she left out the "security" part around strangers. People reacted in weird ways when they found out she prevented hackers, and the last thing she needed was some guy she'd met once in a bar contacting her to break into some company's computer system.

He raised his eyebrows and looked her up and down, and her earlier excitement ebbed. "Really? Cool."

Points to him for not voicing his disbelief someone who looked like her could perform her job. "What about you?"

"I own a small contracting company upstate."

Well, that could mean anything, but since she refused to pursue him beyond this evening, it was irrelevant.

"Want to get out of here?" He pointed to the door.

She knew him all of ten minutes. She wasn't stupid. "I just got here." She smiled to take the edge off her words. "It's noisy up here, though. Maybe we can move toward the back?"

With a nod, he grabbed his drink, nudged his friend, and pointed to a corner table. Eden and Abby followed. She sat next to Taye and listened as he described his job.

"So basically, you contract out small construction jobs?" It explained his hands. They were nicked and calloused, as one would expect from a guy who used them to build things, but they were smaller and more square than Ted's. Ted's? Why was she comparing this guy to Ted?

"Exactly. Basement remodels, bathroom renovations, things like that."

Well, at least he was easy to talk to—and cute. "You enjoy it?"

"Yeah. What about you? Do you like programming?"

"I love it." Putting in her earbuds, drowning out the world, and creating or solving a puzzle was heaven. Her biggest puzzle, though, wasn't some company's firewall. It was Ted—what made him tick, and why the heck she reacted to him. She squeezed her hands into fists. This was not what she planned. She needed to focus on Tray…Taye! Her face heated in embarrassment, and she hoped he wouldn't notice. "I love the challenge each opportunity presents and the satisfaction when I figure out a tricky line of code. From your glazed expression, I think I've lost you."

He chuckled, a huskier sound than Ted. She didn't

want to think about him any longer. Taye's arm snaked around her shoulders, and she stiffened. This is what she'd always liked, the brief connection between strangers. But now? For some reason, his embrace trapped her.

"Hey, easy," Taye said.

She took a deep breath as he withdrew his arm. "Sorry, I don't know what came over me. It's okay."

But when he put his arm back, it wasn't. She couldn't protest again without sounding crazy. Her heart sped up, and she looked across the table at Eden and swallowed hard. Eden was occupied with Paul, fingers entwined, gazes locked.

She leaned against Taye and sipped her drink, trying to eradicate whatever funk she'd gotten into and return to her normal, fun-loving self.

"Want to dance?" If the music was going to pound, she might as well make use of it. When Taye nodded, she led him onto the small dance floor.

They gyrated to the beat of the dance tunes, his body kept time to the music, and it was only a matter of time before he pulled her toward him, and they danced closer, their bodies undulating together. His pupils dilated as her body rubbed against his, and sweat popped on the nape of her neck. The music was loud, the aroma of alcohol strong.

She couldn't do this.

This wasn't her. Well, it was usually, but tonight, it couldn't be.

"I'm sorry." She pulled away with a gasp and rushed to their table. Grabbing her purse, she told Eden she needed to leave.

"Wait," Taye said, "I'll walk you home."

Outside, she gulped air in the relative silence. Taye was a nice guy. She should have been interested. "I'll be fine on my own."

And she rushed away.

Chapter Six

Once again, Abby found refuge in front of her computer screen. This time she holed up in her bedroom to forget the disaster at the bar. She buried her thoughts in lines of code, but the glow from the computer screen in her dark room reminded her of the dance floor. She turned on the bedroom light, but its glow illuminated her bed, where, if she'd acted differently tonight, she and Taye might be. If not at this moment, sometime in the future.

Sinking onto the bed, she sighed. She liked to have a good time, and she wasn't interested in commitment. Why did she run away?

Ted's face intruded, and she groaned. The man was her boss. She couldn't afford him in her personal life, more so because he was sexy as sin.

Ted sexy?

Oh holy hell.

She grabbed her laptop and frowned at the screen as she attempted to type code. She had a job to do. The money from this job would ensure she'd never have a life like her mother's.

Ever.

An hour later, she'd written half as much code as she should have, but at least she focused. Sort of.

Her phone rang, and Eden's number flashed across the screen. Jabbing at the answer button, she hit speaker, and continued to type.

"Hey, Ede."

"What happened to you?"

No clue. "Bad timing." Liar.

"Really? Taye was hot."

"Yeah." Talk about an understatement.

"That's it? 'Yeah?' "

Abby closed her eyes. But instead of Taye's open and freckled features, Ted's chiseled ones appeared. She sighed. "I'm tired, I guess."

"You, tired? Since when?" Her tone indicated her disbelief.

"Since I started this new job." She bit her lip. It made sense she'd be tired from a new job, right?

"Oh, so that's the way it is," Eden said.

"What do you mean?" She scratched her neck, not liking Eden's tone.

"You're entranced by someone at work."

Entranced. Entranced? "Oh please. I'm not entranced. I'm busy." Yup, busy, busy, busy.

"Not busy enough to skip our weekly bar night."

She made it sound so…cheap. "I like hanging with you, Ede."

"Aw, and here I thought you liked playing wingman. Or having me be yours."

Abby laughed. "Next time, I promise."

"Good. Sweet dreams…about the mystery office man."

Eden hung up, and Abby swore under her breath as the call ended.

It was an off night. She wasn't entranced. There was no "mystery" office man. She wasn't like her mother.

****

However, her refusal to become entranced was tested on Friday night when she stepped outside her apartment.

Ted leaned against his car. She'd assumed he would have sent one, but not with him in it. And she never expected him to look as good as he did against it. White, open-collared dress shirt, unbuttoned at the neck, emphasized his tan skin, and she fought the desire to touch him. Tailored gray dress pants with a rigid crease down the middle of each leg left her imagination to fill in the lean, muscular legs she'd seen at the sporting goods store last week. All he needed was a finger hooking a jacket over his shoulder, and he'd fit right in on the cover of *GQ*. Speaking of shoulders, his filled out the shirt and oozed sex appeal. She averted her gaze from them. What would they feel like?

And the car? It was a Bentley, all sleek silver lines and high polish. Its power and luxury sent shivers down her spine.

She swallowed at the sudden dryness of her throat. A glass of water before she left her apartment would have been wise. Actually, if she were determining wise moves, a tumble with Taye would have been the best. It would have taken the edge off. It must be why she looked at Ted as if he were the "fudge-" to her "-sicle."

She met his gaze.

His blue eyes twinkled, creases appeared at their corners, and his mouth twitched.

Dammit. She should have realized a man who couldn't hear well would be a keen observer. And he'd observed her studying him.

"Like what you see?" he asked. His voice

weakened her knees.

"You have a beautiful car." She ran her hand along the hood. It was warm and sleek.

He opened the door, and she climbed in. When they were both settled, he pulled away from the curb. Not knowing how well he could hear her when he faced away from her, she remained silent.

It was better that way.

"You look nice," he said as he drove.

Nice? She'd hoped for something stronger from him and berated herself for the flicker of hope. This is a business dinner.

"They'll be impressed," he added.

Impressed with my clothes? What kind of client is this?

He must have seen her puzzled look. "They'll be impressed with a female programmer with your qualifications."

It made much more sense, although it irked her. At the traffic light, he turned toward her.

"I'll try to live up to the reputation of my gender," she said.

He nodded. "I'm sure you will."

They rode the rest of the way in silence and ten minutes later, pulled up in front of Cioffi's. Abby's heart pounded as she uncurled her fingers. Dinner couldn't be as uncomfortable as the car ride.

****

Ted entered the dimly lit restaurant and swore under his breath. Dinner would make their awkward car ride seem like a piece of cake.

Dim overhead lights added ambiance. Candles illuminated each table. Although the tables in the center of the restaurant were able to seat four, tables for two lined the perimeter of the room. Silver damask tablecloths and wine-colored plush chairs added to the romantic vibe.

This was a restaurant for romance, not for a business dinner, and he'd bet a million dollars Carol chose it for that specific reason.

He didn't know how to conduct business and hold an intelligent conversation in shadowy light to prevent lip reading. He thought there might be music playing in the background, making it harder to hear.

Abby's gaze had raked his body when she'd walked out of her cottage, and he was surprised he hadn't burst into flames. She was…stunning. A simple black dress and heels drew his attention to her curves. And her lips? Wine-colored, soft, and luscious. Thank God he'd kept his gaze on the road. Every time he'd stolen a glance her way, he had to refrain from panting.

Not a good look for a man, and a terrible idea for a boss.

He was supposed to be beyond surface finery, but boy she tested him.

"Give me a minute." He walked to the maître d'. "Is there any chance you have a private room?"

The maître d' frowned. "We do, but it needs to be reserved in advance."

Ted clenched his jaw, took a deep breath, and spoke. "Is it available now?"

The maître d' opened his reservation book. "It seems to be."

"I'd like to reserve it now, please." He plastered a smile on his face.

"But I have plenty of tables out here for you two."

"Actually, it will be four of us."

He raised his brow. "There's a charge for the room."

"I'll pay it."

With a nod, the maître d' led them to a small private room in the back of the restaurant. It was decorated in much the same way as the rest of the restaurant.

"Can we turn up the lights?"

If Ted requested the maître d' to dance naked, he couldn't have looked more horrified.

"But it will ruin the ambiance."

"It's a business dinner. I don't need ambiance. I'm sure the delicious food will more than make up for it."

A little pacified, the maître d' raised the dimmer switch a millimeter, handed them menus, and left, mollified by the wad of bills Ted thrust at him. As soon as he left the room, Ted rose and raised the dimmer switch all the way up.

"Well, that's a relief," Abby said. "I thought I would have to figure out my food by touch." She winked.

Ted heaved a sigh of relief.

Carol walked in and reached for Ted. "There you are. Oh!" She pulled up short. "You invited a guest." She flared her nostrils and shot daggers at Abby.

Ted stepped away to avoid her embrace. "Abby, this is Carol Timmons. She's the VP of technology for Sentec. Carol, this is Abby Marlow. She's our newest programmer, and she's fantastic. I thought this was a good chance for her to meet the two of you." He craned his neck. "Where's John?"

Carol held out her hand to Abby. "Nice to meet

you." Turning her ruby-red smile to Ted, she continued. "Family emergency." She looked around the room. "I was convinced they'd lost our reservation. This is private, although kind of bright."

Ted cleared his throat. "Yes, I thought we'd disturb everyone else less if we sat here. I wish you would have called me about John's emergency. We could have rescheduled."

With a toss of her head, Carol removed her wrap and sat in the chair Ted held out. "We all still have to eat, don't we?" She motioned to both Abby and Ted. "Relax. The food is amazing. John said he'd catch up with you at the conference." Carol focused on Abby. "So is this the wunderkind Greg told me about?" she asked Ted as she reached for his hand.

Ted pulled his hand away. Abby tensed. Remembering how she'd gone out of her way for him, he nodded. "She's talented at what she does."

"I'm sure. In the meantime, I've heard the veal chop is divine."

Ted rubbed his chin. He ignored the menu and focused instead on reading Carol. Since their last date, he'd spoken with her several times, letting her down gently but firmly when she suggested they make plans. He hoped she wouldn't make a scene.

With a start, he realized the waiter stood at his shoulder. "Ah, I'll have the veal chop."

"Rushing through the meal already?" Carol asked. "I thought we were ordering drinks."

Ted's face burned. Dammit, he'd missed what the waiter said. Abby moved, and he looked at her. She smiled. Was she reassuring him or fed up? He shouldn't care.

"I'm ready to order now," Abby said. "This way we won't be interrupted in the middle of our conversation."

She'd addressed Carol, but kept her gaze on Ted, and his tension eased. Okay, maybe it wasn't awful. He released a breath, and she nodded as she ordered her complete meal, including drink and appetizer.

When the waiter left, Ted turned to Carol. "Since this is the first time Abby's with us, why don't you fill her in on what Sentec does?"

Carol narrowed her gaze. "Okay, business before pleasure." She began her spiel, which Ted already knew. He focused on other things. Like Abby.

As usual, the scent of strawberries wafted around her. It must be her shampoo, as he couldn't imagine a grown woman spraying strawberry perfume. Besides, the scent was subtle and fresh, not cloying like most perfumes. It did funny things to his insides, things he shouldn't contemplate.

He shifted in his chair and sipped his water. The chilled beverage doused some of his discomfort. The longer she spoke to Carol, the more animated Abby became, which was a change from the Abby he was used to. With him, she was more guarded. Maybe it was because he was her boss, or maybe she was extra careful when she spoke around him because of his disability. He frowned. Did she take exception to him because of his hearing loss? He hoped not. She was easier to understand than other people. She'd adapted to the "always look at Ted when you speak to him" rule, and she enunciated each word. Except when she was upset. He hid a grin. She might be more difficult to understand then, but she amused him. The more he thought about it, the more he liked the idea of her accompanying him to the conference.

"So it looks like you were right," Carol said.

The waiter returned with their orders. "About what?" Rosemary and thyme replaced the scent of strawberries and although his veal looked delicious, he missed the fruity scent.

"Abby."

He froze. He'd kept his daydreams to himself, right?

Carol gave him a calculating glance. "About Abby's programming skills, of course. I'm impressed, and I'm sure John will want to go ahead with the new proposal."

He tasted his veal, as much to collect his thoughts and let his muscles relax, as a chance to savor the flavor. "Very good. I'll follow up with him this week, and if he's in agreement, my people will draft the contract."

"Excellent," she said. "Make sure Abby's on the team."

Ted glanced across the table. Abby's cheeks flushed. "Of course."

"Good. Now, Abby, tell me about yourself," Carol said.

Ted swallowed, his gaze shifting between Carol and Abby. He stiffened, unsure of Carol's motive. He focused on the woman's body language instead.

Abby cocked her head to the side. "What would you like to know?"

She was evasive. He supposed if he were in Abby's shoes, at dinner with the boss and a client, he'd be wary too.

"Well, let's see." Carol tapped her lips with well-manicured nails. She reminded Ted of a predator stalking its prey. Should he step in?

"Where did you go to college?" Carol asked.

The question was harmless, and Ted relaxed.

She raised her chin. "MIT."

"Impressive. What made you come out to the West Coast?"

"The Silicon Valley. I know there are other areas to work in computers, and remote work is pretty easy, but there's still nowhere better than here for jobs."

Ted observed Abby's body language this time. Her hands gripped her knife and fork, and she cut her meat in precise strokes.

"Is your family out here?"

Abby's face was inscrutable. "No, I'm the only one. But I've made some great friends here, and I'm happy."

"Are you dating anyone?"

The merlot he'd drunk started to go down wrong, and he forced a swallow before he spit it out. "Carol, I'm not sure it's the best question to ask in this situation."

Abby had rescued him several times already. It was his turn, no matter how much he wanted to know the answer to the question.

"I don't mind the question." Abby looked at him. "I don't do relationships."

The taste of the wine turned bitter, his stomach burned, and he set his glass on the table.

Carol leaned forward. "What do you mean?"

Abby crossed her knife and fork on her plate, the epitome of Miss Manners. She dabbed her lips, and for a moment, he was jealous of her napkin. "It means I want to establish my career without outside influences to derail me."

He couldn't find a single fault with her logic. He should be ecstatic he'd found such a devoted and talented employee. She was focused and confident, and he would reap the benefits.

Except the dinner he ate sat like a lump in the pit of his stomach.

Chapter Seven

Abby's mind raced. Carol was a successful businesswoman, had worked her way up the corporate ladder, and dealt with many of the issues female corporate executives handled. Her line of personal questions was inappropriate and unprofessional.

And the "come hither" looks she gave Ted? They would be more appropriate between two people who were attracted to each other. Abby sensed no chemistry between the two of them, at least not on Ted's part. Ted looked at Carol the same as he looked at Abby. In fact, he recoiled from physical contact with Carol. She hated being thrown into whatever game the two of them played. Carol looked at her like she was the world's tastiest dessert and Ted, like she was the disappointing ending to a much-loved book.

There was something off about Carol's behavior, starting with her choice of one of the most romantic restaurants in the area for a dinner meeting. *Is she trying to set professional women back a thousand years?* Carol's interest in Ted was a no-brainer. He was gorgeous and successful. But Carol was a puzzle. Her body language and questions were aggressive. Her gaze reminded Abby of a bird of prey. She'd spent the entire dinner glancing between the two of them, smirking and asking veiled questions. She shouldn't be jealous, but her actions and mannerisms were not in line with a woman at a business dinner. And there was her latest question—are you dating anyone?

Seriously?

Regardless of how Carol chose to behave, Abby needed to remain professional. She shivered.

Carol sipped more wine. "I remember being like you."

We are nothing alike. I would never treat another colleague this way, and I'd mentor someone starting out in the industry. "And now you are a senior executive," Abby said. She was more concerned with Ted's behavior. He'd invited her to this business dinner, yet other than a brief protest about Carol's inappropriate question, he hung her out to dry.

"Yes, I am." Carol studied her wineglass.

Why is Ted silent? She needed him to speak to get the attention off her and turn the topic of conversation in a new direction. Hell, while she'd deny it with her dying breath, she'd appreciate a little help here. When he refrained—it appeared being a whiz at reading body language had no bearing on reading minds—Abby spoke. "So will you be at the tech conference, Carol?"

"I'll be there for a day, but John will be there longer. Ted, we should make plans to get together." She reached across and touched the back of his hand. Abby's stomach heaved.

His eyes were icy shards of glass as he withdrew his hand from Carol's reach. "We already have an appointment scheduled, Carol."

Carol looked down her nose at him, took a large gulp of wine, and mentioned other companies she wanted to visit during the trade show. She leaned in close to Ted, and Abby's jaw hurt from clenching it.

Ted was pleased with her work performance. He never would have taken her to a client meeting if she wasn't up to par. Yet somehow, right now, he seemed disappointed in her. She'd done everything he'd asked her to do. She'd come to dinner. She'd let him pick her up and drive her to this restaurant when she could have driven herself. She'd spoken to Carol and impressed her with her knowledge. He'd left her hanging.

Her stomach plummeted while her pulse increased. Was he disappointed in how she answered Carol's questions? They were intrusive. He couldn't possibly think she needed to answer them. That was taking "the client was always right" maxim a bit far. What happened to sticking up for your employee? Her cheeks burned, and she gulped a glass of water.

"Can I get you anything else?" The waiter stood next to Abby, but looked at Ted. *Yes, an easy exit.* She gritted her teeth and prayed her boss would end this meal.

"Just a check," Ted said.

Abby exhaled in relief.

The waiter nodded.

Carol turned to Ted. "I'm glad we did this," she said, "although I had hoped we might have dessert."

Ted shook his head. The two of them were having a conversation she wasn't a part of. As if this dinner could get any more awkward.

Carol turned to Abby. "It was wonderful to meet you." She handed her a business card. "I hope we can get together at the conference."

Abby reached into her purse and pulled out one of her own. It was the professional thing to do, even if she'd be happier to never encounter this woman again.

"I'd like that."

Once Ted took care of the check, Abby followed them out of the restaurant. She shook hands with Carol, who stood on tiptoe, pecked Ted's cheek, and walked away. Ted stiffened, took Abby's elbow, and crossed the street. She walked with him to the car, when she would have preferred to run away. When his car beeped and the doors unlocked, she grabbed the door handle and climbed inside. Closing it, she put on her seatbelt and folded her arms across her chest.

Between his inaction and Carol's landmines, she'd had enough.

****

An idiot could figure out she was angry again. But why? Ted swallowed his disappointment and confusion and took a deep breath to release his own pent-up tension. Carol was more difficult than usual. He jogged around the back of the car. Carol would never change. Instead, he needed to figure out what he did wrong.

Without a word, he started the car, felt the thrum of the engine beneath his feet, and pulled out into the street. Five minutes later, he pulled into a parking lot, turned off the car, and turned on the inside overhead light.

"Let's talk." He pushed his seat back and turned to her, resting an elbow on the steering wheel.

"Talk about what?"

She was too brilliant to play stupid, but he humored her.

"Why you're angry at me. I never encouraged Carol and—"

"Who says I'm angry at you?"

Every luscious body part of hers but her mouth.

"As I've said before, I read body language. Yours screams 'anger.' "

She scowled, and his hands itched to wipe away the crease between her eyebrows. But she didn't do relationships, and he was her boss. Even if he hadn't sworn off flings, touching her would not only tempt him to break his resolution, but put her at a distinct power disadvantage. He'd never take advantage of a woman.

"Never mind."

He scowled. "Are you blowing me off?"

"You're my boss. You pay me too well to indulge in anger. I'll get over it."

He ground his teeth together. "You're right. I'm your boss. As such, I want to know why you're angry with me."

She looked askance. "Really?"

He nodded and waited her out.

"I don't like being left hanging out to dry."

What. The. Hell. "Excuse me?" He must have misheard her.

"I don't like being put in an uncomfortable situation."

He heard her. "What did I do?"

She inhaled, and her chest rose and fell beneath the little black dress she wore. His confusion disappeared.

"You compl...ignor...how ina...priate Carol was wi...her...tions to me."

Blinking, he cleared his thoughts. He'd missed most of what she said, but caught the gist of it. He needed to focus. Dammit. He couldn't tell her how attracted to her he was, something Carol probably picked up on, leading to her behavior at dinner. He was

Abby's boss. But he needed to tell her something.

She shook his arm, and he turned toward her. Her anger was banked and concern deepened her eyes to a darker gray. "What's wrong?"

He looked away. "You're smart and independent, and I thought if I stepped in, it would look—both to you and Carol—like I didn't trust you to be able to take care of yourself."

This time, pressure on his arm made him look at her again. "So you were trying to show me how much confidence you had in me?"

He winced. "Yes. Although listening to your point of view, I can see why my strategy may have backfired." His heart pounded. He couldn't stand the idea he'd made her feel less than the brilliant woman she was. "I'm sorry."

"I don't understand why Carol acted like that in the first place. Is she like that all the time?"

Of course not. But Abby didn't know he and Carol were once a couple. She had no knowledge about his attraction to her, either. A wholly inappropriate attraction, but which he was having a difficult time denying. He could tell from her stillness she waited for him to explain more. This close to her, he couldn't think straight. With a sigh, he continued. "Carol has always been…difficult. But she's good at her job, and she's a client. And sometimes you have to put up with difficult clients." He rubbed the nape of his neck. "I should have explained more about her to you ahead of time. I'm sorry."

Up ahead, a group of teenagers walked along the sidewalk, their exaggerated motions telling him they talked and laughed. A car pulled into the parking lot, circled, and pulled away again. He wished he could as easily escape.

She tugged his elbow, and he dragged his gaze to her once again. "Thank you."

Tension left his body, and his muscles loosened.

"And I apologize as well," she said.

He leaned forward, curious now. "For what?"

"You're my boss, and I need to remember I can't let my anger out at you every time I'm annoyed."

"Even if I weren't good at body language, your feelings are easy to read." He held his breath. Would she read between the lines and know how often he'd observed her?

She bumped his shoulder. "Hey, you're not supposed to agree with me."

Some of his tension subsided. "Isn't the first rule of dealing with women, 'always agree with everything they say?' "

"You're impossible."

Throwing his head back, he laughed. The release was good, but he sobered quickly. "All jokes aside, I'm sorry."

She studied him for a full ten seconds—he counted—and he wondered what conclusions she drew. "Okay."

Such a simple word, but such a complicated relationship.

****

Later that evening, he signed onto his computer for a videoconference with CAST. The four members— Caleb, Alexander, Simon, and he—were friends since college, and Ted always looked forward to their regular calls. Tonight's was to discuss their next charitable project. He adjusted his screen so the three other men's faces were easy to see. That in itself was new. Simon, who'd been burned in a fire, always kept his face hidden, forcing Ted to develop special technology that allowed his friend's words to scroll across the screen. But ever since Simon met his girlfriend, Meg, the man had changed and no longer hid from the rest of them.

"Well, look who's here," Alex said. "Simon, have you actually come up for air? Or did Meg leave you?" His friend was joking, and Simon smiled.

"Jealous, Alex?" Alex was an architect, and his projects took him around the world. Each time he landed, he showed up with another woman on his arm, but never anyone who lasted.

"Nope."

Ted noticed a flicker of something in Alex's gaze, but before he could think about it further, Caleb spoke.

"Okay, guys, settle down. What's our next project?"

Caleb was the serious one of the bunch, rarely showing his feelings, and always keeping them on task. However, Ted recognized the occasional flicker of emotion in his friend's gaze. Maybe because he was hard of hearing and relied on body language and other cues, but Caleb wasn't as emotionless as he led others to believe. Ted also knew the man would do anything for those he cared about, even if he wouldn't admit it.

"I'd like to look into something with technology," Ted said. "There has to be a benefit it can provide to some underfunded or underprivileged group. Maybe a school or something."

"Any specific ideas who?" Simon asked.

"I haven't had a chance to look into it. But I'll

poke around at the conference and see what I can find out."

After they agreed to explore the idea further, Simon asked him to remain online, and he waved goodbye to the other two, who disconnected from the call.

"What's up, Si?"

"I was going to ask you the same thing," Simon said. "You seem a little off. It's not like you. You're usually the most focused of the group."

Ted rubbed his temples. Between the full meal, the conversation with Abby, and the late hour, he was exhausted. All he wanted was to blow off the question. But Simon was his closest friend.

"There's this woman."

Simon's face stretched into a grin. "Of course there is. Meg will be pleased."

"Meg doesn't need to know anything about this. It's not going anywhere." Ted's ears heated.

"Why not?"

"It's complicated." He wished it wasn't, but he couldn't see his way out. Computers he understood. He thought he'd understood women. He'd been with enough of them, although none seriously. They'd never looked past his hearing issues, and he'd kept them all at a distance. Then Abby appeared, the one woman who took no issue with his hearing and the one woman he couldn't have. She was his employee. He had no idea how, or if, he could navigate a personal relationship with an employee without the appearance of not giving her a choice in the matter. Their positions were too unequal.

"How? You've never been one for complicated."

"I know. But lately? I might be changing my mind." He'd seen how happy Simon and Meg were, and he wanted that kind of relationship. "She intrigues me, except she isn't into relationships." And I can't initiate one with an employee.

Simon's face contorted, and it was unrelated to the burns and scars that marred it. The bastard was trying not to laugh.

"Stop it, Si. I'm serious."

Simon held up a finger to wait and pulled away from the screen. Ted adjusted the volume and, at full blast, he could hear the faint sound of laughter. Dammit. He turned the sound to its normal level and drummed his fingers on the desk while his so-called friend regained control.

"Are you finished?" Ted asked when Simon returned to the screen.

"Yes. How did you manage to find the one woman who isn't into relationships?"

"I hired her."

Simon's jaw dropped. "Are you kidding? Why are you thinking of her as anything more than an employee? Are you trying to get sued?"

"Yeah, I thought a lawsuit would add a little spice to my life, asshole. She's brilliant and beautiful. She makes me laugh. She doesn't have an issue with my hearing." He wanted to look away from the screen at his last statement, but he refrained. If anyone would understand, it was Simon.

Comprehension dawned on his friend's face. "Oh, man, that's rough."

Ted snorted. "Just a little."

"So what will you do?"

"I have no idea. Look, I'm not an asshole. If we pursued a relationship, and it failed, I'd have no problem separating personal and professional. I'd never put her job at risk. But I can't ignore that others wouldn't understand, and I can't guarantee she wouldn't be uncomfortable. The scale is so uneven; I shouldn't talk to you about this, much less think about it."

But he couldn't help thinking about it. About her. His cock jumped every time her image entered his brain. But he was her boss. If somehow, she decided she wanted something from him, she was worth more than a quick lay, even if he couldn't have her.

"I don't envy you."

Ted ran a hand through his hair. "I'm up Shit's Creek."

Simon nodded. "Yeah, you are. Good luck, my friend."

They hung up, and Ted lay in bed that night as images of Abby floated through his mind.

What will happen when you have to see her at the tech conference?

He grabbed his pillow and smothered his face. Professional relationship. It was all he could hope for.

He would have to ignore her unless absolutely necessary.

Chapter Eight

Abby's phone rang on the way to work Monday morning. With a roll of her eyes, she answered it. Her mother would continue to call otherwise. She put her on speaker in the car, gritted her teeth, and said hello.

"So how's the new job?"

"Good. I'm getting a lot of experience." The key was to keep this conversation short.

"Any interesting men?"

Abby gripped the steering wheel. Her mother wouldn't be her mother without asking that question. "No."

"Strange, I looked up the company, and the CEO is hot."

Terrific. Now her mother was a research whiz? "Mom, I won't date my boss."

"So you work for him?"

"He's the CEO and owner, Mom. Everyone does."

"Well, you could do a lot worse."

"What do you mean?" Why was she asking her mother questions? She should figure out a way to get off the phone. She switched lanes, keeping an eye on traffic.

"Don't get lippy with me. I have more experience with men than you do. They're all interested in only one thing. It's your job to make sure you get the good end of the bargain."

Abby took a deep breath as she pulled into her parking space and locked her door. Her mother's experience with men was nothing to be proud of. She'd suffered through more failed relationships than most liposuctioned reality-show divas. The attempt to give her advice was ludicrous.

"I know, Mom. I won't jeopardize my job."

"You wouldn't have to work if you got lucky with the CEO. He could take care of you for life."

Or fire me. "I know, Mom." Thanks to her mom, her motto was only date men who could support themselves, only ever one at a time, and always leave first. Ted, who qualified in the "support themselves" category, was off-limits.

"Well, think about it."

As usual, her mom made no sense and refused to listen. "I will, Mom. I've gotta run. Love you."

"Love you too, sweetheart."

Entering the building, she considered what her mom said. She'd never risk financial instability like her mom. And her mom would never understand why she'd prefer to be without a man than with the wrong one.

****

Ted paced his office, which became more like a cage every damn day. Three days had passed since he spoke to Simon. Three days since he'd decided to avoid Abby. Three days since he'd been able to accomplish anything.

He'd shut his door two and a half days ago so no one could observe his distraction, and he still felt vulnerable.

With a roll of his shoulders, he focused on the latest security update he needed to review. What he wanted was to toss the computer off his desk, but he'd have to explain to his finance guy what happened.

Ignore her, my ass.

"Greg!" he yelled into the phone and hung up without waiting for a response. The light above his door blinked, and he yelled again. "Come in."

Greg looked at him like he was ready to placate an angry child. Ted's anger increased.

"Why haven't we set the daily schedule for the tech conference?"

Greg stretched out in the chair across from Ted. Other than the twitch of a muscle in his jaw, he looked relaxed.

Ted's fury increased.

"I'm not your secretary," Greg said. "You arranged that with Marge."

"Well, Marge is gone. And Sherry hasn't grasped the finer points of conference management." Or his own special needs, which he wasn't about to broadcast.

"I know."

"So I need you."

"Can't."

Ted rose behind his desk. "Why the hell not?"

Greg rose and leaned over the desk until his face was inches from Ted's. This was new. "I'm the lead programmer. I'm not playing secretary because you're frustrated."

Ted wouldn't have been surprised if Greg swung around and clipped him in the jaw. In fact, he contemplated smacking himself as soon as Greg left. But right now, he needed to make amends, and unfortunately, it involved admitting Greg was right.

He backed away from his desk. "Yeah, okay. I

deserved that, not you. Sorry."

Greg nodded and sat across from him.

Ted exhaled. "What the hell am I supposed to do?"

"About the conference or about your 'horny and frustrated' problem?"

Ted glared at him, and Greg snickered. "Get the PR firm to take care of it. It's their job, isn't it?"

Of course it was. The fact Ted had forgotten about them showed how distracted he was. As for his own accommodations, he'd figure those out once he spoke to the PR people. "Yeah, you're right."

"Whoa, twice in one conversation. I'm on a roll." Greg turned when he'd reached the door. "You need to fix the 'horny and frustrated' part too, you know. Come out with me tonight. I'm meeting friends. It'll be good for you."

Ted wanted to resist the pull. Maybe Greg was right. Maybe a hookup was what he needed.

Chapter Nine

Ted lay in bed early the next morning, filled with regret. The rumpled sheets smelled of sex and the warm body next to him who tried to calm his horniness. The pounding and thudding of the music in the club echoed long after he'd left with this woman and added to his frustration.

Well, okay, he wasn't horny any longer, but he wasn't satisfied. The random woman he'd slept with didn't make him forget about Abby. The dull ache deep inside was still there, the itchy feeling something wasn't quite right. He wanted to run.

He turned toward the woman who shared his bed. He'd met her at the club where Greg took him. The club was dark with flashing lights. He'd missed most of the conversation around him. The music pulsated, and his body vibrated. The drinks flowed, and the women flirted. This one, in particular, smiled at him, seeming without concern over his lack of conversation and inability to follow along. He'd taken her to bed like any number of random women in the past. Only this time, sex with her fueled his desire for a relationship.

She stirred. "That was nice," she said. She rose and pulled on her bra.

He should have wanted to pull her back into bed. "Yeah."

Turning to him, she raked her gaze over his body.

"You're a man of few words. I like that."

He watched her clothes slide over her body, hugging her curves, and his mouth should have watered. But all he could think about was Abby. When the woman finished, she grabbed her phone, and his phone buzzed. "I texted you my number. Call if you ever want to do this again."

She left, and he fell against the pillow.

Shit.

She'd satisfied his need and proved he was at the mercy of his baser instincts. Great. He'd caved. He'd decided he was ready for commitment, and as soon as the going got rough, he abandoned his principles and climbed on the bicycle, or in the sack, as the case may be. Only it was as unsatisfying as ever, and his problems were still there.

Greg was wrong.

****

Abby reviewed the schedule for the tech conference and figured out how to best manage her time. The days were packed. Two days of workshops, one day of media interviews and panel discussions, and one day on the trade show floor. She glanced between the schedule and the list of workshops and tried to figure out a way to get in all the ones she wanted to attend. At least their hotel was nice. After long days, she'd be able to relax in comfort.

She compared Ted's schedule to hers. After all, the primary reason she was there was to assist him. Prior to seeing the schedule, she assumed she'd be free to attend whatever workshops she wanted and only be required for client dinners, media interviews, and appearances on the trade show floor to answer questions from potential customers. But now she wasn't sure.

Turning toward his office, she groaned. Once again, his door was shut, indicating he shouldn't be disturbed. How was she supposed to help him without knowing what he expected? She'd have to email him.

"Got a minute?" she asked his secretary, Sherry.

Sherry popped her gum. "Sure, what's up?"

"Any idea when he'll be free? I need to go over the conference schedule with him."

"Not a clue, but I'll let him know you need him when he comes out. If he ever does. He's been a recluse all day."

"Tell me about it. I don't suppose you have any idea about his plans for the conference?"

Sherry shrugged. "Sorry, I wasn't here last year when he went."

As Abby was about to return to her desk, Ted's door opened, and he stuck his head out. Their gazes locked, and Ted retreated into his office.

Was he avoiding her? She looked at Sherry, who shrugged. He'd come out of the office for the first time today, made eye contact with her, and disappeared again. What else was she supposed to think? Confusion bubbled inside her. Walking over to his door, she knocked and opened it a crack. Ted sat at his desk, staring at his computer screen.

She waved, and he looked at her.

"Got a minute to go over the conference schedule?"

"Not now."

Seriously? "When would be a good time?"

"I'll let you know. In the meantime, can you get me a copy of the code you're working on? I'd like to take a look at it."

"Sure. Can I use the computer?"

He nodded, and she walked around his desk.

She ignored his spicy scent she hadn't missed until right now, typed a few words on his computer, clicked on a few files, and opened it. "Here you go. Want me to explain anything?" She waited, annoyed at the part of her that wanted him to ask her to stay.

"No, I've got it."

Maybe she could convince him. "Okay, but you should know I have some concerns—"

He held up a hand. "Email them to me. Thanks."

She stiffened at his dismissal. It was borderline rude, and it wasn't like him. They'd gotten along fine, but now? Why was he being so cold? She tried to tamp down her response and look at things another way. She'd spotted some odd script in the part of the code she reviewed and wanted to point it out to him before she continued with her part. But if he wouldn't talk to her now, she'd have to leave it.

At her desk, she spent the rest of the morning worrying over his review of her program and wondering how to make the tech conference work. Wondering if she should even bother to go. By lunchtime, she still hadn't heard from Ted.

Walking over to Greg's desk, she waited while he finished his phone conversation.

"Don't worry, Carol," he said. "We'll work it out." He hung up the phone and started when Abby sat next to his desk. "Yes?"

"Everything okay with Carol?"

His face flushed. "Oh, yeah, she…don't worry about it. What can I do for you?"

It was weird. "Do you know anything about a code discrepancy in the Sentec project?"

Greg frowned. "What discrepancy?"

"I found some odd script in the current code. I warned Ted about it when he asked to take a look at my work, but—"

Greg's mouth dropped. "Ted's got it? I haven't seen it yet."

"I know, but he asked, and I couldn't say no."

Greg gripped the pen in his hand. "Don't worry about it. I'll go talk to him after lunch. I'm sure it's fine."

At least Greg was on it. Some of her tension loosened. This was why she liked small startups. Everyone looked out for everyone else.

****

Ted opened his window to clear the air of the lingering strawberry scent from when Abby was in his office. He needed to get a grip, and he never would if every breath he took reminded him of her. Staring at the project Abby gave him, he closed and opened his eyes, hoping he'd somehow find the ability to concentrate. The flash of the light over his door was a welcome distraction.

"Ted, can I talk to you a minute?" Greg stood in the doorway.

Ted waved him inside. "What's up?"

Greg looked serious. "We have a problem."

Ted steepled his hands on his desk. Just what he needed on top of everything else. "What kind of problem?"

"Sentec seems to have a security breach."

Ted swore under his breath, and Greg stiffened.

Since Endicott oversaw Sentec's security, Greg's "we've got a problem" was a huge understatement. "Where is the report?"

"I'm putting it together now."

"Any idea where the breach came from?" All thoughts of Abby's code disappeared.

"My preliminary research indicates us."

Ted slammed his chair back, and Greg jumped. Ted pounded the desk with his palms. "Are you kidding me? How can you be sure it's not us finding vulnerabilities and exploiting them for our analysis?"

Greg clenched his jaw. "Codes are different."

A wave of nausea hit him. If his company's software was the problem, all of their clients could be impacted. They'd have to recall the product, come up with a fix, handle the media's attention at the conference...

"Okay, not a word of this to anyone. Not a single mention of this at the conference. Nothing gets out until we know what's going on. Got it?"

Greg nodded.

"Are you able to look into this from the conference, or should you stay here?"

"No, I can take care of it from the conference, Ted, don't worry."

Ted nodded. "Stay on it and update me."

"I hear you're reviewing Abby's code?" Greg asked.

Ted narrowed his gaze. Greg's posture was off. "Yeah, I want to see what she's doing."

"Probably a good idea. She's new and now with this potential problem, well, you can never be too careful."

Ted frowned as Greg left, and his stomach lurched. His company was everything. It was his livelihood; his proof he wasn't stupid, like his father said; his purpose in life. A security breach, especially an internal one, would jeopardize his life's dream.

Chapter Ten

The one-two rhythm of Abby's feet hitting the ground soothed her. The spread of endorphins through her brain as she jogged the running path helped her overcome the last vestiges of her anxiety. Ted hadn't talked to her all week. No one had mentioned the coding discrepancy. She inhaled the early Sunday morning air, cool, damp, and salty on her lips, and let her tension float away. Rather than continue along her usual route through her neighborhood and south toward the city, she ran toward one of the trailheads toward the rolling hills. Though there were few people around at this time of the day, something about the packed dirt beneath her feet, instead of concrete, while birds chirped their wake-up calls soothed her.

She settled into her normal pace. Passing a few early morning dog walkers, she nodded a silent greeting and continued through the yellow and gold trail. The light changed from muted purples and grays to pale greens and yellows as the sun rose.

"On your left!"

She leaped off the path into the brush at the edge. A bicycle whizzed by, skidded, and halted a few feet ahead of her.

She approached the rider, ready to yell at whoever was careless enough to ignore her. When he removed his helmet, she gasped. "Ted!" The tension she'd worked hard to get rid of returned in a whoosh.

He tucked his helmet under his arm. "I think we're destined to run each other off the road or bang into each other or something."

"What are you doing out here?" she asked. His blond hair was dark with sweat, and his cycling shirt showed off every cut of his muscles. And his biker shorts? If she weren't already panting from exertion, she'd pant from lust.

Wouldn't that be awkward?

"I often ride in the mornings, although this is off my usual course."

She pointed at his bike. "It's not…"

He squinted and after a moment, his face lit up. "…from that store? No, I told you I won't shop there. This is my old one, which works fine." He frowned. "You always run alone?"

She pointed to a nearby jogger. "I'm not alone."

"But you're not with anyone."

Standing this close to him, she wished for things she shouldn't. "No, I'm not."

"How far are you going?"

"The end of the trail and back." Or however long it took to get him out of her mind.

He put his helmet on. "Come on, I'll keep you company."

"It's not necessary." Clearing her mind would be impossible with him next to her.

"It's safer this way." He looked down the trail.

His desire to protect her sent warmth curling up and down her spine. It had been a long time since anyone was concerned about her. All of a sudden, the idea of company appealed to her. Touching his arm—

and trying not to squeeze his bicep like you would if you tested the ripeness of a peach—she waited for him to turn. "You're welcome to join me if you want. If you can keep up." She winked and raced away, his bark of laughter a brief punch in the silence behind her.

She no longer kept an easy pace, easing into the morning. This time, she sprinted hard. The slight whir of his bike wheels warned her as he reached her a few moments later.

"You're pretty fast, but I'd suggest you slow down."

She turned toward him. "Out of pity for you?"

His lips twitched, and his nostrils flared, but he kept his humor reined tight. Instead, he cycled next to her, his head turned slightly toward her. "The only pity I ask for is please don't make me carry you home when you're too tired to continue."

"Wouldn't dream of it, sir." She made sure he could read her lips.

He grinned, and the last of her tension disappeared. He accepted her teasing.

"Oh, you'll pay," he said.

He rode ahead, and she thought for sure he would leave her in the dust. But he turned around, a gleam in his eye, and returned to her side. When they reached a part of the trail farther on, he pulled ahead a little and skidded in a puddle, splashing her legs. She gasped and looked at her mud-spattered shins and ignored the twinkle in his eye.

"You play dirty—literally."

Ted stopped while she paused to clean her legs off. Given the opportunity—two could play this game—she took her mud-streaked hands and wiped them on his chest. She drew in a breath and realized her mistake. Sure, she'd repaid him for splattering her with mud, but a sudden awareness of his body overrode her satisfaction. His muscles were hard, and she wondered what the rest of him felt like. Her pulse pounded in her ears, and her gaze shifted to his lips. What would it be like to kiss them?

She jerked and pulled her hand away. No. She jumped at the strangled sound from the mouth she'd considered kissing and raised her glance to his eyes. His surprise mirrored her own.

Mistake, mistake, mistake! An internal voice blared a warning. She'd intended for it to be like when she and Max, her best friend from childhood, challenged each other as kids. In fact, when he teased her, Ted reminded her of Max—something about the glint in his eye and the "need to win" coupled with concern. But she hadn't counted on the sexual component.

She closed her eyes. She was not like her mother. She wasn't.

"Abby?"

She stilled. Maybe he couldn't see her. Right, and maybe unicorns are real.

"Yes?"

"Open your eyes."

She opened them.

"Let's get breakfast."

****

What the hell happened? She almost kissed him.

Ted replayed the last thirty minutes in his mind. Whether he played it backward—from the breakfast invitation—or forward—from nearly running her over with his bicycle, the results were the same.

He was a glutton for punishment.

Somehow, he'd caught up with the woman all good sense told him to leave alone. Instead of keeping his distance, he'd welcomed her touch, her mouth inching toward his. Even after witnessing her reaction, he was taking her to his favorite breakfast spot instead of going home.

"Have you been to Bert's?" he asked.

She kept walking.

He'd spoken out loud, right? Clearing his throat, he tried again. "Have you been to Bert's?"

She whipped her head around and made eye contact. "What? Oh, sorry. No."

His cheek twitched at the role reversal. It was a nice change to have someone else miss what was said.

"From the front, it's a hole in the wall. But it's got a great back patio, and the breakfast is amazing." The outside was quiet too. He never had trouble hearing there.

"Sounds nice." She bit her lip, and he wished he could see inside her brain to know what she thought. "I'm not sure breakfast is a good idea, though."

Neither was he. "Are you not hungry?"

"I'm always hungry."

The trailhead was ahead, and unless he convinced her soon to have breakfast with him, she'd disappear and the really-bad-idea-why-am-I-doing-this-chance would be lost. Maybe he should let her. Then again...

"Is it against your religion to eat out?"

She paused. Her face reminded him of a storm— her eyes were bullet gray, and her cheeks puffed like rolling clouds as she caught her breath—and he couldn't stop staring. For once, he didn't watch someone's lips, trying to make sure he understood them. Her face was expressive, and her thoughts announced themselves in her eyes. She was scared. Of what? Him?

"No."

"Why is breakfast a bad idea?" he asked. Other than the fact he should stay as far from her as possible, of course.

"We'd be eating together."

He tapped the handlebars of his bicycle. She was right, they would. Which was the exact opposite of what they should do. "Do you steal food off people's plates?"

Her lips curved, and a glint appeared in her eyes. "Sometimes."

"Me too. I won't steal yours if you don't steal mine."

"But we'll be together," she said.

He looked around them, at the trees, either end of the trail, and at the sky. "Psst, we already are."

"Just breakfast?"

"Just breakfast." He was hungry. They needed to eat. Afterward he would ignore her until the conference.

Fifteen minutes after reaching the trailhead, they walked onto the patio of Bert's. Abby's mouth dropped, and the ten-year-old inside of him considered for a moment crumpling a napkin and trying to make a basket. Lucky for him, the twenty-seven-year-old side of him won out.

"Impressive, isn't it?" While the front of the building was boring—plain windows and lettering, and the inside was a typical-looking café with the requisite tables and chairs, the owners put all of their creative juices into designing a beautiful landscaped garden oasis, with flowering trees, bushes in all hues of green, blue, and yellow, and vibrant flowerpots. A stone wall enclosed the space, and above the wall, mountains loomed in the distance. It was amazing. Simon would love the wide-open spaces and the greenery.

The only thing better than the view was the food.

As the waitress handed them menus, Ted frowned at the laminated list. "I can never decide between the Belgian waffles with bananas or the cinnamon French toast," he said.

"Get them both." Her gaze widened as if she challenged him, and he relaxed for the first time since he'd almost knocked her over.

"I am," she said.

He frowned, sure he misheard her. "Are you for real?"

"I told you, I'm always hungry."

"I will too," he said. He needed to see this. If she could fit it all in, so could he.

Usually, he tried not to notice her body. This time, he couldn't help it, and he stared at what was visible above the table. She was tiny. Pronounced cheekbones, fragile shoulders, slender arms…he'd ignore her breasts for this one moment…where did she plan to put it all? He thought about all the times he'd looked at her in the office. There was always some sort of snack on her desk. Maybe she ate a big breakfast and snacked during the day. She hadn't eaten much at the disastrous dinner with Carol.

When the waitress brought out their food, he watched Abby dig in. She was precise in her strategy—

a bite from one followed by a bite from another. The movements of her lips mesmerized him, and for the first time in his life, he wished he were a fork.

"You're right, these are amazing," she said between swallows. "I can't decide which I like better."

In the time it took him to eat one of his orders, she polished off two. Could he blame his lack of speed on his sexy table companion? Her food consumption flabbergasted him. "Don't you have a stomach ache?" he asked.

"No, do you?" Her forehead wrinkled with concern.

He pushed his plate away. "No, but I haven't eaten as much as you."

"You know, it's not polite to comment on a woman's eating habits."

He shouldn't, he would regret it, but he said it anyway. "I thought I wasn't supposed to think of you as a woman."

She stilled, and he cursed under his breath.

He'd taken a chance he could get away with voicing his thoughts, and she'd take it as a joke. But—

Her fork clattered to the plate, she tipped her head back, and laughed.

He wasn't good at describing sounds. Not in great detail, anyway. But her laugh? It was the kind he couldn't help but join in, the kind that filled him with joy, like a giant bubble in his stomach. It was the perfect pitch for him, not too high and not too low. It was outsized, like her appetite.

If he let his own pleasure seep through and joined her, the sound of her laughter would be drowned out, and he wouldn't be able to hear her. He liked hearing her as much as he liked being with her, which was a problem he'd think about later. For now, he sat and enjoyed.

****

She was in a lot of trouble, she thought that night as sleep escaped her. No, a lot wasn't strong enough. Gargantuan heaps of sticky, gooey trouble. If she were to put it into computer science terms, she was about to enter into syntactic garbage—objects or data in a program's memory space unreachable by a root set. In other words, lusting after one's boss should be syntactic garbage, unreachable by an employee.

His deep, scratchy voice sent shivers down her spine. She wished he would touch her intentionally. His sense of humor made her wish she could spend her time making him laugh, rather than coding for clients.

Despite all the reasons why it couldn't work—she was his subordinate, she needed this job and the salary it paid her, she refused to turn out like her mother—her libido rebelled against her.

For those reasons and more, she should turn and walk away. Find another job. Move to a different city. Become a skier, instead of a runner, so he couldn't follow her up a mountain on his bike.

The next morning, she marched into work and knocked on his office door. His broad smile greeted her, and she swallowed. Stay firm.

"Can I talk to you a minute?" Perched on the edge of the black chair across from him, she folded her hands in her lap to keep them from shaking. "I shouldn't go to the tech conference."

He leaned forward with a frown. "Why not?"

I'm attracted to you. "I don't think I'm the right

person for it."

He stilled a moment, then rose, and came around to the other side of the desk. Seated across from her in one of the two chairs, he rested his elbows on his knees.

Denim jeans emphasized his leg muscles, the same leg muscles she'd seen yesterday in all their bare glory on his bicycle. She'd memorized every sculpted line of his thighs and calves in secret. Darn it.

"Are you talking about the conference in general or assisting me, specifically?"

His voice was neutral, as was his face, except for a tic in his jaw.

She swallowed. She was in over her head. No matter what happened, she would suffer the consequences. If she went with him to the conference, she was at risk of losing her convictions. If she stayed home, she risked losing her job and some of the respect she'd earned. What computer security programmer objected to attending a computer security conference? How the heck was she supposed to answer?

Assisting you. "I don't think it's a good idea."

He leaned back, and his face went blank, but she wasn't naïve enough to think he had no reaction to her words. She was pretty sure, if the clenched fist in his lap and the protruding vein in his neck were any indication, he had quite a strong reaction at the moment.

"I see."

No you don't. "I'm sorry. But I've got programming work, and I don't see how I'll have the time to get it all finished. You were right in the first place—I shouldn't go. I think the responsible thing is for me to stay here."

"Responsible." He pronounced the word like he sucked on a lemon.

She nodded.

He'd stared at her mouth the entire time she spoke, and she'd been careful to face him so he could understand her.

Or at least, what she wanted him to believe.

Yet he remained silent.

After what she'd swear was an hour but was probably only a few seconds, he spoke. "Responsible people keep their word."

"Responsible people keep their jobs." Her face heated.

He raised an eyebrow. "We'll compromise. You'll come to the conference, but just for the conference."

"What does that mean?"

"It means I'll find another assistant. You'll have plenty of time to finish work, and you'll benefit from the learning experience."

He was her boss, and his tone brooked no arguments.

She walked to the door. She wouldn't have to spend the entire conference at his side. As she left his office, she wondered why she felt horrible.

Chapter Eleven

Ted avoided Abby for the rest of the week, which is what he should have done from the beginning. Breakfast was a mistake. No matter how much he enjoyed her company, how much he thought she enjoyed his company, she was having second thoughts and sending him mixed signals. Backing out of the conference was her poor excuse to avoid him, and he'd seen right through it. He'd given her a plausible excuse to go without being tethered to him, and she'd jumped on it.

So he ignored her. He ignored her supple fingers as they flew across the keyboard. He ignored her long, straight, black hair gleaming beneath the lights. He ignored her laugh, which he heard too often for his own good. He ignored her silver eyes, shimmering like mercury.

He focused on conference prep—perfecting his speeches, coordinating his schedule with his PR people, and checking his travel arrangements.

He missed Marge. While he was capable of doing everything, she excelled at letting him know when his tone was off in his speech, or finding quiet and well-lit interview rooms. His new secretary, Sherry, was clueless.

So he'd try not to worry about what other people would think of him.

Except... His father's words echoed in his mind: stupid, stupid, stupid. His cheeks burned. He hated making a fool of himself. No matter how many times he told people he was hard of hearing, they assumed he wasn't as intelligent as they were. Sometimes it worked to his advantage—he could manipulate people who underestimated him—but he hated it.

Therefore, instead of looking forward to this conference, he dreaded it. Abby backing out exacerbated his anxiety. He should have told her to stay home. In fact, he should stay home because of the Sentec issue. No matter how many programmers he put on the problem, as CEO, he should stay home and oversee their work. Or try to fix it on his own. How could he have a meeting with Carol at the conference without all the facts? If only he had scheduled fewer presentations and appointments.

The day before the group left for the conference, Ted called a meeting with the conference attendees— Greg, Tom, Cory, and Abby—to go over last-minute coordination. His heart knocked against the walls of his chest at the thought of being close to Abby, and he paced the room. *This is ridiculous.*

She entered the conference room, and his breath caught. He opened his mouth to inhale more oxygen, closed it, and motioned everyone to sit. His chest tightened.

"We need to double-check coverage for client meetings," Ted said. He focused on his tablet instead of the beautiful woman at the table with him. The last thing he wanted was multiple meetings with the client, him, and Abby. Lucky for him, there was only one meeting Abby was scheduled to be alone with him.

"Can we discuss workshops?" Greg asked. "I have to finish some work during the conference. I'd like you all to attend as many as needed and get me the notes. Not to mention the workshop I'm giving." He winked. Abby smiled. For the first time since she'd walked in, she looked comfortable.

"Ted?" Greg asked. "Hello?"

Ted jerked. "Sorry, I was distracted. Of course we can." He clenched his hands into fists, he examined the list and made sure at least one of them attended any workshops they needed to improve their knowledge. "Don't forget, we can always get copies of the material."

"It's never the same," said Cory. "I'm out on the trade show floor on these days." He pointed to the schedule on his tablet. "Who will be covering when I'm not able to be on the floor?" After they coordinated coverage, Ted rang for Sherry.

"Where is the final interview schedule from public relations?"

"Right here," she said. He looked at the schedule and added it to his file.

"Okay, company plane leaves tomorrow at eight a.m. sharp," he said. "See you all there."

Greg turned toward Abby. "Get the airport information from Sherry."

Ted expelled a breath as soon as everyone rose to leave. Except for his one error—allowing Abby to distract him—he'd remained professional. Other than the first few minutes where he'd needed a moment to adjust to her presence, he fared pretty well. Maybe he could handle this after all.

"Greg, can I see you a minute?"

Greg nodded and remained in the room after everyone else left.

"I looked over Abby's work, but with all the conference prep, I'd like another set of eyes. Can you review it?"

"Of course. I was going to suggest it." Greg raised his chin.

Ted half expected him to preen like a peacock. He exhaled. "Good. In the meantime, I need you to keep me updated about the potential breach while we're at the conference. It's not ideal, but we can't have a client dinner without knowing more detail."

"Don't worry," Greg said. "I'll take care of it. Trust me."

The next day, the stench of coffee, engine oil, and carpet chemicals assaulted him as he entered the private airport lounge with his luggage and laptop case. After he checked in and handed over his bags, he strode to the coffee bar and ordered the largest they sold.

"I'll have the same, please."

He froze at Abby's scent.

Careful not to bang into her—it was the start of all of his difficulties—he turned around and nodded as he took a sip of his coffee, as much to distract himself as to imbibe the caffeine.

She followed him to the pleather club chairs and sat across from him. Should he talk to her? He could hide behind his CEO title and read. Instead, she picked up her tablet and disappeared behind it. He couldn't decide if he was relieved or offended.

Greg, Cory, and Tom arrived at the same time. "Did you guys see the weather forecast?" Greg asked.

Ted shook his head. Abby peeked over her book.

"They're calling for storms later in the week over New York."

Ted scrolled through the weather app on his phone. "Yeah, but not until after we're scheduled to leave. We should be fine." Abby clutched her tablet.

Their flight was called, and the five of them walked to the jet. They mounted the stairs on the jet way, and Ted greeted the pilot and co-pilot before he settled into one of the plush, buttery-yellow leather reclining seats. He eased into the comfort of the chair. Unlike a commercial jet, this plane had three groups of four seats around glossy zebrawood tables. He placed his laptop on the table in front of him and stared out the window. The background noise of the engines would make it next to impossible for him to carry on conversations with anyone, and accustomed to this, Greg, Cory, and Tom huddled together over their tablets and phones around their own table.

Movement to his right distracted him, and he turned.

Abby sat alone. After closing the window shade, she buckled her seatbelt and faced forward, her jaw clenched, every muscle on high alert. The engine revved, and the plane got ready for takeoff. She jerked, squeezed the armrest until her knuckles whitened.

Her long lashes fluttered over her pale cheeks. She was terrified.

With a sigh, he crossed the yellow and blue-carpeted aisle and sat next to her. Conversation was useless, but he reached over and clasped her wrist to calm her with his presence. Before he could process how delicate her wrist bones were, she'd flipped her hand and squeezed his in a death grip.

****

Abby hated flying. Scratch that. She hated taking off and landing. The actual flight part was okay, provided it was smooth. If she were logical about it, she should love to land, since the alternative was what frightened her in the first place. But she couldn't be logical right now. She was on an airplane, holding hands with a man she needed to avoid.

She wasn't sure which was worse—the plane or the man. His scent permeated her nostrils. She'd breathe it in if she were able to relax her body. His sculpted bicep touched her shoulder, and heat spread along her arm. She'd lean into it if she wasn't terrified of moving.

The motors roared as they got ready for takeoff, and she gripped Ted's hand harder.

Airplane. Ted. Airplane. Ted.

Crap.

"You forgot to mention you owned an airplane." She tried to redirect her thoughts. There, opening her mouth to speak didn't cause any catastrophe. She allowed his scent to fill her lungs and stifled a moan. Maybe breathing was a bad idea. She held her breath.

He remained silent but rubbed the inside of her wrist with his thumb. Jolts of electricity shot up her arm, and she gasped. So much for holding her breath.

"You don't have to sit with me," she said. "I'll be okay." The airplane surged forward, and she jumped.

Trying not to embarrass herself, she focused on his touch—just the right amount of pressure, back and forth at the base of her hand. Her skin warmed. Her stomach fluttered. At least, she thought her stomach fluttered...maybe it was about to explode from airsickness, even if she wasn't yet in the air?

She cracked one eye open and checked for airsick bags in the seat pocket.

Ted turned to look at her and gave her a small smile.

"Whose idea was it to fly in a stupid tin Tupperware container?" she asked. "I'm pretty sure I've stored leftovers in things bigger than this."

His face crinkled in confusion for a moment before he blanked his expression. Pulling his hand out of hers, he returned to his seat as the plane began its ascent.

What bothered him all of a sudden, and how come no one yelled at him for getting up while the "fasten seatbelts light" was lit? Must be the perks of owning a plane.

Greg sat next to her. "You okay?"

He wasn't Ted, and she missed his comforting presence. She took a deep breath. Now they flew on an even keel, and Greg would have to do. "Yeah, for now. I hate takeoffs and landings."

He nodded. "You've got about five hours until you have to worry again. If you want company, come on back."

She thought about it as he left, but she wanted to know what was going on with Ted. He hadn't spoken to her while he sat next to her, yet he held her hand, until he shot out of his seat and stalked to the front of the cabin. The man ran hot and cold better than her Kohler faucet. The plane jostled, and she flinched. There was no way she'd leave her seat. She craned her neck to look over at Ted, but he was bent over his tablet, and she couldn't catch his attention. She looked around, but there wasn't anything to toss his way, either, and she might miss.

—Thanks for sitting with me during takeoff.— she texted.

He looked over at her and nodded.

—Is there a problem?—

Ted clenched his jaw and jabbed at his phone screen.

—I don't like being called stupid.—

—I know.—

—Why did you say it?—

—I didn't. Can we talk instead of text?—

He turned to her, and his face was a stony mask. With a sharp jab of his finger, he pointed up and at his ear. He shook his head and focused on his tablet. His shoulders were stiff, jaw clenched.

Why is he angry?

Guilt washed over her. He couldn't hear over the sound of the plane engines. Which meant he missed everything she'd said earlier.

But calling him stupid? Her mouth dropped.

—Wait. I called the plane stupid. Not you.—

A flush crept up his neck, and his ears turned bright red. He stared straight in front of him. His shoulders rose and fell. When he turned to her, a trace of confusion lingered in his gaze. He blinked, and it disappeared.

—I'm sorry I called the plane stupid ;)—

His features relaxed, and his fingers flew over his keyboard.

—It doesn't have feelings.—

She shrugged. He did, though.

—I think it's time for me to find another word. Guess I know now why you ignored me.—

This time, when he looked over at her, his gaze

was wary. She'd never seen such expressive eyes. When she resumed ignoring him, she'd have to pay attention to other people. Maybe she'd missed something.

—What did you say earlier?—

—You never mentioned you owned your own plane.—

—It's the company plane.—

—It's your company.—

He smiled.

—I said you could go to your seat, and I'd be fine.—

—You looked scared.—

—I hate flying.—

He worried his lip between his teeth.

—Is that why you wanted to skip the conference?—

She'd never tell him the full reason.

—One of them.—

Doubt rolled across his face. He ran his hand over it and resumed typing.

—Is that why you called my plane stupid?—

She nodded.

—Technically I called it a 'stupid Tupperware container.' I've stored leftovers in things bigger than this.—

He grinned, and for a moment she forgot why she planned to ignore him. It transformed his face, creased his cheeks, and created a bubble of ease around him.

—Don't you know not to make fun of the size of your boss's plane?—

—You said the plane doesn't have feelings.—

—Touché.—

The plane hit a patch of turbulence. She gasped,

grabbed the armrests, and dropped her phone. Squeezing her eyes shut, she breathed in through her nose and out through her mouth. She'd read somewhere it helped. On what planet did gasping like a guppy help?

A click, followed by a squelch of leather and pressure on her hand made her open one eye. Ted was there.

Again.

This time, he pried her hand off the armrest and cradled it in his. If she liked him, she would find his grip and his presence reassuring. Maybe even lovely.

She opened her mouth to speak, realized her mistake, and typed one-handed on her phone.

—*Isn't the fasten seatbelt sign lit?*—

He shrugged.

—*My plane, my rules.*—

—*Oh, so now it's YOUR plane.*—

His mouth twitched.

—*Stop sassing the boss.*—

—*Yessir.*—

She leaned against the soft leather seat as the plane bumped and pitched. Gritting her teeth, she focused on Ted's hand around hers. It was warm, all-encompassing.

"Relax."

Ted's voice was a whisper, but it resonated low in her stomach. She peeked over at him. He looked away from her, so he couldn't read her lips. The engines were still noisy, which meant he still couldn't hear.

Her chest expanded.

He didn't talk to her because he expected her to answer him. He talked to her to make her feel better.

Her stomach dropped, and although the plane still bounced around, she was pretty sure it wasn't from the plane's motion.

How the heck am I supposed to resist this man?

****

His hand was numb. Abby had clenched it for the past two hours, and he'd spouted nonsense for the same amount of time, trying to keep her calm. The turbulence stopped about twenty minutes ago, and she'd fallen asleep.

On his shoulder.

He shouldn't like it. He concentrated on her, rather than his body's discomfort.

He liked the weight of her on him, the scent of her hair wafting around him, the sigh of her breath as she rested. He also liked the dichotomy she presented.

In his large hand, her small one was delicate. But she was strong.

On the airplane, she was fearful. Around the office, she was feisty.

She was cognizant of his hearing difficulties. But she treated him the same as everyone else.

She'd said her fear of airplanes was one of the reasons she asked to skip the conference.

What was the other reason?

He'd assumed she disliked him. However, she made no attempt to avoid him.

He closed his eyes. He might as well enjoy this unexpected intimate time with Abby. When she woke up, they would resume their working relationship and their distance. There was something nice about this warmth and closeness as they traveled. Almost as if they were in a relationship together. His breath caught.

When he thought about a relationship, Abby was the one who floated through his mind. She was brilliant and funny. When they were together outside the office, they had no trouble talking to each other. She fascinated him, and he wanted to know all the little things about her—her favorite color and food, what made her sad, was she ticklish and where, who her favorite author was. He was attracted to her, and he suspected the feeling was mutual.

He groaned. It was time to have a conversation with her. Clear the air, get it out in the open. Figure out once and for all whether they could have a relationship, and how it would work.

But not while they were fifty thousand feet in the air. If they had this conversation, he needed to be damn sure he understood everything.

He shifted in his chair, and she woke with a start, rubbing her hands over her face and hair. She looked at him, face flushed, and emotions flitted across her beautiful sleep-clouded eyes—embarrassment, desire, and fear. She reached for her phone.

—*Sorry I fell asleep on you.*—

—*Guess I shouldn't count myself as a scintillating conversationalist.*—

Her smile smacked him in the chest with its intensity. Suddenly, his desire for conversation with her took on a whole new importance. If he was lucky, he could get those smiles all the time.

This plane couldn't get on the ground fast enough.

Chapter Twelve

The jet landed and, in no time, they found their luggage and were settled in the limo. As it drove into Manhattan, Abby craned her neck to stare at the skyscrapers, the gray and silver edifices silhouetted against the bright blue sky.

"First time in the city?" Greg's voice interrupted her, and she nodded. She refused to look anywhere but out the window. She might miss something.

When they stopped at a traffic light, her mouth dropped at the sheer number of people crossing in front of them.

Ted, as expected, remained silent, but when she turned to look at him, his mouth was curled in a slight smile, as if he found her fascination with the city amusing.

They pulled up in front of their boutique hotel. It was elegant and hip at the same time. A bellhop in silver with purple accents rushed to open the door of the limo, while three others waited with luggage carts, and a doorman held open the front door of the hotel. Jazz music played, piped outside from a hidden sound system.

This was more like what she expected.

She followed the others into the hotel and up to the sixth floor. Eggplant-colored carpet muffled their footsteps as one by one they reached their rooms, and silver wall sconces with purple bulbs lit their way. When she swiped her keycard, her door unlocked. Ted held the door wide as she pulled her suitcase inside.

"I'm across the hall, and Greg is next to you," he said. "We'll meet for dinner in an hour."

She admired the ultra-modern decor of her room—black marble desk and dresser, silver accents, white marble bathroom, and a huge silver and purple tufted bed. She bounced, testing the mattress. After unpacking her clothes and storing her toiletries in the bathroom, she walked to the window overlooking Manhattan. Cars and buses drove in tandem like blood running through veins and arteries. People swarmed street corners. Clouds reflected off windows and raced across the sky.

A shiver of anticipation ran along her spine. She'd always wanted to see New York. She'd wanted to go to this conference for years. Two of her dreams were about to come true. Thank goodness she changed her mind about the conference.

And maybe I'll survive this close to Ted.

When the knock sounded at her door, she was dressed in black jeans, a white sweater, and suede high-heeled boots, and ready for dinner. In the hallway, all the guys waited. Ted leaned against the wall, a little apart from the others. Taller than the rest of them by several inches, his gray button-down shirt gave his blue eyes a silver tint. His black jacket draped from a finger over his shoulder. A ghost of a smile played across his lips, and as she closed her door, he pushed away from the wall, nodded to her, and walked next to her out of the hotel and down the street to the restaurant.

When they arrived, Ted held the door open. She walked inside and stopped short at the sight of arcade games lining the walls, wooden tables and chairs in the center of the room, and a well-stocked bar on the side. Ted bumped into her, and she wobbled. He grabbed her upper arms to keep her on her feet and spun her around.

"What's wrong?" he asked.

"It's an arcade," she said. Classic rock music played in the background.

"A barcade," Cory said. "They're awesome, and I thought since it's my night to pick a place, it was just what we needed. Ted agreed, and I rented out the place for us."

She bit her lip as she considered her question. "It's noisy…" She'd lowered her voice so the others couldn't hear, but enunciated so Ted could understand.

He nodded. "I've been here before. I love video games. It'll be fun. Let's check out the place for a bit before we eat."

Dropping coats onto chairs around a table in the middle of the room, they scattered. When Abby spotted Super Mario World, she rushed over. She ran her hands over the controls until Ted's face in the glass reflection made her turn.

"I used to love this game," she said. The overhead music played and though the place was empty, she spoke in a slow and clear manner to him.

He nodded, beer bottle in hand. "Think you can beat me?"

When she raised an eyebrow in challenge, they went to the token dispenser, and each returned with a pile of tokens, two of which he slipped in the slot. She beat him the first time and crowed with delight.

He gulped beer. "Rematch."

Once again, she beat him. She wanted to jump up

and down, but he was her boss. Maybe it wasn't a good idea to savor the victory in a public display and show him up. Before she could decide, Greg walked over.

"Care to see if you can beat me?" he asked. Ted took Greg's whiskey glass and retreated a step to watch.

She beat him twice. Ted remained silent, although amusement showed on his face, while Greg mumbled about revenge. But she was hungry and refused another chance to play. Instead, she ordered food at the bar, adding it to the tab Ted started. Everyone followed her and while their orders were prepared, they continued to play. Ted waited with her at their table, where the noise level was a little less.

"You're good," he said. "At the game."

"I spent hours at the arcade on weekends while my mom worked. Mostly watching, sometimes playing." It depended on how strapped for cash her mom was. Her face burned at the memory of her mom in the bar next door, waiting tables and getting extra money slipped in her blouse for a quickie in the back room. Of course, Abby knew about it because of the time she'd gone to find her mother when she had a headache. She walked in on her mother and some guy doing...well, whatever. She raced away. Later, her mother made sure to give her more money for the arcade games.

Ted leaned toward her. "You look uncomfortable."

She shook her head to rid her mind of the memories. "Sorry, bad memory."

"Yet you like the game."

She wanted to avoid her history, but she needed to say something to alleviate the awkwardness. Something in Ted's expression made it impossible for her to remain silent. It was like an invisible string tugged at her reserve. "Playing the game reminds me of my mom when I was a kid."

"Parents can be challenging." His jaw clenched, and she wondered at the story behind his words.

Greg came over. "Dinner's here." He sat next to her.

This was twice he'd interrupted her and Ted. If she were more suspicious, she'd think he kept them apart on purpose, but she chalked it up to coincidence.

Cory sat on her other side. While most of them talked about the last time they were in New York, ate their burgers and fries, and challenged each other's expertise or lack of with the video games, Ted's head swiveled back and forth between each person, depending on who spoke. He remained silent, a crease between his brows, his response a half step behind. After a few minutes, he focused on his food instead of the conversation.

Abby clenched her hand around her fork. The stainless steel dug into her palm. Despite Ted's nonchalance when they arrived, with the loud music in the background, the poor lighting in the room, and the multiple conversations at the same time, he struggled.

Memories of their flight flitted through her mind. He'd helped her when she was afraid. He was her employer, but he might be her friend. And friends helped each other.

She caught his gaze across the table and held it. As his face relaxed, she could see the tension leave his body.

"Tough crowd," she mouthed.

He rolled his eyes. "You're not gloating."

"I like to keep my triumphs quiet."

Ted threw his head back and laughed.

"What's the joke, Ted?" Cory asked.

Ted's gaze passed from Abby to Cory and again to Abby. "Have you played Super Mario World with Abby?"

"Not yet."

"You should."

Cory turned to Abby. "After dinner?"

"Sure."

As Abby beat Cory for the fourth time, she grinned at Ted.

Friends. She could handle friends.

****

Ted settled into bed and removed his hearing aids for the first time all day. The cottony stillness soothed him, and he sighed in relief. Being around people without a break meant he was "on" all day. He was exhausted.

He made sure his phone was on vibrate and moved it under his pillow so he'd feel his alarm in the morning. Should he text Abby? His hands itched, and he clenched his fists and slid them beneath the blankets. He couldn't get her out of his mind.

He'd spent the entire day with her, and still, he wanted to talk to her. Her sense of humor cheered him, and he admired her competitive drive, which he'd seen during the video game. She wasn't obnoxious when she won, but she was proud. He admired her.

And the part of her life she'd let him see? He wanted to know more. What made those shadows cross her face?

The sheets, which were cool beneath his bare back when he'd first lain on them, were warm now, and despite the cold temperature outside, his room was stuffy. He flung off the covers and stalked naked to the window.

Based on other people's complaints, nights in New York were noisy. The city that never slept made its presence known to visitors who tried to sleep, and only those accustomed to ignoring horns and sirens could tune it out.

He was lucky. From this distance, he heard the faintest of hums, and only right next to the window. No, the noise wasn't what kept him awake, it was the lights. Through the gap in the curtains, bright white lights shone from neighboring buildings. Police cars and ambulances sped by, red and blue lights flashing.

But if he were honest, Abby kept him awake. His skin heated at thoughts of her, but there were no clothes for him to shuck. He returned to his bed.

His phone vibrated. He looked at the screen and hoped it was Abby.

—You might want to be careful.—

Ted frowned at Greg's text.

—Careful?—

—With Abby.—

—What do you mean?—

—You two looked pretty cozy today.—

—She was afraid on the airplane.—

—And you rushed to her rescue.—

He'd seen her fear and sympathized. What was wrong with that?

—I don't see a problem.—

—You might be right, but you should still be careful. Mixing business with pleasure is dicey.—

He stuffed his phone under his pillow. Greg was

right. He needed to be careful, and they needed to have that conversation.

Chapter Thirteen

Ted's eyes ached from focusing on people's lips, his neck muscles were rocks, and it was only day one.

Shit.

He leaned forward and shook the outstretched hand, shifted his focus to the person's face, and concentrated on his mouth. The trade show floor was noisy, which made conversation an auditory maze. The lighting created shadows in odd places and lip reading was tricky. Most of today's floor time was networking—greeting people and showing off different technology. Interviews with the media, as well as meetings with potential clients and partners, would start tomorrow. He'd have to ensure they retreated to one of the quiet rooms he'd reserved ahead of time. The muscles in his back tightened, and he closed his eyes to gain his center.

His pulse raced, and his eyes flew open at the touch of a hand on his elbow.

Abby.

Desire flooded through him as her pale pink lips curled in a hint of a smile. What would it be like to kiss her?

"Need any help?"

He froze. With kissing her? Her smile faltered and reality intruded.

"Why would I need help?" He turned away. He

needed to get ahold of his emotions. Her hand tugged at his elbow. He clenched his fists and turned.

Her gaze shifted between him and somewhere past his left shoulder. "You might not, but your computer does."

Brushing past him, she stalked over to the computer displayed on the podium. The screen flashed. It shouldn't.

Shit.

Her fingers tapped the keyboard in a flurry of movement and in less than thirty seconds, she'd tamed the flashing screen. Before he could thank her, or apologize for his outburst, a hand on his shoulder drew his attention away from her, and Cory directed his focus to another nameless executive. He glad-handed, nodded, and hoped he said the appropriate thing, but this time he was distracted. In the back of his mind, all he could think about was Abby.

When he was finally alone, Abby was leaving the trade show floor, and he rushed after her.

"Wait." He suspected the entreaty came out more like a demand.

She spun around, lips pressed together, as if she restrained herself. Like he should have.

"Yes?" she said.

He had to hand it to her, she conveyed enough tone in one word, even he could hear it. It wasn't desire. She was annoyed with him. "Where are you going?"

"The next panel discussion."

With a frown, he checked the schedule on his smart watch. "It's not for another hour."

"I want a good seat."

He raised an eyebrow at her, expecting her to

blush, or look sheepish, or something.

She betrayed nothing. *Damn, she's good.*

"You have some time. Walk with me."

She stiffened. Being the good employee she was, she fell into step with him, but remained silent.

A strange sense of disappointment filled him.

His watch buzzed, and he read Cory's text.

—*Where are you going?*—

Ted's fingers jabbed the small keyboard. —*Out.*—

—*We need you here.*—

—*I'll be back*— Ted said.

He squinted at the bright natural light of the outer hallway, but his tight muscles loosened in relief at being off the floor, and he breathed once again. Striding along the corridor, he found a corner with chairs. He motioned to the seat adjacent to his. He thought she would refuse, but she perched on the edge—she obeyed him, but with reluctance.

"I'm sorry I snapped at you." He clasped his hands in his lap.

She stared. "Okay."

He tried to figure out how to lead the topic of conversation toward the two of them and the relationship he wanted to explore.

"You're wrong, though," she said.

Frowning, he sat again. "About what?"

"You need my help."

His vision narrowed, and a watery roar filled his ears. He thought of kissing her, and she wanted to "help" him?

"—Ted!"

Her shout brought him up hard and cleared away some of the pounding in his ears.

She held up her hands as if in surrender. "Don't fire me yet. Please."

He hadn't thought of firing her. At this point, she must know it was the furthest thing from his mind.

She gave him no chance to speak. "You have a multi-billion dollar company you created. You're smart. Brilliant. And your clients and employees value you. Nothing I say next is meant to call any of that into question, okay?"

He nodded.

"This place is huge. It's hard for me to hear, and I have two good ears."

His mouth relaxed of its own volition.

"The last time you were at this type of conference, you had an assistant with you. She paved the way, from what I understand, and made things easier for you. But you don't have her this time."

He took a breath. "You said you wouldn't."

At least she possessed the grace to look away. "I shouldn't have refused."

"Why did you refuse?"

"It's not important. What is important is you should have an assistant this time. It can be anyone you want. Not because you're not capable, but because it's easier."

"I want you." Would she recognize the double entendre? By her blush, she did.

"I still don't think I'm the right person for you, but I'll help you."

"And you still won't tell me why you wouldn't before?"

She shook her head. "Give me your schedule for today."

She was bossy, but she was right. And she spoke to him in more than one-word sentences. He showed her his schedule, and she entered it into her phone.

She met his gaze, and he relaxed.

"You have nothing scheduled for the next hour. What are your plans?" Abby asked.

"I should be on the show floor." The thought filled him with dread.

"I'll go with you, and we can leave in forty-five minutes for the next panel. You know, travel time," she said with a wink.

Maybe this wouldn't be bad. At least he'd get to be with her. They returned the way they came. Right before they entered the hall, she stopped.

"That's my phone. I'll turn it off."

"Anyone important?" he asked.

She shook her head. "It's my mother. I'll call her later."

"No, you should talk to her. I'll meet you inside." Once again, he entered the hall alone.

****

"Hi, Mom." Abby tried not to drool at the way Ted's long-sleeved oxford shirt emphasized the muscles of his retreating back.

"Hey, baby, where are you?"

"I'm at the tech conference. I told you about it."

"Oh, with your sexy boss. Mmm, must be fun. I'll bet you're getting lots of alone time with him."

Abby cringed. Her stomach clenched, and she swallowed as bile burned her throat. "I told you, Mom, I'm not interested."

"What, he's not successful enough for you?"

"Of course he is. He's tops in his field, and he's

116

richer than God." She rubbed her forehead. This conversation was pointless. "Did you call for a reason, Mom?"

"Yeah, I thought of coming to visit you while you're in New York. I figured I'd take a bus, and you could meet me and maybe sightsee."

Her mother lived in a dream world. "Mom, I'd love to see you, but I have to work. I don't have time to sightsee."

"Come on, they can't keep you busy all the time."

"My boss needs me. Why don't we talk after the conference, and we can find time to see each other? Okay?" Somewhere far away from Ted.

"Well, I'll look into the bus anyway. I can entertain myself, and I'm sure you can get away for a meal or something."

Her mother hung up before Abby could answer. Her headache blossomed into a full-fledged migraine. She squinted as she put her phone away and returned to the trade show floor. As usual, it was packed, and she wove her way in and out and around the masses until she reached the company booth. All she wanted was to curl into a ball in a dark room, but Ted stood in the middle of the space. People surrounded him. He needed her, which is why she'd given in and agreed to assist him, though every fiber of her being said to resist the pull of her mother's DNA. When he noticed her, his face brightened, and he strode toward her.

"You're back," he said.

"My mom wants to visit."

He frowned. "Bad timing. They expect a snowstorm at the end of the week."

She'd forgotten about it. It was the best news she'd

heard all day. "I'll tell her," she said. "Do you reach out to people or wait for them to approach?"

"I try to answer people's questions as they stop by."

"How about you let me run interference?"

With a quick nod, he followed her over to where people hovered around the computer terminals. A guy pushed forward and held out his hand to Ted.

"Caden McCurdy. Tell me about your penetration testing."

Abby put a hand on each of their arms and faced Caden. "I'm sorry to interrupt." She turned toward Ted. "When you're finished talking to Caden about penetration testing, I need you to meet someone over there." She enunciated her speech and watched his face brighten with understanding.

Ted explained to Caden how they kept their firewalls secure. Abby interjected a few times to clarify things for Ted, under the guise of relating it to her own programming.

After five minutes, Caden nodded and walked away. A woman and two men asked about cloud security. Once again, Abby asked questions when necessary. Her head was splitting, but Ted seemed more comfortable. She squinted and continued.

When they left, Ted's face softened. "You're a big help, but I'm concerned about you. You don't look well."

"It's a headache."

"How long have you had it?" He reached into his back pocket and withdrew a container that looked like it held contact lenses. He knocked out two pills. "Ibuprofen." He handed them to her.

"It started during one of the panels and got worse after I got off the phone with my mom." She winced and hoped he'd think it was from the pain. She hadn't meant to say that—it would create questions she didn't want to answer.

"Problem?"

She stared at his loafers. "It's nothing I'm not used to."

His index finger grazed the underside of her chin, and she raised her head.

"I missed what you said," he said.

Her cheeks heated, as much from realizing she'd messed up by not looking at him as in reaction to his touch. His skin was cool against hers, and she wondered what his hands would feel like on the rest of her body. Ugh. Too much talk with her mother caused this line of thought.

"I said I'm used to it. Every time she and I talk, it's a painful reminder of who I don't want to be. I won't let it interfere with my work."

"I'm not worried." His blue-eyed gaze pierced hers and, for a moment, she got the impression he could see her soul. When she remained motionless, he nodded and glanced at his watch.

"We should leave for the panel," he said.

With a nod, she walked to the hallway, grateful for the crowded show floor. If he couldn't walk next to her, he couldn't talk with her. She suspected one of these times, he wouldn't let her dodge his questions as easily.

****

Ted should have passed the rest of the afternoon in the panel sessions. Physically, he sat in his seat in the front row. He watched the mouths of the panelists and took notes on the main points and questions he'd ask later. But his focus was not on cybersecurity. It was on Abby and the secrets she kept. He started to think his own company's security protocols, some of the most stringent in the world, were nothing compared to her secret-keeping capabilities. He focused on her, instead of the panel discussion.

He would have enjoyed it if he could admire her physical beauty. She took his breath away. Maybe he should start carrying around a paper bag. Black, glossy hair begged to be touched. He wanted to trail his lips over every inch of her creamy skin. Long lashes framed silver eyes that noticed more than she should. Strawberry scent filled his nostrils. He longed for her when he shouldn't.

She's my employee.

She's more than that.

They were friends.

He had no worries about his lack of hearing. She understood, treated him like anyone else, and her ease at accommodating his hearing issues often surprised him. Around her, he'd started to believe it was no big deal when he confused words or sounds or missed entire conversations. She made him believe everything was okay.

Now, how to fix the "employee" problem?

Clapping motions startled him. Shit. The panel was over, and he hadn't focused on anything. Out of the corner of his eye, Abby's laptop screen caught his eye. Thank God Abby took notes.

"Greg texted me. We're getting together for dinner tonight in an hour," Abby said while they collected their things.

As they walked out of the room, Greg rode up the escalator toward them. He waved, but his face hardened, and his muscles tensed.

"Abby," Greg said in greeting. "Ted, can I talk to you a minute?" Usually Greg bantered, but right now, he was serious. Ted's stomach tightened as he wondered what security breach information Greg wanted to discuss. From his body language, it looked bad.

He nodded to Greg and turned to Abby. "Email me a copy of your notes."

"Sure. I'll see you both at dinner."

"What's going on with the security issue? Find out something?" Ted asked Greg as Abby walked away.

Greg waited until Abby left. Ted clenched and released his fist. He'd put Greg in charge of finding out what was going on. Out of all his employees, he trusted Greg the most. They'd known each other for years. Greg was as invested in the success of the company as anyone. Why was he stalling?

After Abby faded into the crowd, Greg pulled Ted into the empty conference room and shut the door. "You need to watch out when it comes to Abby."

Ted jerked. "You can't suspect her for the data breach."

"That's not what I'm talking about. I overheard her on the phone earlier today."

"Eavesdropping? Isn't that a little beneath you?"

Greg had the grace to flush. "I walked by, and she was loud."

He didn't know that about her. "So what?"

"She spoke to someone about you."

His blood warmed. Was it when she talked to her

mom?

"She mentioned how successful and rich you are and bragged about how much time she spends with you."

Ted's hands chilled. "Are you sure you heard right?"

"I walked right behind her as she said it."

She'd never acted like his money was important. But Greg heard her, and he wasn't hard of hearing.

"Maybe she referred to the success of the company."

"It's not the impression I got, and I'm concerned."

"She's never cared about how much money I have. Maybe you should focus more on the Sentec breach and less on eavesdropping." He winced. Even he knew how harsh he sounded.

Greg raised his chin. "I'm telling you what I heard. I know you're interested in her, regardless of how you try to hide it. Your gaze follows wherever she goes. I see the way you light up in her presence."

Ted's heart pounded in his chest. Was Greg the only one who noticed or were there others? Here he thought he'd been discreet. He had to back off, no matter how attracted to her he was.

Chapter Fourteen

Abby would give anything for some computer code right about now. Code she understood. Code behaved in specific ways all the time. Unlike Ted. She walked behind the group out the door of the restaurant. He ignored her when they arrived, sat at an angle at the table so talking to him was difficult, and resisted her attempts to get his attention.

"Ted!" Out on the sidewalk, she shivered from the cold as she raced to him and tapped his arm.

He jumped.

She maneuvered in front of him. "Is there something wrong?"

He frowned at her and remained silent.

Her face heated at the awkwardness. Her mouth moved as fast as her feet. "You don't act the way you normally do, not to me, and I don't know what happened…"

She stopped at the shuttered look on his face. His nostrils flared. "Never mind," she said and turned.

"Wait."

She paused. "Please talk to me."

He ran a hand through his hair, looked around, and gestured to her to follow him. Stepping toward an entryway, he opened the door and pulled her into a drugstore. Blinking, she looked around at the bright store with rows of medicine, groceries, batteries, and toys. He pulled her down an aisle and into the clinic area, where there were chairs.

She sat across from him and bit her lip. Her stomach fluttered. How in the world was she supposed to understand this man?

He sighed and looked away. After a moment, he faced her once again. "Greg heard you talk about how rich I am." He spat out the last few words.

She squinted at him—maybe it would clarify things. Right now, he made no sense. "What? When did Greg hear me say that?"

"Earlier today. You were on the phone."

Abby ran through her day. The phone call she'd taken was with her moth…oh no. She sank against the chair and held up a hand. "Wait. He missed the context."

Ted folded his arms across his chest and leaned back, like he was ready for a show. And she was the third-choice understudy.

She paced the waiting area, the weight of his stare on her. Her mother was none of his business. But he thought awful things about her.

Music played, the sound filtered into the store through speakers. How was she supposed to convince him?

With the truth.

Sort of.

"I talked about how successful you are as the CEO of a major computer security corporation. I was trying to explain to my mom how great my job is." In a roundabout way and for reasons she'd never tell him.

He looked at her and something shifted. His posture straightened, and for a moment, she thought what she'd said made him proud. But that couldn't be right. *Crap, he likes me.*

"Really?" he asked.

She nodded. It was a "sort of really." Her mother wanted her to reel him in, like some prize fish from deep in the ocean. In her mother's view, her worth was dependent on her ability to catch the big fish. She wanted Abby to take advantage of him for no other reason than he was rich.

She wanted to rail at the irony. Her entire life, she'd focused on financial independence. If she were to listen to her mother, she could have financial security, which in her mother's mind was better than independence. Only the one man who could ensure she'd never want for anything ever again was her boss.

A longing filled her chest, and she looked out over the store, decorated for Valentine's Day. Was he a romantic, card-sending man or not? And why did she care? *Crap, I like him, too.*

Abby shifted her focus to the paper cutouts of Cupid and hearts suspended from the ceiling.

"I hoped Greg misunderstood. I couldn't ask you without sounding…too personal," he said.

"There's one more thing," she said. "If we're honest with each other." He nodded, and it gave her the courage to continue. "This is the second or third time you've believed the worst of me. You've jumped to conclusions about me without giving me the benefit of the doubt, or at least confronting me about it. I know you're my boss, but I don't deserve that treatment."

Ted ran a hand across the nape of his neck, his skin flushed. "I have a knee-jerk reaction to when I think I'm being taken advantage of, but you've never behaved like that, and I should have believed in you. It won't happen again."

He was good at apologies. If they were a couple, their fights—and making up afterward—would be fun.

Once outside, the cold air bit into her skin. It refreshed her. Or maybe it was the knowledge she'd convinced Ted to believe her.

"It's too early to go to sleep," he said. "Feel like exploring?"

She nodded, and they walked around Times Square. Everything fascinated her—the people, the stores, and the theaters. Cars honked, people bustled by, and a rainbow of lights blinked. And, of course, there was Ted. He walked next to her, and she felt his presence though they were apart. But heat radiated off him, and his scent tickled her nostrils. She was in big trouble.

As they approached Rockefeller Center, he turned. "Want to skate?"

"I don't know how."

"I'll show you."

Skate with Ted? "Why?"

He rolled his eyes. "It's fun."

Fun. With Ted. Her internal dialogue sounded like a children's primary reader. "Okay."

Ted ushered her over to the skate rental and paid for them both. Finding an empty bench, he handed her the skates. "Don't lace them too tight, but don't let them gap, either."

She'd never be able to balance, much less skate on them. And skating with her boss was not going to lessen her attraction. Not sure why she agreed to this, she slipped her feet in the boots and laced them, covering the laces with the Velcro straps. Her leaden feet fell to the side when she stuck her legs out in front of her.

"Let's go." Ted stood.

Let's go? How the heck did you stand on these things? He held both hands out, lips only slightly quivering, and waited for her to place her hands in his. When she touched him, warmth spread through them up her forearms. His grasp was firm, and he tugged her to her feet without incident. They walked to the ice.

Now what?

"Ready?"

His voice was low, his breath warm, and somehow intimate, though they were in such a public place. He took her hand and led her into the rink.

I'm gonna fall, I'm gonna fall, I'm gonna fall.

Or not. He slid his arm around her shoulders. His embrace was heaven, and he skated with ease. The entire right side of her body was in constant contact with his. Her nerve endings zinged, and her skin heated.

Either way, she was in trouble. As she put space between them, her feet went out from under her, and she gasped.

She was falling for her boss.

****

Ted grasped Abby as she started to topple. Pulling her tight against him, he skated them to the rail and leaned against it, giving her time to get her feet back under her. Greg was right; Ted shouldn't hold her like this, but no one was around and with Abby everything felt right.

And he was enjoying her body against his. He stifled a groan. Soft breasts, delicate bones, strawberry-scented hair. He wanted her, more than he'd ever wanted another woman.

She'd bragged about his success to her mother? For a man who'd grown up with a dad who called him stupid, Abby's brag was more of an aphrodisiac than any sexy model ever could be.

He hugged her to him on the pretense of making sure she remained upright and waited for her to pull away.

Her lips moved, and he studied them, unable to hear her with the background music, the whoosh of air as they glided, the voices of the skaters, and traffic noise. He thought she said "thanks," and he nodded. When she started to speak again, he took his finger and placed it over her lips. They were velvety soft and pink, and he would have given anything to kiss them.

Instead, he shook his head. "I can't hear you. And lip reading is exhausting." He expected the usual shame to creep in. Maybe because she was out of her element here on the ice and relied on him. She clutched his hand as he guided them slowly over the ice. Maybe it was because he saw no pity. In fact, desire flashed. She blinked, and it was gone. But he'd seen it.

He could spend their entire time together wondering what conversations he missed. He could worry about what she thought, or about whether or not the CEO of the company should skate this close to his employee.

Or he could skate.

He held her close again, and they circled the rink. The cold air reddened her cheeks and nose. His hands should have been cold without gloves, but they weren't. Holding Abby, melding their bodies together, created a furnace between them. He was surprised the ice beneath their blades didn't melt.

They circled the rink once, twice, three times, and on their fourth turn, snowflakes fell. The sky glowed from the reflection of the lights on the clouds, which were so low, it seemed as if the tops of the buildings supported them. Abby shivered. He drew her close again as he stopped at the railing.

"Cold?" he asked.

She shook her head no.

If she wasn't cold…he leaned toward her, and her eyes darkened. Her lips parted, and his heart thumped in his chest. He wanted to kiss her more than he wanted to be able to hear the sound of his name on her lips.

She reached out and traced her finger across his cheekbone. When she pulled back, there was liquid from a melting snowflake on the tip, and a blaze of heat across his cheek.

"…never…snow…"

He caught the gist, and his shock at her comment broke the spell. "You've never seen snow?"

She shook her head. He wanted to ask her where she'd grown up, but this wasn't the place because of the noise of the tourists. Besides, it was late, and if he weren't careful, he'd do something he shouldn't.

Like kiss her next to the golden statue in Rockefeller Center.

He steered them toward the exit, and they returned their skates. Moving away from the noise of the rink, Ted took a deep breath when he could hear again.

"You want to walk in the snow or cab it?" he asked.

The look of joy on her face was contagious as she

held her hands out to collect snowflakes. He'd grown up in Ohio. Snow was nothing new to him, although he remembered how much he'd loved to play in it. He'd built huge forts in the snowdrifts, where sound was muted and light filtered through the flakes. The snowy walls offered a natural barrier and allowed him to dream of days when he'd be far away.

Like now.

Only this barely qualified as snow.

"I want to walk a little if you don't mind," she said.

He fell into step beside her. "They're calling for a blizzard, and it smells like one."

"Will we be able to get home?"

"This is New York. It can't stop functioning because of snow."

She shuddered. "I don't want to fly in a snowstorm."

"Me neither."

They walked the long trek to their hotel on city streets still not prepped for a blizzard. The snow melted on contact, and while some people looked up and noticed the flakes, most people ignored them.

Except for Abby. When they stopped at street corners and waited for the crossing sign to appear, she stuck her tongue out to taste them. He refrained from warning her how dirty New York snowflakes probably were—she enjoyed them too much, and he didn't want to ruin it. As they walked past well-lit restaurants and theaters yet to spit out their patrons, she held out her hands to touch the flakes. Meanwhile, he fought the urge to smooth them out of her hair, or trace them over her eyebrows.

By the time they got to their hotel, he was cold.

Abby brimmed with energy.

"You look like you could walk another thirty blocks," he said.

"In the snow? Absolutely."

"You realize this doesn't count as snow, right?"

"Is it white?"

"Yes."

"Is it cold?"

"Yes."

"Is it falling from the sky?"

"Yes."

"It's snow."

He grinned. "If you say so."

"How can you think it's anything else?"

They stood in the lobby of the building. Ted was loath to separate from her. He leaned against a pillar, hands in his pockets. "Where I'm from, this amount wouldn't make the weather report."

"Where is that?"

"Ohio. You?"

"Florida."

"Ah, it explains your lack of experience."

She raised an eyebrow. "Ohio is famous for snow?"

"We got our share of blizzards. I was a snow-fort expert."

"You were?"

He nodded. "I'd sit in them for hours."

"By yourself?"

"My friends disliked the silence." He never noticed a difference, and he liked the eerie bleached light and purple shadows. "I think they missed out on the smell."

"The smell?"

"Snow has a smell. Can't you tell?"

She frowned.

"Well, if this turns into a storm, you'll have to go outside and inhale. Trust me."

"Thanks for the skating tonight. I'm glad we cleared the air."

As he watched her walk away, his stomach clenched at the sudden emptiness Abby left in her wake. His hands ached to touch her, and he fisted them at his side. Could they move to the next level without jeopardizing their professional lives?

****

When Abby opened the curtains the next morning, the snow swirled in front of her window, streaked past building façades, and piled on corners. Her breath frosted the glass, and she looked in amazement at the streets below. Cars, which whizzed by yesterday, crawled along and fishtailed around turns despite their lack of speed. People hunched against the cold and slid along icy sidewalks. Even New Yorkers waited for lights to change and cars to stop before they crossed the street. The anticipated storm was here.

At breakfast, amid the aroma of frying bacon and percolating coffee, conversation about the storm was the main focus. Everyone pulled out their phones, checked their schedules, and double-checked their appointments.

"The conference is still slated to continue, for now." Greg lifted a forkful of eggs to his mouth. "Although they offer assistance with travel arrangements to anyone who wants to go home early."

Abby swallowed her coffee. *Get on a plane any earlier than necessary? No, thank you.*

"I'm planning to stay." Ted buttered his toast. "I still have meetings to attend. But if anyone wants to leave today, I'll have our plane available for you."

Cory and Tom looked at each other over their empty plates. "We're finished after lunch."

"I'm finished by three." Greg pushed his plate away.

"So go straight to the airport. You can take off by four." Ted's fingers flew on his phone keyboard. A waitress stopped with a refill of coffee, but he covered his cup with his hand.

Greg turned to Abby. "Want to come with us?"

She looked between Greg and Ted as she shook a packet of sugar. Clearly, Greg wanted her away from Ted. Did he see the attraction spark between them, or was he jealous Abby would have Ted's ear? The smart thing would be to go with Greg. He was her boss. But the thought of being stuck for six hours on an airplane with him filled her with loathing. He'd tattled on her to the CEO of her company. Under ordinary circumstances, she was afraid of flying. In a snowstorm? Her stomach lurched in fear. Time with Ted, on the other hand, sounded much more appealing, if no less dangerous. Snowflakes fell, and she swallowed as she glanced out the window. She should leave. He tempted her too much. Plus, the weather would get worse, and the sooner she left the better. But she was here to help Ted. If he stayed, shouldn't she?

Ted turned his head. "You decide."

She took a deep breath. "I'd rather wait out the storm. Also, there's a seminar I don't want to miss…"

She thought a spark of something flashed in his gaze, gone almost as fast as it appeared. "If you change your mind today, you can always leave with them."

Greg nodded, his jaw clenched. "I'll check in with you before I leave."

As everyone rose to go, Ted turned to her. "You don't need to stay for me. I know you don't like to fly."

"Pretty sure I'll like it less in the middle of a snowstorm."

He grinned. "True."

Abby bundled up and trudged with the others to the convention center. Although the hotel was a few blocks away, the bitter wind whipped around the buildings, froze her cheeks, and formed icicles on her lashes. Snowflakes stung her face, and the wind took her breath away. Her feet slipped on the sidewalk, and Ted reached for her. His rescues were becoming habit. She wanted to thank him, but it was too cold to stop and turn toward him.

By the time they entered the convention center, she was frozen, and the warm air cocooned her as she stamped the snow off her shoes and shook it from her hair. They coordinated schedules, arranged meeting times, and went off to start their day. Today was her busiest yet. Between her schedule and Ted's, there wasn't a moment to breathe. She'd have to figure out lunch later.

She touched his arm. "I'm off to a panel now, and I have a meeting with Greg. I'll meet you on the trade show floor afterward, okay?"

"Okay. I'm on the floor most of the afternoon, and I have interviews and potential client meetings all morning. I'll see you here when you're free."

"Will you be okay on your own?" She held her breath as she asked, expecting his pride to burst forth and his temper to flare.

But all of her previous reassurances must have made an impression. He nodded. "I'll be fine."

As she sat in on cloud security, she listened with one ear to the panelists and the other ear to the people around her who commented on the weather. Her phone, along with a hundred others, dinged with a weather warning.

Afterward, she met with Greg, who took her around the trade show floor and introduced her to a variety of industry professionals. While most of the conversations revolved around introductions and technology, a portion also discussed the weather. People were split about whether to leave early or remain until tomorrow. When they were finished, Greg walked her to their booth.

"What do you think?" he asked. "Are you willing to risk being snowed in here?"

More than anything, she wanted to confront him about what he'd said to Ted about her. But Greg was her boss, and she couldn't jeopardize her job. And maybe the snowstorm would turn into nothing. "I think I'll stay. There's the client dinner tonight with Carol where Ted needs my help, and there's one more session I want to go to tomorrow."

He looked at her, and she tried not to fidget under his scrutiny. She'd suspected for a while Greg disapproved of her working this closely with Ted, and his behavior now confirmed it.

"Are you Ted's assistant now?"

"You know we agreed I'd help him out."

Greg clenched and unclenched his jaw. "I'm concerned about how it looks for Ted and for the company."

"What do you mean?" Greg had warned Ted about her phone call with her mother. Did he still think she was after his money?

"Mixing business and pleasure is tricky, and I wouldn't suggest it, especially early in your career. In addition, we hope to go public in the next year or two. We can't afford a hint of a scandal."

She glared. "I have no intention of causing a scandal for the company."

He looked at her again for several seconds and nodded. "Make sure it doesn't become an issue."

Abby's gaze tracked Greg until he disappeared into the crowd, and her stomach squeezed at the threat. Greg was her immediate supervisor, and she wanted to protect her job security...no matter how sexy the CEO of said job might be. However, she disliked how he spoke to her. She brushed off the awful feeling the conversation caused. She needed to find Ted. She walked toward their booth and spotted him immediately.

Greg was there, huddled with Ted. She thought Greg's lips formed "Abby," but she couldn't tell for sure. A moment later Greg left, and someone else corralled Ted. He looked miserable. The strain on his face was evident. His posture was stiff. He needed a break. The din distracted her. How must he feel?

She had already reserved an interview room for Ted—well lit, quiet, and off the trade show floor. After texting her trade show liaison to direct all clients there, she walked over to Ted and interrupted the conversation.

"Excuse me." She gave a look of apology to the

three men next to Ted. "Ted, you need to get to your next appointment."

Confusion crossed his face, but he nodded. When the men stuck out their hands, he shook them and turned to Abby. From the expression on his face, it was clear he was exhausted. Squeezing his upper arm, she faced him and enunciated her words. "Come with me."

With a nod, he followed her to the room she'd reserved. The room was bright, per her instructions, so he could see to read lips, with a table along the back with snacks and drinks. A conference table sat in the middle, with connections for all kinds of technology products. She pointed to a chair, and Ted sank into it. Not wanting to exhaust him further, she texted him.

—You have 20 minutes to yourself. Relax. I'll let you know when the appointment is about to start.—

He whipped his head up from his phone and pinned her with his gaze. "I thought you said I needed to get to my next appointment?"

Crap. Would he object to her managing him? Her fingers flew across her keyboard.

—We forgot to agree upon a secret handshake for when you needed a break, and you looked like you needed one.—

He laughed and like a deflated balloon, all his tension disappeared. "My mistake."

She nodded and walked toward the door.

"Where are you going? And stop texting me; you can talk to me in here."

"I was going to give you some privacy until your appointment."

"It's not necessary."

"I would have thought you'd appreciate the alone

time."

He ran his hand across the nape of his neck. "You could use a break as well."

She might not be a body language genius, but she recognized his tells when he was uncomfortable. And he was uncomfortable with her leaving him here alone.

Interesting.

She sat at the conference table and placed her bag on the table. Rummaging around inside, she caught movement out of the corner of her eye. He'd stretched out in the chair, his khaki-clad legs up on a second one, head leaning against the high-backed headrest. The long-sleeved navy shirt with the company logo in the corner fit well enough to emphasize his chest muscles, especially when he folded his arms in front of him. His eyes were open, body facing both her and the door. Not how she would choose to relax, but if it worked for him…

Every time she moved, he followed her with his gaze, but if she turned to him, he looked away.

"Am I disturbing you?" she asked.

"No, why?"

"You're watching me. I thought you were going to rest."

"I'm resting."

She arched an eyebrow at him, and he looked away for a moment.

"Don't worry about me," he said. "You won't disturb me."

Don't worry about the gorgeous man staring at me? Right. Pulling out her laptop, she checked emails, reexamined the schedule, and looked at weather reports. The trade show floor was still packed when she was out there a few minutes ago, but the forecast called for a major storm, and airports already experienced delays. She would sit out the storm. There was no way she'd get on an airplane in a major snowstorm, even if the FAA let the planes take off.

With five minutes to go before the first interview, she put away her laptop and rose. As expected, Ted watched her.

"Ready?" she asked.

He let his feet fall to the floor, sat straight in the chair, and arranged his computer and other paraphernalia in his space at the table in a fluid motion Abby wouldn't have been able to picture if she wasn't there. It confirmed what she'd thought—he wasn't resting.

"Want me to sit across from you or next to you?"

"Across," he said. "If I'm stuck, I'll glance at you."

"And I'll text anything I think you need."

His eyes twinkled. "Managing me again?"

"Who, me?" She winked and left to get the first client, her face warm at the chuckle behind her.

Chapter Fifteen

Ted groaned as Abby shut the door of the private conference room behind the last of his appointments of the day. Four hours of interviews, client meetings, and client pitches. Four hours of eyestrain as he stared at various colored lips—pink, beige, red—and various shaped mouths—thin lines, puckered, plump, and hidden in facial hair. The last was the most difficult, but without Abby, he would have been lost.

She'd helped him throughout, often jumping into the conversation to give him a moment to rest. No matter who else was in the room, he was always aware of her. Right now, she sat across the table from him.

His wrist buzzed, and he read the texts that came in—one from the rest of his team who were about to board their flight, and one from Carol, canceling dinner.

It was just as well. He wanted to sleep for a thousand hours.

His wrist buzzed again. Abby. He frowned. Why did she text him?

—I think we're free until dinner with Carol.—

"Why—" He started to ask her, but the expression on her face, one of understanding and concern, without a trace of pity, stopped him. Floored him. Filled him with appreciation at her consideration. As with the rest of her actions throughout the day, she made things easier on him. Though he'd never admit it, he was grateful not to read any more lips, not even her delectable ones.

"She canceled," he said.

—I guess you're off the hook.—

With anyone else, he would have packed his things and gone to the hotel room, where he would collapse onto the bed and fall asleep. Or gone to the gym and worked out until his body was as tired as his eyes were. But Abby? This was the perfect opportunity to find out if she knew anything about the Sentec breach. And maybe discuss her feelings about interpersonal relationships in the office. The second topic of conversation was less likely, but he'd still be a fool to let her go.

"I need some air," he said. "Want to go for a walk?"

She looked at him like he was insane, then typed: *—You realize there's a snowstorm outside, right?—*

"Yes."

—They've canceled flights, people are staying in, and you want to go out?—

"I thought you liked the outdoors."

—I like jogging, not sliding on icy sidewalks and getting pelted by razor-sharp pieces of frozen water.—

"Where's your spirit of adventure?" He goaded her and loved her reaction. Sitting across from him, blinking at him, her eyes reminded him of mercury— never still and changing depending on her mood. He suspected if he weren't her boss, she'd jump out of her seat, place her hands on her hips, and actually tell him he was insane. But she kept her body in tight control. Only the whiteness of her knuckles as she gripped her phone, and the turbulence in her gaze told him he had her.

Until she pushed away from the table, marched around to him, and poked his upper arm. Beneath his oxford, his skin burned at the contact. When he met her fierce gaze, she nodded, strode to the door of the conference room, and shut off the light when he was right behind her. The show floor was almost empty. People with any sense left earlier in the afternoon.

Her strawberry scent wafted around him, disorienting him for a moment. When he realized she'd left him behind, he hurried to catch up. Without hordes of people around the different booths, they traversed the floor quickly, reaching the lobby area. The tiny drill sergeant next to him kept her pace until his nose pretty much touched the glass of the front door. If his other employees could see him now. He smiled, distracted once again, until her movement caught his eye. She tapped a finger on the window. His gaze shifted from outside to her and back again.

"You want to go for a walk in this?????"

Although it was now dark outside, the brightness of the snow and the contrast of light against dark showed how the snow whirled in circles. Drifts formed on the sidewalk, snow accumulated in the street, and the only people outside huddled against the building as they waited for a taxi or smoked.

"We'll never find a taxi in this weather," he said. "Bundle up. We'll have to walk the six blocks to the hotel, like it or not."

She opened her mouth, closed it, pulled out her phone, looked at it, and put it in her bag.

What did she hold back?

With a nod, they returned to where they'd stored

all of their coats and bags.

Bundled like Eskimos, they opened the doors of the convention center, hunched their bodies, and braced against the wind. Ted reached for Abby, and she took his hand. Why did he hold it? To help her against the wind. Employees shouldn't be allowed to blow away in the storm—she wasn't Mary Poppins. *Yeah, right.* It was unrelated to his insane desire to keep her close, to touch her.

And it was slippery. The city hadn't yet sent its plows through, and no one had salted the sidewalks. At the corner, wind from all directions swirled around them. He pushed Abby behind him to protect her as they turned the corner. The six blocks, which were bracing earlier in the week, were exhausting now. By the time they reached their hotel, he was frozen.

He turned to Abby, and his mouth dropped. Covered in snowflakes, she looked like a glittery snow angel, sparkling and rosy.

"Don't you dare laugh at me."

Laugh at her? She was beautiful. Her cheeks and nose were red; her eyes glittered as much as the snow droplets on her hair and eyelashes. For the first time since he'd admitted his attraction to her, he didn't want to touch her. He'd melt all the snow and ruin the effect.

She folded her arms across her chest and tapped her upper arm. Her mouth quirked. "Maybe I should stare at your ears?"

He jerked, before his entire body relaxed and warmth flooded through him. She'd teased him like a normal person, not like an employee. It felt damn good.

"Touché," he said.

By now, the snow melted to water, and Abby

shook out her damp hair. He wanted to reach out and grab a hank of it, wind it around his hand, bury his face in it. Instead, he stuck his hands in his pockets and looked over at the bar.

"Want to get a drink?" he asked.

Her gaze roved between him and the bar. "Let me change into dry clothes."

Good idea. His pants cuffs were wet, his thighs caked with snow.

After changing into jeans, he returned to the bar, ordered a whiskey, and waited for Abby to arrive. He nursed his drink and looked around. It was small and New York hip, in blues, violets, and blacks with silver accents. There was background music, which he couldn't identify. A few guys sat with drinks, but the place was mostly empty.

The amber liquid was dignified, dry, and warmed him as it slid down his throat. He sputtered when Abby walked to him and sat on the stool next to him, his nerve endings alert, body tight. She'd changed into a red shirt with a wide neck and a pair of curve-hugging jeans. If he thought she was beautiful before… He should stop drinking right now and keep his wits about him, but instead, he took another gulp and flagged the bartender. Turning to Abby, he asked, "What do you want to drink?"

"Whatever you're having." He liked the implied trust and ordered her a whiskey.

She nodded her thanks and took a gulp as her gaze traveled around the room.

There was less noise here. He should talk to her, take advantage of her momentary lapse in employee/employer correctness.

Her mouth lifted.

"What are you smiling about?" he asked.

She pressed her lips together, but she couldn't prevent the sparkle in her eyes. "The last time I drank whiskey in a bar, my friends and I played truth or dare."

Some of the dullness in his brain went away. "Which friends?"

"College friends," she said. "There were six of us on full scholarship, working three jobs, and taking classes. We bonded over caffeine in the morning and various kinds of alcohol on our little time off."

God, her mouth was beautiful. "And you played drinking games?"

Her gaze shifted, and he watched her eyes turn various shades of gray. They were like storm clouds rolling across the sky, and he wondered what she thought.

"Yes, I had a friend, Nate, who liked to assign different games to different drinks. Whiskey was 'Drink or Dare.' "

She took another sip, and her mouth curved around the rim of the glass.

"How did it work?"

"There's an app with categories of dares. We'd take turns putting someone in charge of choosing the category—for instance, fantasy dares, college dares, etc. We'd go around the table, and you either took the dare or drank."

He'd never felt old before, but learning about a drinking game app made him feel ancient. Any moment his bones would start to creak, and his hair would turn gray. He took another gulp of whiskey, and his body warmed.

"What kinds of dares were there?" he asked. "Give me an example."

"I'm sure you can use your imagination," she said. "Walking up to someone and saying some random thing. Removal of clothing items."

"And did you drink or dare?"

"It depended on the night."

The last of his reserve evaporated. "Want to try it now?" he asked.

"With my boss?"

"We're already drinking together." It would be a great way to find out what she knew about the Sentec breach. If anything.

"I don't have the app."

He leaned forward. "So we'll adapt. I'll ask you a question; you either answer or you drink. Then you can ask me a question." If he worded his questions right, he could satisfy Greg's concerns and also find out more about Abby as a person.

"I think this could get awkward."

"You can stop at any time," he said. "I won't get you wasted. In fact, you can switch to water if you'd prefer." She was tiny. He'd bet her alcohol capacity was much less than his. He'd have to remember to pace himself, as well as not pressure her to drink too much.

"Whiskey's fine. For now. But I reserve the right to change the subject."

He pushed his glass to the center of the table and folded his arms. "What are your thoughts about Sentec's security?"

Her body jerked. Did his question surprise her? "You're asking me a work question?"

"It's our common experience. I thought you would

be more comfortable, at least to start."

When she bit her lip, he clenched his hand beneath the table as he fought his body's reaction to her sexiness. Right now, he needed to focus on the business side of things.

"The company or the code?"

"Either." He studied her—her expression, body language, and of course, her lips.

She leaned forward. "I have some concerns."

He studied her, looking for subterfuge, or anything that looked off. She was sincere. "About what?"

She fiddled with her glass. "There are some lines of code that don't add up."

If she were the problem, it would be in her best interest for her to answer as she had. Except his question was general enough for her to comment on other aspects of the company. "Such as?"

"I think there might be some weaknesses that could lead to a breach."

She focused on him. Her body was tense but without a hint of guilt.

"Can you be more specific?"

"I gave you my report. I'd be happy to show you what concerns me, but I'd rather wait for you to look at it first. But I also gave it to Greg."

Her body language gave him the impression she kept nothing from him. Was she uncomfortable? Yes. But there could be many reasons for her discomfort. His gut told him she wasn't the source. He was still worried about the breach, and he'd have to find out who might have caused it, but he'd bet his fortune it wasn't her. He'd talk to Greg and dig further later. Without alcohol to soften his edges, and when his body stopped humming with desire.

"Besides," she added. "It's my turn to ask you a question."

He nodded. What would she ask him?

"What's your biggest fear?"

He coughed. What should he say? Heights? Needles? "Failure." Swallowing, he watched her astonishment mirror his own.

"That surprises me."

"Why?" He was a glutton for punishment.

"You're a success with your own company. What's left?"

So many things. He stared into his whiskey tumbler and watched the light reflect off the cut crystal. He had buckets of money, but what good was it without anyone to share it? Sure, CAST helped him feel good about his investments—philanthropically, he was a success. But the days passed alone, and he wanted to belong to someone. Someone who valued him for who he was. There was a part of him that started to think maybe she was the one.

****

Abby waited for his answer. Individual spotlights over each booth lit the space enough for him to read her lips. At least, she assumed he was able to read them and hear her since he hadn't indicated a problem. He hadn't gotten the telltale frown between his brows, hadn't pasted the blank expression across his face when he misunderstood. Why was he silent?

She'd never been around anyone more successful than him. Other than the times when he couldn't hear, he oozed confidence and ability. And the times he couldn't hear? He successfully hid his disability.

Therefore, what was left?

"My personal life."

He spoke in a low voice, and she almost missed it.

"What do you mean?"

He rubbed the nape of his neck, pulled at his collar, and swirled his whiskey in his glass. The amber liquid sloshed around the sides of the glass. It mesmerized her.

"It's hard to have a personal life when you work all the time. On the rare occasions I go out, most women date me for my money."

Or his body. All his lean muscle mass, chiseled features, and fluid grace. But she wouldn't say it. "I never thought of failure that way."

"Why not?" he asked.

It was a foreign concept. "I guess because growing up with a mother who went through men like kids go through shoes, I always focused on other things like grades and my future." Nerves made her jittery. Here she was with her boss...so many things could go wrong. "My mother was broke and depended on men for everything. I never wanted to be like her." Attraction warred with fear and tightened the muscles in her stomach. "To me, you can't be a failure if you're successful at what you do."

What would Ted think of her confession? She couldn't bear to look at him, to see the pity in his gaze. She took a drink and glanced around the room. There were a couple of men—one at the bar, another at a table in the corner—and none of them appealed to her like Ted. She looked up when he reached for her hand. Surprise and sympathy—not pity—glowed in his eyes. She exhaled. His grasp was warm and firm and sent prickles of desire running down her arm.

"I'm sorry," he said. "I've been hard of hearing since I was a child. I had a ton of ear infections, and the doctors put tubes in my ears. Unfortunately, there were complications and my ear drums tore, causing more of a hearing loss."

"The doctors couldn't fix it?" She appreciated his getting personal so she wouldn't be the only one, and she should probably stop, but she couldn't resist getting all the information she wanted.

"No, they were afraid I'd lose all my hearing. Although, at this rate, I'm not sure it would have been much of a difference." He swallowed. "People often mistake my lack of hearing for lack of intelligence."

She squeezed his hand. He returned the squeeze and quickly released her.

She wrapped her hand around the whiskey tumbler and stared into the depths of the amber liquid. The cool glass against her Ted-warmed skin helped clear her mind. If she wasn't careful, she could fall for him. Hard.

"I always vowed I'd never be dependent, like my mother, on a man," she said. She should walk away to stop her heart from falling. But she suspected it wouldn't work.

Ted reached across the table and tipped her chin, and she repeated what she'd said. She was tempted to lower her head once more to feel his skin against hers, but it would be foolish.

"I saw what happened each time my mom chose a man who had no feelings for her. I never wanted to see the same hollow look in a man's eye when he looked at me. I never wanted to have to be with someone in order to feed myself or my child. So I learned to code." And never got serious with a man.

Ted's gaze shifted away from her mouth, and the room faded away. His blue eyes shone with compassion and understanding. They pulled her in, like some silky blue rippling cord connecting her to him. His pupils darkened, his mouth parted, and his phone buzzed, breaking the connection as he looked at the text.

She wasn't about to fall for her boss. Too late. Tipping her glass, she drowned out her conscience with the rest of the whiskey.

"Hey, I thought we were playing." Ted turned his phone over.

"We weren't good at it, and I'm starved." Must be why the butterflies in her stomach were fluttering, right?

"Do you want to have dinner?"

With him? More than anything. "I think I'll go upstairs and order room service and maybe watch a movie. We're leaving tomorrow morning?"

He nodded. "Let's meet downstairs at nine."

She refused to look back, to think about what might have been. Otherwise, she'd never keep her hands off him.

****

Ted paced his hotel room, finding no solace in the silence. Alone, he'd removed his aids. Yet the snow falling outside his window reminded him of his potential folly.

They should have left with the rest of the team earlier in the day. Taking off tomorrow would be dicey, which meant there was a chance they'd be stuck here together for longer than anticipated. He'd been able to get to know Abby better personally. His attraction to her grew with each layer he peeled away, but could he afford to focus on his personal life when he needed more information about the security breach? He'd told Greg he'd use this opportunity to find out if Abby was responsible. Since she wasn't, he should move on, too. The success of his company depended on finding and stopping the breach. What the hell kind of computer security expert was he if he took time off from his responsibility to spend more time with his sexy employee? Why the hell did he call her sexy?

She is.

Some days he wished his lack of hearing applied to his ability to hear his inner voice. He sighed. He'd call Greg in the morning and have him forward all his notes, as well as start to focus on other programmers. His gut burned at the idea of someone trying to ruin his company.

His watch buzzed. At two o'clock in the morning? He looked at Caleb's name. Ah, California time. The text was to all of CAST.

—When are we talking next about our ideas for our next donation?—

—Back in CA tomorrow hopefully. Can discuss anytime.— Ted answered.

—Up late, jetlag?— Caleb asked.

Ha. More like Abby-lag. *—Yeah.—*

—How's the snow? I miss skiing.—

Caleb owned a ski house in Colorado. Ted had visited it a time or two, and it was gorgeous.

—There's a lot. Not sure about travel tomorrow. And trying to get to the bottom of problem.—

—Good luck and be safe. Maybe you should stay

put.—

That was Caleb, always the caretaker.

Ted paused, the kernel of an idea planted in his mind.

—I have a potential idea for investment. Need more research before I discuss.—

—Sounds good.—

When he and Caleb stopped texting, Ted grabbed his computer and stretched out on the bed. The glow from his computer screen was the sole light in the room and through his open curtains he could see the snow continue to fall. Something Abby said earlier struck a chord. Caleb gave him an idea. If he couldn't sleep tonight, he might as well be useful.

Chapter Sixteen

At nine the next morning, Abby's sleepy little boutique hotel was anything but sleepy. The chic lobby overflowed with people trying to check out and get help with transportation in the middle of a snowstorm. The concierge, hotel desk staff, and the bellhops lost their New York blasé attitude and were harried. This did not bode well.

She scanned the crowded lobby and spotted Ted behind a mass of people at the front desk. His hand covered a yawn. She flashed a quick smile and joined him in line.

"Bad night?"

He nodded. "I couldn't sleep."

Despite her confused thoughts about Ted, the whiskey had relaxed her enough to sleep once she settled. Either she'd drunk more than he did or he had other things on his mind.

The people in front of him stepped forward, but he reached for her and turned her toward him. "My pilot won't fly in the storm, so we can't leave, unless you want to try to get a commercial flight."

"In this storm?" She raised an eyebrow. "I don't want to fly in this weather, but you can if you want."

Something flickered in his gaze. "Let's extend our hotel rooms, and we can figure out our next steps."

When it was their turn, the desk clerk scanned her

computer. "You were due to check out today, and the rooms have already been taken. I've got one room. Everything else is gone. It's yours if you want it."

Abby turned to Ted. "What do you want to do?"

"Let's take it and see if there are any other hotels in the area with available rooms."

They got the key from the clerk and sat on the zebra-print sofa in the lobby. Abby pulled out her phone.

"I'll call them," Abby said. Fifteen minutes later, she faced him. "There's nothing within thirty blocks of here. I don't know how we'd get to anything farther with the ice and our luggage." Her stomach churned. How were they supposed to stay in one room?

Ted placed a hand on her arm. "Let's take our luggage to the room. We'll figure out the rest when we get there."

The elevator was crowded. People chattered about the inconvenience of the storm. It stopped on each floor, and they exited on the fourth. Swiping his new key card against the electronic lock, Ted held the door open for Abby to enter.

She walked halfway into the room and stopped dead. Her body flashed hot and cold.

There was only one bed.

****

If he weren't focused on the shape of her backside in her jeans, and the wiggle of her hips as she walked, he would have plowed right into her when she stopped in the middle of their room. But he avoided a collision in time. He peered beyond her into the room.

In the middle of the room sat the king-sized bed.

A bed they'd have to share.

This was not part of his plan. No matter how much better he wanted to get to know her, no matter how much time he wanted to spend with her alone, forcing her to share a bed was not his plan. He swore beneath his breath. At least, he thought he did. But she remained unfazed. He was safe.

Safe from her knowledge of how the thought of sleeping in the same bed with her made all the blood rush to his groin. Not safe from her, though. Not at all.

"There's one bed," he said. No one could knock his keen powers of observation.

She nodded. He touched her shoulder, and she turned around. "Uh, yeah." She was pale, and her gaze darted back and forth, as if somehow willing a second bed to appear.

They walked further into the room, and he squeezed the handle of his bags. The leather dug into the palm of his hand. He focused on the bed they were somehow supposed to share. Heat traveled through his body, and his throat dried. No matter how large it was, any bed with her in it was too small.

He swallowed against the bitter taste in his mouth. He should walk out, find a private space, and call Greg. Focus on business instead of her. But he couldn't.

You like her.

He needed time away from her to call Greg and to let his body cool off.

He handed her the room key and backed away. "You take the room," he said. "I'll figure something else out."

"That's ridiculous. You take it. I'm sure they'll have a cot, or extra blankets or a pillow, and I can crash on the couch in the lobby."

His muscles tightened. "There's no way in hell I'll let you stay in the lobby, even if they allow it, while I take this room."

She took a step back. "Why not?"

How could she wonder about this? "I don't leave women in the lurch."

She arched a brow. Her mouth was pinched, and he'd swear fiery daggers shot from her eyes. She hated being singled out for her gender as much as he hated being reminded of his difficulty hearing. "Women? Going sexist on me now?"

He tapped his fingertips on his thigh and ignored how sexy she looked when angry. "So what? You're not sleeping in the lobby."

Her face whitened. "I can't sleep in the bed with you."

Why the sudden fear? He couldn't sleep there with her either, but he wasn't afraid. Lustful, maybe, and aware he shouldn't be, but scared? He tried to calm his voice and swallowed his exasperation at the futility. "It's a king. There's plenty of room. Or maybe they have an extra cot."

She paced. Her lips moved. He frowned. Although it was the two of them in the room, for some reason, he couldn't hear her. She must have whispered. He clenched his jaw and wished she'd stay still long enough for him to read her.

"Stop," he commanded.

She jumped. He must have yelled louder than he intended. Volume was a pain in the ass to control.

"Sorry, what did you say while you paced?" To anyone else, it would have killed him to admit he couldn't understand them, but he'd grown comfortable with her…to an extent.

Her apology appeared in her gaze. "I can't sleep there with you."

Heat flooded through him. "You said that already. I don't see much of a choice. Can you call downstairs to ask about a cot?"

She nodded and turned away. Two minutes later she turned back. "They're all taken. I can't sleep here with you."

"We don't have a choice," he said.

"But…I work for you."

She covered her mouth, and he fisted his hands in order to hide the urge to pull her hand away…or kiss it. He inhaled sharply, choked, and turned away to cough. When he recovered, he scanned the room and stared once again at her stricken face. She was his employee, and she was in a terrible predicament—stuck in one room, with one bed, with her boss. Sympathy welled. He needed to help her, no matter how much he desired her.

"Look, let's call the airport and see if there's any way we can fly home," he said. "Maybe another pilot will be available." He'd fix this, even if his heart pounded with desire. Her hand on his arm stopped him.

"There's no point. Even if flights take off, there's no way I'll get on a plane now. I won't fly in a snowstorm."

Heat ricocheted up his arm at her touch. "Let's see if they have any extra blankets, and I'll make a pallet on the floor," he said. "You can take the bed."

She looked at the floor. "You can't sleep there. I'll sleep on the floor."

He glared. "No way. You're not sleeping on the

floor."

Her gray eyes flashed, and the silver specks in their depths reminded him of an icy lake. "More of your 'lurching women' problem?"

Lurching…oh. He struggled not to laugh. He needed to keep the upper hand in order to win this argument.

"Something like that," he said.

She waved her hand like she swatted a fly. "Whatever, floor or bed it doesn't matter. I can't sleep here. People will talk."

She turned as if she was about to bolt, and he reached for her. Her body was soft and warm. The scents of strawberries and mint wafted around him. Her jet-black hair was swept in a messy bun, and the flyaway strands stuck out at all angles. Probably shouldn't mention it, though.

He raised an eyebrow. "What people?" Swinging his arm around, he showed her the empty room. "We're the only ones here."

"Work people."

"How will they know?"

"You won't tell them?"

He withheld a snort. "My assistant and I sharing a room? Right, doesn't sound fishy at all." She wasn't the only one concerned about reputation.

"I'm not your assistant. I'm an assistant security programmer, who happens to be assisting you on this trip."

He shook his head at the irony and turned away. Usually he was the one with the bug up his ass about needing any help. Yet she argued about her title? Her hand on his arm made him turn to her again.

159

"Look, you don't understand what it's like as a woman."

He raised an eyebrow. "You're right, I don't. But," he continued, "I know what it's like to have unwanted gossip about my abilities—or disability. I've worked damned hard to cement my reputation, and I'm not about to risk it, either, which is why I won't tell anyone."

Relief softened the curve of her mouth before she pulled up short. "But then it's a secret, and if it gets out it's worse."

He folded his arms across his chest. "So what's the solution?"

She sank onto the bed, which barely dipped under her weight. "I don't know. But we shouldn't both be here."

She was right. "And under normal circumstances, we wouldn't be." He sat next to her, careful not to crowd her, but close enough to hear her. He chose his words with care. "There's a snowstorm outside, and all the hotels are taken. We have the last room, and we don't have a choice. If it gets out, which I doubt it will, these are extenuating circumstances."

"Extenuating enough for me to survive the gossip and keep my job?"

If word got out, he'd ensure she suffered no consequences. He'd somehow put the onus on him. "Yes."

She looked at him askance, and he returned the look. After a moment, she relented.

He bumped her shoulder. "Okay now?"

She nodded.

Was he? He was about to share a bed with the

woman he was falling for.

****

Oh God, now what? Abby lay in the bed. In the dark. Next to Ted. Listening to him breathe. Just the thought boggled the mind. Her boss was gorgeous. He was intelligent. He was single. And he lay next to her. Okay, if you wanted to be technical about it, he lay about eighteen inches away from her, but she doubted those inches would count for much if anyone found out. Whoever said size didn't matter had never tried to sleep with their boss.

And there was the crux of her problem. There was no way she would sleep with him next to her. She took a deep breath, calmed her nerves, and inhaled a whiff of minty toothpaste and soap. Her stomach clenched, and she moaned. Since when was toothpaste and soap sexy?

The bed jostled, and the bedside lamp glowed. Ted looked at her. "Did you say something?"

Tell me he didn't hear me. She frowned and covered her mouth.

He leaned over and pulled at her hand. "I can't read your lips behind your hand."

Now he was much closer than eighteen inches.

She sat and faced him, legs crossed. It mortified her to have to maintain eye contact with the man she lusted after when they were in bed together.

"No. Wait. You sleep with your ears in?"

He raised his hands to the sides of his head. "My ears?" Comprehension dawned. "You mean my aids?"

His cheeks formed a large dimple, like a parenthesis, on either side of his mouth when he smiled, and Abby stared, fascinated.

"No, I don't sleep with my ears in. The bed

vibrated."

"Oh." Too bad the vibration wasn't from some other activity. In her mind, she slapped herself for the thought. She was not her mother.

He tipped her head. "So you said nothing?"

She shook her head.

"But you're not asleep."

"No." *I never will be, now that I know what your bare stomach looks like.* She'd seen a glimpse of it when he'd removed his button-down shirt to go to sleep. His T-shirt rode up before he'd pulled it down. Someone said tech geeks were flabby. That someone was wrong. This tech geek was wiry, lanky, but well built, with sculpted muscles. Not an ounce of flab. And below that? Well, she wouldn't look.

Her gaze wobbled.

She shouldn't look.

Her throat went dry.

"Problem?"

"No," she whispered, dragging her gaze to his face. Was it her imagination, or were his cheekbones a little ruddy?

"Well, you should try to sleep. If you need music or something, feel free. It's not like it will disturb me."

He smiled again, and there was something soft about it. It wasn't like those he'd given earlier to others, the kind that only stretched his lips. This one reached his eyes, which in this half-light looked crayon blue. He remained seated, watching her. She lay down and curled on her side.

Once she was settled, he shut off the light.

Sure, she'd try to sleep. And if she couldn't, instead of sheep, she could count his ab muscles.

Chapter Seventeen

Ted woke the next morning from the vibrations of Abby walking around. Cracking his lids open, a sliver of light escaped beneath the closed bathroom door. The scent of strawberries poured from it. He inhaled. It was feminine and light and…her. His cock stirred. The little top and pajama pants she wore last night had almost killed him.

He lay in bed and remembered how the light blue top accentuated her breasts. Her blue and green plaid flannel pajama pants rode low, showed a small swath of skin, and drew attention to her hips. Her rear? Good God, he'd wanted to cup it in his hands and squeeze. Instead, he clenched his hands at the image of her leaping into the air with a scream. And the totally deserved sexual harassment lawsuit he'd face.

His stomach twisted. Twenty-four hours later, common sense had smacked him on the head. He grabbed his computer and connected to his work server. Then he reached for his phone and texted Greg.

—*Abby isn't responsible for the security breach. Expand the search and let's talk when you get this.*—

He looked up the airport. No matter how much she hated to fly, he owed her the chance to get home as soon as possible. Although the storm itself passed, massive delays and advisories were posted. Highways around the airport were closed, and the governor declared a state of emergency. There was nothing to be done about travel now.

He reached for his aids and put them in. He never removed them in front of other people. He'd never spent the night with a woman without them. But Abby was no longer "other people." The scent of strawberries grew stronger as he approached the bathroom and put his hand against the door. Inside, he heard noise, but it was hard to distinguish—a shushing sound meant she was in the shower. He hardened as images of her naked, with water sluicing down her body, took his breath away.

Rushing to the bed, he pulled his laptop out of its case, put it on his lap, opened his email, and channeled every stereotypical geeky aspect of his personality. Anything to distract from thoughts of her. Plus, it helped to hide his reaction. After he read the same email three times, he slammed his laptop cover closed.

"Problem?"

He jumped as Abby walked in. Her hair was wrapped in a towel, and she was dressed in jeans and a sweatshirt. Her feet were bare, and his gaze traveled to her blue-painted toes. Wrenching his gaze away, he looked at cheeks rosy from the shower. A lock of wet hair escaped from her turban, and a droplet of water shimmered in the hollow of her collarbone. He should have stuck with the toes.

"Uh…"

"You swore at the computer. Anything I can help with?"

"Nah, I'll grab a quick shower, and we can go to breakfast."

"All yours." She pointed to the bathroom, and he

swallowed the question he longed to ask—want to join me?

The invitation would be stupid. And get him sued. With a groan that rumbled in his chest, he locked the bathroom door, entirely unsure if it was to keep her out, or him in.

Feminine things covered the countertop. Nothing was messy, but her pink toothbrush rested in a glass next to his. Her travel bag, quilted, colorful, and pretty, was on the opposite side of the counter from his. And in the shower were bottles of who knew what kind of female-scented things. He was better off not checking. He stepped into the shower.

And jumped right out again when he realized he'd forgotten all about his aids. She and her feminine things distracted him. He might have more money than he could ever spend, but he wasn't a proponent of sending $10,000 down the drain.

Between distraction, trying to pay extra attention, and attempting not to think about the beautiful woman who was on the other side of the tile wall, his shower took three times longer than usual. By the time he was finished, dried, and dressed, his stomach growled.

"Ready for breakfast?" he asked as he walked into the room.

She nodded and hopped off the bed, shut off her computer, and joined him in the hallway. Her hair was still wet, and the sight of her braid was intimate, for some reason. His normal vision of her was at a bank of computers with the other programmers, and although she dressed better than any of them, this was different. His body hummed with heightened awareness.

The lobby was filled with people, and the hotel

Jennifer Wilck

restaurant was packed. The hostess led them to a small table right near the buffet line, where Ted paused.

"Are there any other tables further away from here?"

"I'm sorry, sir, but this is our only available table right now."

With a sigh, he sat.

"Can I get you anything to start?" She handed them menus.

"It's fine," he responded. Which, by the confused look on her face, was not the correct response to her question.

"How about coffee?" Abby asked, and Ted looked at her with relief.

The waitress returned a moment later with the coffee pot and poured.

"Are you ready to order?"

"Just milk," he said.

Once again, she looked confused.

"I think we need a few more minutes," Abby said. "And can we have skim for the coffee?"

Ted rose, chest tight. "I'm going to the room."

"No." Abby reached for his arm.

He looked at her hand, pale against his darker skin. Was she really going to force him to explain it?

She shook his arm, and he looked at her. "Stay. Please."

"It's too noisy."

Pulling out her phone, she typed. A second later, his wrist buzzed.

—*Please stay. I'll handle the waitress.*—

—*I don't want you to have to handle the waitress.*—

166

He was truculent, but he didn't care.

—Ok, you can continue to play who's on first until she gives up, and you starve.—

—Not a lot of people would talk to their boss this way.—

—Lucky for you.—

She'd provided the same assistance for him at the conference, and he'd appreciated it. But his defenses were primed now. It was personal. He let out a deep breath. This was his life. He was still embarrassed, though.

—You win.—

His gaze flicked between his screen and her face, looking for some reaction to his text.

His watch buzzed again.

—Shall we get in line for the buffet?—

With a quick sip of his coffee, he rose and held her chair. When they'd chosen their food, they put their phones on the table face up and ate. An old woman walked past and grumbled.

"Such a nice-looking couple, and you're not paying attention to each other. You two should talk to each other, not bury your faces in cell phones." She walked off.

—Do I want to know what she said?—

Abby leaned on her hand, shoulders shaking. When she calmed, she typed what the woman said. His mouth opened.

—Come on, it's funny.—

Abby was right, and he smiled as he dug once again into his breakfast. Afterward, they sat in the lobby, and he checked in with the office. Greg still hadn't responded to him, nor had he returned his texts or calls. When Ted was finished, he texted Abby.

—Everyone got back but it was a bad flight.—

—I'm glad I wasn't on it.—

Thank God for small favors.

—Flights won't take off before tomorrow.—

—Want to go explore the city?—

A long walk in freezing weather sounded like just what he needed.

****

Outside the hotel, Abby shivered in the sharp, biting air. Ted touched her shoulder, and she shivered for a different reason. Her attraction to him was off the charts.

"Is it too cold for you?"

Although she wasn't hard of hearing, he looked at her every time he spoke. He made her feel like she was the most important person in his world, and it was one of the things she liked about him. She dug her hands into the pockets of her parka and raised her shoulders. "As long as we don't stand in one place too long, I'll be fine."

The sidewalks were salted, but slush and ice piled along the corners. Crossing the streets was messy, and much of the time they walked single file. Since they couldn't talk, she had lots of time to think. And most of her thoughts were consumed with guilt.

She should have returned to California with the rest of the team. Instead, she'd shared a room with her boss. Her mother would be proud. Hell, she'd probably want to take out an announcement in the local paper and show it to all her friends. "My Daughter Shagged a Billionaire."

They walked crosstown on Thirty-Fourth Street,

stopping to check out Macy's, veering off to traverse Times Square—this time in the daylight—and playing tourist. In order to get out of the cold, they entered St. Patrick's Cathedral, and she admired the stained glass and flying buttresses. Their footsteps echoed on the marble floors, but everyone's hushed voices kept the noise levels low.

"This stonework is amazing," she said.

Ted nodded. "I sometimes wonder what we'll leave behind after we're gone."

"What do you mean?"

"Well, we create code to protect companies. If we are successful, no one is aware of our part. What kind of legacy is it?" he asked.

"True, but our code protects the work the companies create. In a way, we enable their creations to endure."

"So we're the caretakers." A half smile played across his face. In the ambient light of the church, his face was defined with light and shadows. It gave him the look of one of those marble statues found in museums. Abby fisted her hands at her sides to prevent her palms from stroking his cheeks.

"But what happens to the caretakers who shirk their duties?" He drew her toward one of the polished wooden pews.

"What do you mean?" The seat beneath was hard, but it was a relief to sit after their long walk.

"What kind of legacy do we leave when we abuse the trust our clients have and use our expertise to steal secrets?"

She frowned. The conversation took a weird turn. "It's no different than when anyone breaks the law, or abuses someone's trust. I think we're remembered for what we've accomplished—good or bad—as much as for how we've made people feel."

"And how do you want to be remembered?" His voice deepened, and he leaned forward.

She looked at the soaring arches, listened to the echoes of footsteps on the marble floors. All around her were tourists, including many who prayed in this awe-inspiring cathedral. Their sincerity was palpable. *For being something other than my mother's daughter.* "I want to be remembered for doing my best, for always trying to improve, and for learning from my mistakes."

Ted grabbed the back of the pew in front of them, his knuckles white. "And have you made a lot of mistakes?"

"Everyone does, don't they? I think sometimes, despite our best intentions, we can't help ourselves. Hopefully, nothing serious enough I can't fix, though."

His grip loosened. He looked around the cathedral, and she followed his gaze. Despite the weather, or maybe because of it, more people entered, and it was crowded.

"Shall we go?" she asked.

With a nod, he rose, and she followed him out. They exited the cathedral, headed toward Fifth Avenue, and turned south, jostling tourists and maneuvering through the snow. Ted was tall and broad, but he wouldn't push his way through people as they tried not to slip on the icy sidewalks. Despite the cold weather, everyone was out. Catching up to him, she touched his elbow. She directed him to follow her, and they walked to the New York Public Library.

They walked with care up the icy steps, Ted taking

Abby's arm. His concern for her touched her. Desire flared. At the top of the steps, she leaned against one of the gray stone columns and caught her breath, but he joined her, arms on either side of her, his body shielding her from the few brave tourists who entered or left. This close to him, his eyelashes provided a dark outline to his eyes, his cheeks were ruddy from the cold, and his minty breath warmed her face. Out of reflex, she curled her hands around his hard biceps. His jeans brushed against hers, an invisible string tangled between the two of them, pulled her toward him. The air crackled.

She blinked. His lips were parted, pale, and looked like silk. She wondered what they'd feel like against hers, her neck, her…with a huge effort, she dragged her gaze away from his lips.

His neck enticed her more. The skin was a bit rough, and right below his Adam's apple was the hollow she wanted to touch. More than anything, right now, she wanted to touch it. She lifted her hand off his arm and stopped in midair as he swallowed. Was he as turned on right now as she was?

His pupils dilated until they were outlined in electric blue. He tipped toward her, his nose brushed against hers, and he paused.

He was going to kiss her.

One of his hands moved to her cheek, stroked it, and sent shivers down her neck. He brushed a strand of escaped hair and hooked it behind her ear. She whimpered at the touch of his fingertip on her earlobe and turned her face into his hand. Cupping her neck, he drew her closer to him, angling his face as he brought his lips toward hers…

"Oh, excuse me." Someone knocked into them, waving an apology as they continued down the stairs.

He pulled away, and she rested her head against the stone pillar, gulping great amounts of cold air.

"What are we doing here?" Ted jammed his hands into his pockets.

There were many ways to answer his question, and they all depended on her bravery. "It's supposed to be a beautiful building. I thought we'd go inside where it's quiet and explore."

He stared at her for several beats of her heart. She couldn't read his expression. Did he not understand her? Did he wish she'd talked about their almost kiss? Did he admire the stonework behind her?

Without a sound, he took her hand in his and led her into the library. His stride was longer than hers, and she raced to keep pace with him. They'd never held hands while they walked, and all the while she jogged next to him she thought about his palm touching hers. It was maybe thirty degrees outside, yet his bare hand warmed hers.

And the other parts of her he'd light on fire with his touch.

He pulled her through the main lobby, up the stairs, and to the left, giving her no time to admire anything. They raced along the long hallway and stopped outside of one of the rooms. It was empty. He opened the door and pulled her inside. Finding an out-of-the-way nook, he led her over and leaned her against the wall.

Determination and desire burned as he lowered his mouth and claimed her lips for his own. One hand cradled the back of her head, the other rested on her waist. He pulled her closer. Finally. His mouth was soft and firm and sure. She whimpered against his lips, and he pulled away.

"Did you say something?"

She bit her lip. "Don't stop."

His nostrils flared, and he covered her mouth again with his own, tasting, nipping, licking, until she parted her lips, and he thrust his tongue into her mouth. He was minty and warm, and she was going to turn into a puddle. She moaned. Relief and desire mingled together, filled her with a need strong enough her knees wobbled. Wrapping her arms around his neck, she held on, stroked the soft skin below his ear, and ran her hands through his hair. His body against hers formed a wall of solid muscle. She was safe and warm.

When he pulled away, hours or days could have passed. Foreheads touching, they both panted and neither one let go.

"Wow," she said.

Ted pulled back, took his finger, and pressed it against her mouth. He pulled her against him and wrapped his arms around her. They were like bands of steel, and she burrowed into him.

"Don't talk," he whispered. "I don't want to hear you say this won't work. I want to hold you against my heart. Feel how hard it beats? That's you. I've wanted you for so long."

Her eyes prickled at the emotion in his voice, and she gripped him tighter. It wouldn't work. She couldn't be this lucky, but she'd never felt this way, and she'd denied her attraction for so long... She would give anything to try. When she thought she could control her voice, she tapped him on the back. With a sigh, he pulled away.

"I won't say it," she said. He closed his eyes as her hand touched him, and he kept them closed until she reached his jaw. "I want you too."

****

She wanted him. He had no doubt she said it. He heard her words, and he read her body language. Even if she remained silent, her eyes said it. Their gray irises—they were soft now—glowed, and her pupils were huge. He hardened. God, he wanted her. More than he'd ever wanted anyone. The knowledge she reciprocated his desire made his more potent. But they were in a public library, and sex in the stacks had to be frowned upon.

Besides, when they had sex, he wanted it to be perfect. On a beach on some tropical island with crystal blue waters and pink sand. Or in a glen of heather on the moors after a picnic. Maybe in a room filled with candles and roses and... Hell, how about their hotel room?

He looked at her, and his chest swelled. Who was he kidding? Anywhere with her would be perfect. But he didn't want to wonder about professionalism. He wanted to focus on her. He pulled her against his side, wrapped his arm around her, and together they left. She leaned against him, and he inhaled her scented hair. Her other arm was wrapped around his waist, and he sighed with pleasure.

"Ready to return to the hotel?"

She swallowed. "How will this work?"

He gave her a squeeze. "We'll figure it out, okay? But for now, let's enjoy ourselves."

Chapter Eighteen

In the hotel room—the totally inappropriate hotel room with one bed for the two of them, Ted braced. Abby would be uncomfortable. She might change her mind. Whatever her response, he had to accept it, no matter how eager for his kiss she'd been in the library.

She walked toward him. She grabbed his wrist, and he stared. He would never be able to be near strawberries again without thinking of her. Her soft pink lips parted, and she lifted on tiptoe, one hand on his chest for balance. The spot of contact burned like a brand through his shirt, skin, muscle, and bone, straight to his heart, which he'd swear skipped a beat. Or two.

"I want you," she said. "Right now."

Surprise and desire slammed through him, and he pulled her toward him, crushing his mouth to hers. This woman who avoided relationships wanted him.

Their breaths mingled, their tongues tangled, and when she wrapped her arms around his neck and stroked his nape, he groaned. Lifting her, never breaking contact, he held her against him, and she wrapped her legs around his waist. He tangled one hand in her hair, squeezed her bottom with his other, and staggered backward until he hit the bed. He sank onto the mattress.

Stroking his cheeks, she shifted and pressed her knees into the bed on either side of him. He focused on her touch. When he slipped his hands beneath her sweatshirt and touched her velvet-soft skin, heat surged through him, and he hardened in his jeans. With a whimper, she pulled away. His jaw dropped as she pulled her sweatshirt over her head. He devoured her with his gaze—creamy skin, bright pink underwear, tiny waist.

He was greedy; he needed to touch her. He cupped her breasts, ran his thumbs across the silky material of her bra. Her nipples hardened beneath him. She swallowed, the column of her throat moving, as he skimmed her delicate collarbone with his lips. He licked his way up her neck, and she let her head fall back. When he reached her ear, she shivered, and he moved from her cheeks to her nose, where he nuzzled against her. Her hands shook as she gripped his shoulders and rocked her hips against him. He bucked beneath her, then froze, afraid of knocking her off him and ending the exquisite torture. But she took up the rhythm again. He closed his eyes and pressed her against him, hard.

His hands slid up her ribcage and around her back, and he hesitated at the clasp of her bra, but she mouthed the word "no," and he stilled.

"You first," she whispered. She ran her hands down his sides and tugged at the hem of his shirt. Slipping her hands beneath the fabric, she brought them around to his front, skimmed his body as she brought them to his chest. His skin ran hot and cold beneath her touch, and he let go of her so she could pull off his shirt.

She stopped. Her hands rested against his chest muscles. He ran his hand over her body and across her jawline to lift her chin. When their gazes met, a flush tinted her cheekbones a dusty pink. Leaning toward her, he took her lower lip between his teeth and sucked. She inhaled. Chest to chest, her warm breath puffed against her lips, and as his hand slipped around her neck, her pulse throbbed against his palm.

He wanted to tear off the rest of her clothes and throw her on the bed, yet at the same time, he wanted to slow down, to memorize every touch and scent of her. Her fingertips trailed from his chest to his back, up his neck, and massaged his skull.

Running his lips across her mouth, he trailed toward her ear, nibbling on the lobe, before following the taut tendon of her neck to her collarbone. What he would give for champagne to drizzle in its hollow—hell, he'd use water if he could bring her with him to get it. He never wanted to be more than a hairsbreadth apart from her.

She arched her back. Her breasts tilted toward him, and he buried his face in them. With another glance at her face—her closed eyes, a half smile on her lips—he reached around and unclasped her bra at last. A short intake of breath was her only reaction before he focused his attention on her perfect breasts. He took one in his mouth, laving her with his tongue, then moved onto the second one, inducing more panting and hip rocking in her than he thought he could bear. His hips rocked in tandem. Sweat trickled down his temple, and he doubted how much longer he could last.

She tugged at the clasp of his jeans. "Please." Her whispered breath fluttered against his ear.

He nodded, and she set the button free. His hands fumbled for her jeans, and they pulled away from each other long enough to shed the rest of their clothing. At the foot of the bed, both naked, he held her at arms-length to admire her pale skin, small waist, and flared hips. Getting his fill, he returned once again to her breasts.

She reached for him, caressed his buttocks, and pulled him close, and he took one lingering glance at their reflection in the mirror above the dresser—the two of them twined together as one—before he buried his face in her hair.

When her hands slipped between them, and she grasped him, he flung his head back, used all his restraint not to yell with pleasure as he throbbed against her hand. Her clasp was tight. He imagined how it would feel to be inside her...no, he better stop before he came in her hand.

"Abby." His voice rasped, every ounce of control used to extend their pleasure.

"I want you," she said. "Inside me." She rubbed against him. "Now."

He reached blindly for his pants, somehow found his wallet, grabbed a condom, and slipped it on. Lifting her, every nerve ending on hyperalert, knees shaking, gasping for air, he laid her on the bed. He locked his arms, positioned above her, and watched her lips one last time.

"Are you sure?" he asked.

She bit her lower lip, and he waited, staring at her mouth so as not to miss her response. When she nodded, desire flooded through him, and he lowered on top of her. She reached between them and caressed him once again. The head barely brushed her folds. When she raised her hips, he entered, first the tip, and then a little farther as she adjusted to him. Her pupils dilated, her lips parted, and he covered her mouth with his. They rocked together, and when she squeezed his buttocks, he pushed further, before he withdrew and repeated the exquisite torture.

The next time he pulled away, she slammed her hips against him and pulled him close, and finally, he sank into her, reveling in the squeeze of her muscles against him, the oneness of their bodies together, the mingling of their breaths. They rocked together, creating a cadence all their own. Desire built, his gut clenched, and heat suffused his body as he watched her climax overtake her. When he was sure she was satisfied, he allowed his own release, and a million stars shattered his nerve endings, light suffused the dark space behind his eyelids, and the sound of his blood pumping in his veins filled his damaged ears with a rushing tempo. His body slick with sweat, he collapsed on top of her, took her in his arms, and rolled over to cradle her against his body.

Her chest rose and fell in tempo with his own heavy breathing, and he placed his palm flat against it. Wiping a stray lock of hair out of her face, he gazed at her, memorized the line of her brow, marveled at her sooty lashes, and admired her butter-soft skin.

"Wow," she said.

His chest swelled.

"I've wanted you since the moment I first saw you." He traced the slope of her shoulder.

"When you wanted to fire me for staring at your ears?"

He chuckled. "Something like that." Ted lay in bed, his body satiated. "If you want to go, I'll try my best to get you out of here as soon as possible."

She rose on her elbow and looked at him. "No. I want to stay with you."

****

Abby walked naked toward the bathroom on her way to take a shower. Ted's body tightened as he considered joining her there—water sluicing over bare skin, bodies brushing against each other, hands caressing soap over shoulders and down backs—and he groaned. He looked out the hotel window at the snow and ice and pictured rolling in it. Temperature lowered, he flinched as his phone vibrated. It was a text from Greg.

—Looking into the security breach. Will check the security logs tomorrow. Jet lag is getting me.—

His stomach knotted. He had no more hard information now than when Greg first reported the security breach. Why the hell was this investigation taking so long?

—I have a hard time believing anyone I know could be dishonest.—

Especially someone with whom he'd had sex. It presented a bigger problem. Sex meant something. With Abby, it wasn't a fling. He couldn't have sex with her one minute and accuse her of a security breach the next. Which meant he needed to talk to her and hope to God she understood.

—Would it be because you're leading with some part of your anatomy other than the brain?—

A flash of anger sparked, and he stifled it. Greg was one of his closest friends and despite Ted's personal feelings, he was right. He needed to find concrete evidence to counter Greg's accusation. He'd told Abby he wouldn't jump to conclusions, and he refused to lie to her again.

****

Abby stared at her shampoo and conditioner next to Ted's in the marble tile stall. But focusing on anything other than Ted and their amazing sex was impossible.

She turned on the water, hoping to cool off and allow her to function, but the ding of a text interrupted her. She turned off the shower and thrust her attention away from her sexy boss.

Eden, her best friend.

—Hey, are you all right? I heard about the storm.—

Her friend always looked out for her.

—Yeah, Ted and I are stuck in NYC until the storm clears.—

—Oooh, stuck with the sexy boss? What a hardship.—

If she only knew.

—Lol.—

She couldn't tell her how stuck she was with him…or could she? Dancing dots appeared on the screen, and Abby waited for Eden to finish.

—So what are you doing?—

It was time to have a little fun.

—Making out with my boss in the stacks.—

—Funny.—

Maybe she shouldn't have said that…

—Um…—

—Wait, are you serious?—

—Kinda.—

—Call me.—

—Can't.—

—CALL ME NOW.—

She wrapped a towel around her body and sat on the toilet seat, after first locking the bathroom door. Regardless of his hearing issues, she wanted privacy for this conversation.

She closed her eyes and took deep breaths. Dialing Eden's number, she waited for her to pick up on the other end. When she answered, Eden shrieked. She yanked the phone away from her ear.

"Tell me everything!" Eden screamed.

Abby filled in Eden, including their chart-topping sex.

"Congrats, girl. That's awesome."

"I don't know, Ede. I mean, yes, but there are a million potential problems with a relationship with him."

"Like?"

"Like the fact he's my boss. Like the fact if anything goes wrong, I'm the one who has the most to lose. I don't ever put myself in that situation, and I just did. I can't compartmentalize work and personal the way he seems to be able to."

"Now that you've cooled off, do you regret anything?"

Abby paused. There was nothing she wasn't on board with, and Ted would stop if she asked him. "No."

"He sounds about perfect. He's hot, he's brilliant, he's rich, and he's nice to you. Take a cue from him and work on your compartmentalizing skills. Maybe this is a good thing."

"But what if it isn't?"

"You pick yourself up and move on."

"Eden, I don't want to. I worked hard to get this job. It's exactly what I've wanted since I got out of school. If things with Ted go wrong, and I'm fired after only a couple of months...how will I ever find a job I love as much?"

"Life is about more than work, Abby. I know you love the job, and I know how important it is for you to be able to support yourself, but I think you need to give this a chance."

Chapter Nineteen

Abby walked into the bedroom, wrapped in a towel, her hair dripping water down her back. She half hoped Ted would rip off her clothes and repeat what he'd done with her earlier. More than half. Sex with Ted was beyond amazing. Whatever his computer talents and his corporate talents might be, they paled in comparison to his sexual ones.

And now she was experienced enough to know.

Her neck heated at the thought and images of her mother flashed through her mind. She squelched them. She wouldn't think about her mother. Not now, with the hottest man she'd ever been with lying in bed right in front of her.

She walked toward him. Her gaze took in every delicious inch of him, from those muscular legs that wrapped around her, to the bed sheet covering something sexy, to the sculpted chest she'd brushed her lips against, to his neck which smelled of spice, soap, and him, and to his face…which looked worried.

"What's wrong?"

"We need to talk."

Her stomach plummeted. "Don't worry, I'm not a relationship person," she said. "Sex with you was fantastic, but it doesn't have to turn into something more than—"

He held up his hand, and she stopped. She needed

to take a breath, but she was afraid of what might happen.

"It's not what I meant," he said. "And I am a relationship person. However, we need to talk about work."

He did relationships, and he wanted to talk about work?

She dropped her towel and sashayed across the room. No matter how much she tried not to be like her mother, she needed to distract him. The more she thought of it, the greater the chance he would fire her. She was his employee, he was the CEO, there was no way this could work. By the expression on his face when she'd first left the bathroom, he'd come to the same conclusion.

Through the mirror over the desk, she watched Ted stare at her, lips parted. She pulled out her underwear and shimmied into it. He leaned forward, and his chest rose and fell like he couldn't catch his breath.

Good.

She reached for her jeans and cream sweater from her suitcase, and he launched out of bed.

"What are you doing?" he asked.

"You know if we're here too much longer, I'll have to find a laundromat. I overpacked, but I didn't count on extra days here."

She doubted he caught everything she'd said. When a woman was half naked, the last thing a man focused on were the words exiting her mouth. It was fine with her.

This was why she shouldn't mix business with pleasure. However, that boat had sailed, and it was time to make the best of it. Right now, her "best" was to distract him with sex appeal. If distraction failed, they'd…go sledding.

Turning to him, she swayed her hips as she walked and wet her lips with her tongue. He stood in front of her, naked except for his boxers, his arousal on display for her to see. She stopped mere inches in front of him, close enough for her to see beads of sweat on his upper lip. He raised his hands as if to touch her. She sidestepped, walking around behind him and trailing a finger across the wide expanse of his bare back. He shivered at the contact.

"What are you doing?" This time, his voice was hoarse.

Speaking to him while she stood behind him would have been cruel. Instead, she kissed the spot between his shoulder blades and blew against his skin. Goose bumps formed in her wake. His muscles tightened, and his posture would have made a marine sergeant proud.

"Abby?"

She completed her walk around him once again and faced him.

He reached for her, and she stared into his eyes, midnight blue with desire. He tipped toward her like he wanted to kiss her, and he raised his hand as if to cup her jaw.

She handed him her sweater. "Can you hold this?" She hoped he wouldn't hear the desire in her voice. Their fingers touched as he took it from her, and her skin sizzled at the contact.

She shook out her jeans and slipped one leg in. When she wobbled, he reached out and grabbed her elbow. She wanted to disappear into the heat of his embrace, but it would lead to sex, which would lead to the afterglow, which would lead to conversation. Better to go sledding. She steadied her body along with her heart, zipped her jeans, and took her sweater out of his hands.

"Abby, what are you doing?"

His skin was flushed, his voice raspy, and he was still aroused. She shivered as the cream wool dragged against her skin. She was aroused too.

Pulling her sweater over her head, she lifted her hair out of the way and folded the turtle-neck collar.

"Getting dressed."

He frowned.

"You should too," she said.

"Not until we talk."

He retreated from her until the bed separated them and pulled on his jeans. Running a hand through his hair, he exhaled.

Her stomach clenched.

"There's been a security breach in Sentec's firewall."

She frowned. This is what he wanted to talk about? Relief flooded through her, and her heart pounded hard enough she'd swear he could see her chest vibrate. "Must have been why the script looked wonky." Her words tumbled out in a gasp.

"Wonky?" He frowned.

Nodding, she pulled her computer toward her and tapped a few keys, hands shaky. "The information I gave you before we left. I'd started to tell you I noticed something, but you said you'd take care of it."

His muscles relaxed. "Mind if I take a look at the computer?"

Her stomach tightened further. "To see my report

or to check if I'm the guilty party?"

"Technically I don't have to give you a reason, since it's a work computer. Since you're innocent, you shouldn't have a problem with my taking a look."

He was right, but a part of her hated the element of mistrust, especially since they'd had sex. She swallowed and shoved it toward him.

"Here."

His hands dance across the keyboard. Those fingers were much sexier when they danced over her skin.

After a few minutes, he handed her back her computer. "Thanks," he said.

She shut her laptop. "Is that all?"

He grabbed his phone and tapped out a text. When he was finished, he looked at her. "Yes." He narrowed his gaze. "Maybe you can get undressed now?" He stepped closer to her and drew her into his arms.

His warmth and strength almost convinced her to strip, but she needed a break to get over her disappointment. "I have a better idea."

"Better than getting naked?"

His scrunched face was adorable. "For now. Let's go sledding."

****

The excitement on her face was enough for Ted to agree to promise her the moon.

"Let me find sleds," he said.

Despite the discomfort of his biggest hard-on in ages, he struggled into jeans and a sweatshirt. "Wait here," he said. He left the room and leaned against the wall of the elevator as it descended to the lobby. Abby was innocent. Relief made him giddy. He'd texted

Greg, using great restraint and not texting, "Told you so!" Now he could focus on her.

The doors opened to a less crowded area than yesterday. He leaned an elbow on the concierge's desk and waited for her to get off the phone.

"May I help you?"

"I hope so. We want to go sledding."

A variety of emotions crossed her face—annoyance, confusion, and relief. He suspected she'd had a rough morning dealing with customers. "Oh, Central Park is great for sledding," she said. "You can go to Pilgrim Hill or Cedar Hill, depending on your love of crowds and adventure skill level."

"Where can we rent sleds?"

"Um, hmm. I'm not sure. Hold on, I'll check." She stepped away from the desk for a few minutes and returned with a smile. "There's a guy who rents sleds on Cedar Hill. However, in case he's not there, you can use these." She handed him two large room service trays.

Images from college flashed through Ted's mind—he and his fraternity brothers stole cafeteria trays on snowy days and raced down the hill on campus. Simon and Caleb always joined him, and his heart thundered at the thought of doing this with Abby.

"This is great. Thanks."

He returned to the room with the trays. The sight of Abby squeezed his heart. He'd like nothing better than to strip her of her clothes and have wild, passionate sex right here, sledding be damned. But he'd promised her sledding, and he wouldn't disappoint her.

"What are those?" Abby asked when he raised the trays.

"Our sleds."

She frowned. "Excuse me?"

"Well, you want to go sledding, but we don't have sleds. There might be a guy who rents sleds on Cedar Hill, but if not, we have these. I used them in college, and they work."

"If you say so."

"Trust me."

Ten minutes later they were bundled and in a taxi. Twenty minutes afterward they arrived at Cedar Hill. He withheld a snort as he climbed out of the car. Hill? More like a pasture. Bordered by trees, with branches weighted with snow, the meadow was white with sloping…something, certainly not hills…that enabled people to slide. Despite the lack of grade, people were sledding, the most successful ones using saucers or trays like theirs.

The wind whipped the cold air around them, created a rushing noise in his ears, and carried the muted sounds of people enjoying the activity. He turned to Abby, and his breath hitched at the sheer joy on her face. Eyes bright, cheeks rosy, she could have been in a Norman Rockwell painting.

"Look at all of them," she cried. She bent and grabbed a handful of snow, and Ted couldn't decide which he was more attracted to—the sight of her backside or the sparkle in her eye as she formed the snow into a ball.

"Careful." His gaze shifted between the snow and her face. "Remember which one of us is the more experienced snowbird here."

"Snowbird?" She arched a brow as she packed the snow. "You mean the senior citizens who travel to

Florida for the winter, or do those hearing aids let you fly as well?"

He shook his head. Only she could tease him. Something thumped against his chest. Snow stuck to his jacket. She'd thrown the snowball at him.

This was war.

He dropped the trays, scooped an armful of snow, and formed it into a gigantic ball.

"No fair," Abby shrieked. She dodged and weaved in an attempt to avoid him.

He threw it at her. But she was faster than she looked and managed to avoid the majority of the snow, only getting hit on the shoulder. Racing for the trees, she slipped behind a large trunk, and for a moment, Ted lost sight of her. He scooped another ball of snow and made a wide arc around the tree. She'd be less accurate the further away from the tree he was.

Her snowball hit him square in the chest, again.

As she ran away, he threw his snowball and caught her in the back. She stumbled, righted herself, and raced away. Once out of range, she stopped to grab snow, took aim, and threw another one. Once again, it hit him. If she ever decided to turn in her keyboard, she'd have a backup job as an ace pitcher.

He was brushing the snow off and bending to make another snowball when she grabbed him and tried to smash snow into his face. He arched away, grabbed her around the waist, and swung her in the air, her back to him.

"Hey, no taking advantage of the hard of hearing." The trees and people around him blurred while he spun them both around. Between her facing away from him and the wind, he couldn't hear her words, but he could feel their vibration against his chest. There was something right about it, and he hugged her close, for once not caring about what he couldn't hear. When he could no longer stand upright, he sank into the snow, Abby on top of him. She breathed hard, like him, and he stared at the sky until he was no longer winded.

She rolled off him.

"You have lousy aim," she said.

"You have poor timing." He grabbed a handful of snow and mashed it against her face.

Abby sputtered, took his gloved hand, and used it as a towel to wipe the snow off her face. He wished his skin touched hers, caressed her cheek, traced the fine bones of her jaw. The wet snow invaded his thoughts and soaked through his pants, and he hauled them both onto their feet.

"We either need to sled or go back," he said. "Lying in the snow will give us pneumonia."

"Where are the trays?"

They looked around and after a few minutes found them buried in the snow. He took one, handed the other to Abby, and trudged toward the growing crowd of people on the top of the slope. They were able to slide and when the way was clear, he looked over his shoulder at Abby, took a running start, leaped, and landed on the tray, which slid down the hill.

A few seconds later, Abby reached the bottom as well. Her silver eyes sparkled like the snow with sunlight glinting off it.

"Race you to the top." She took off, leaving him speechless. He trudged after her, unable to run in his stiffening, wet jeans. But he enjoyed the view she provided him.

When it was their turn again, she placed her tray next to his and held out her hand. He took it, and together they slid down the hill. Maybe there was a benefit to staying away from the steep ones.

A few more slides, and he was frozen.

"Hey, someone mentioned the Nectar Coffee Shop," Abby said. "Want to get some hot chocolate?"

He nodded, and they hailed another cab. He was cold and warming up with Abby sounded perfect.

****

Abby never knew sledding with trays was a thing, much less how much fun it could be. But like many things with Ted, she was, once again, surprised. As she sat in the extra-warm car and watched the edifices of concrete, brick, and glass pass the car window, she couldn't help wonder what a long-term relationship with Ted would be like. Would they always plan spontaneous activities like sledding on trays to fill her days with surprises? Would he continue to let down his guard about his hearing, enabling her to tease him about it?

They made a quick dash from the car into the Nectar Coffee Shop, and he steered them toward a small granite table beside the window. She unwrapped layers of warm clothes and nodded to the waitress who appeared with a carafe of steaming hot chocolate. Ted did the same. The waitress filled both their mugs, and as Abby sat across from him, the lines blurred between boss and…what? She never stayed with a guy long enough to classify him as anything other than a skill level on the sex scale. They might be friends with benefits, but beyond that? She wasn't a relationship person.

Usually.

"I can hear you thinking." Ted wrapped his hands around his coffee mug. "Which for me is quite a feat." He smiled, and she weakened at the sight of his dimples.

To distract her thoughts, she took a sip of her cocoa. She grimaced as the scalding liquid burned her tongue.

"What were you thinking about?" he asked.

How could she answer his question when she had no idea what she wanted from him? *Coward.* "What made you think of trays as sleds?"

"My buddies and I used them all the time in college."

As a scholarship student with multiple jobs, she'd had no time for sledding. "Where did you go?"

"Harvard."

He was a Harvard man. She'd been at MIT. Plus, she was younger than him by a few years, if she had to guess. Would they have fallen for each other if they'd met in college?

She said, "I guess Harvard grads weren't fond of sleds?"

He laughed, but the waitress approached before she could join in. "Can I take your order?"

Abby looked at Ted and tapped her finger on the menu, on the off chance he missed what the waitress said. But he looked comfortable.

"Sorry," he said. "We haven't looked at it yet. Can you give us a few more minutes?"

When the waitress left, he picked up the menu. "Don't eat too much here. I thought we'd go somewhere nice later."

Like a date? She waited for the dread. Instead, warmth filled her belly, and it wasn't from the super-hot cocoa that had burned her mouth. More likely, it was from the super-hot man across from her. "Okay, I'll get fries."

They placed their order, and Ted refocused on her question. "Sure, some people liked sleds. Those of us on scholarship, though, used what we could find. I'm surprised you MIT kids didn't create some sort of sledding device never seen before."

She shrugged. "I don't know about others. But I was focused on my studies and my jobs. I had no time for anything else."

A flash of understanding passed across his face. "My friends used to try to get me to slack off a lot more than I was willing. We'll have a good time while we play hooky in New York."

The waitress's return with her fries and his soup halted her response. She wanted to ask what he meant by "a good time" because she had some ideas. But he spoke again as he added oyster crackers to his soup.

"I think we should find an indoor activity next. I'm not sure my jeans will ever defrost otherwise."

"I know plenty of activities that don't require jeans."

He sputtered.

"Besides, I'm not the one who forced you to lie in the snow."

He arched a brow. "I'm not sure how accurate your memory is, but okay."

She waved a fry at him and rolled her eyes. "Whatever."

As she munched on the fry, he reached across the

small table and stole one. Without thinking, she slapped her hand on top of his wrist.

"No stealing my fries," she said.

"Stealing? Who's stealing?"

"You are."

"The plate is big enough for two."

"But the plate and the fries are mine," she said. "You didn't ask. You took one. It's stealing. Don't you know stealing is wrong?"

A weird look crossed his face, but it passed, and she refrained from asking about it. Instead, he spoke. "May I have a fry?"

"Of course you may. I'm happy to share."

He sputtered once again, and she winked. "I never said you couldn't eat my fries, but you need to have permission."

"Please, ma'am, may I have another french fry?" His attempt at an English accent amused her, and she pushed the plate toward him.

"Help yourself."

With a flare of his nostrils and a wry look, Ted made a dent in Abby's heaping pile of fries. When they were finished, he flagged the waitress and paid for their snacks, then ushered Abby out to the car. As they drove south on Lexington Avenue, Abby once again looked out the window, fascinated by the people and the buildings as they headed downtown. Ted's thigh touched hers. Heat raced along the side of her body. One fast turn and she'd end up in his lap, which wouldn't be a bad thing. But the ride was slow due to the snowy streets. When they stopped at a traffic light, Abby looked out the window to avoid the man next to her. A sign in the window of a nearby building grabbed her attention.

She tugged on Ted's arm. "Can we get out here?" She pointed to the building—a Boys and Girls Club—and Ted asked the driver to pull over. Once out of the car, Abby raced over to the window, sliding on the ice but not slowing.

"Look," she cried. "They offer coding workshops for teens. I'd love to find out what they do. Mind if we go in?"

Her stomach fluttered with excitement. Something pulled at her, turned her desire to enter to a need, and she rang the buzzer. When the door clicked to indicate it was unlocked, she pulled it open and walked to the security desk. The man behind the desk looked up at her approach.

"May I help you?"

"I saw the sign outside about coding today. Would you mind if we peeked inside?"

The man peered over his gold-rimmed spectacles. "Are you related to someone here? We don't allow strangers inside."

She turned away from the desk and slumped. She should have expected it. As a child, she'd spent hours in places like this. Ted blocked her and tilted her chin.

"What's wrong?"

How could she explain everything to him here, in this public place? Plus, she wasn't sure if she wanted to.

"I learned to code in a place like this. I—" But he'd already turned away. She watched him go to the desk again, reach into his pocket, and hand something to the man behind the counter. The man dialed his phone.

"I have a Ted Endicott here from Endicott Company. He wants to—Right. Okay." The man looked at Ted. "Someone will come out to meet you in a second."

Another man came out into the lobby. "Mr. Endicott? I'm Tony Ruiz, the computer teacher here."

Ted nodded.

"It's fantastic to meet you. The kids will be excited you're here. You're like a rock star to them."

Ted flushed and motioned for Abby to follow the man. He looked to be in his midthirties, with jet-black hair and umber-colored skin. She turned to Ted. "How did you—" But Ted shook his head. They walked along a long musty hallway lined with cinder block walls that carried her back to her teenaged years, when she hung out in a place that smelled and looked similar. The scent filled her with a combination of nostalgia and deep-seated fear. As much as her time there was safe and the best part of her childhood, she was terrified of ever being insecure again. When they entered the computer room, she gripped the doorframe. It was as if she'd traveled back in time. Four computers—none of them new, but all of them functioned—dotted across a table, with groups of kids huddled around each one. The biggest difference, aside from the updated technology, was there were more girls. When she was a teen, she was the only one.

The man flicked the lights, and all the kids looked up from their workspace.

"Hey, everyone, I have an important visitor to introduce. This is Ted Endicott, founder of Endicott Company. He took what he knew about coding and turned it into a multi-million-dollar company."

The kids' mouths dropped, and a gasp filled the room. Ted stepped forward.

"It's great to see all of you interested in programming," he said. He talked about how he started his company, and the kids sat, rapt. Then, he turned his head. "I want to introduce you to Abby Marlow. She's my best cybersecurity expert."

Abby's eyes filled, although whether it was from Ted's introduction or from the kids' reactions, especially the girls, she couldn't say. Instead of speaking, she walked to the first group of kids.

"Hi. Tell me what you're working on."

One by one, the kids showed her their projects. Ted let her take the lead and the spotlight.

"Can you hack things?" One of the boys at the far end of the table asked the question, and all the kids paused.

"Paulie, of course she can't," said a blond-haired boy. "It's illegal."

"Doesn't mean she can't do it," the boy who'd asked the question said.

"She'd never do something like that," said a red-haired girl who looked at Abby with worshipful eyes behind big black glasses.

Abby interrupted the conversation before it erupted into an argument.

"Here's the thing. Anyone with computer coding knowledge can hack computers," she said. The kids elbowed each other. "But that's not the challenge. The challenge comes from not doing it. Paulie is right, it's illegal, and a good computer programmer follows the law. In fact, computer programming is kind of like a superpower. There aren't many who can do what you all can, and it's your responsibility to use your powers for good. It's like…when you see another kid who has something you want. You could steal it, or you could figure out a way to get it on your own, the right way. If you steal it, sure, you'll have the thing you want, but every time you look at it, every time you use it, a part of you deep inside will feel bad because you didn't deserve or earn it. But if you work for what you want, save up for it, not only will you own the item, but you'll be proud of yourself for going about it in the right way." She looked around at the faces turned to her, expressions rapt. "Make sense?"

As one, they nodded in unison. The man who'd introduced Ted pulled her aside.

"That was perfect," he said. "Thank you. I've been trying to teach them enough to continue but not enough to land in jail."

She laughed. "I was them once. Keep doing what you're doing. They need to know life gets better, and they have the power to change their lives."

"I don't suppose you'd care to return another day?"

She looked around the room, thinking there was nothing she'd like more. "Unfortunately, we're returning to California, or I would. But I'll be sure to stop by if I'm ever in New York." She handed the man her card, made one more pass around the computers, and walked outside with Ted.

Their car pulled up front as soon as they exited the building, and they climbed in. Ted turned toward her, an odd expression on his face.

"Do you believe what you told the kids inside?"

The warm glow from spending a half hour with the kids—her younger self—faded. There was an intensity in Ted's gaze she couldn't identify, an odd inflection to his voice.

"Yes, I do." She wondered why this question seemed important.

His body relaxed. "You were great with those kids."

The glow from his praise outshone her curiosity over his motive. "They reminded me of myself when I was their age. I wish we could come here again." She tried not to give too much away, but it made sense a computer programmer would be interested in coding when she was young.

"There probably weren't too many girls working with computer code at the time," he said.

"Nope, I was the only one." Her mom loved when all the boys surrounded her daughter and encouraged her to flirt with them. A sour taste rose in her throat, and she swallowed. She'd pretended to listen to her mom—anything so her mom would let her continue to hang out there.

She needed to cut off this line of questions, though, before she said too much. "What about you? How did you get involved with computers?"

He blinked. "I took an elective in school, and it was one of the few things where my hearing was irrelevant." He stared off into space. "I loved it." His expression softened, and Abby got a glimpse of his more vulnerable side.

Part of her wanted to lean over and touch his cheek. She'd never experienced this connection with any other man. They were more alike than she ever could have imagined, and while he was precious to her, it also scared her. She needed to take a step back, if only briefly. "You know, I should finish some work before dinner. I'm still trying to come up with a fix for the Sentec issue."

He stretched his arm across the back of the seat, and she leaned against it. "I need to check in with Greg. Does he know what you're doing?"

She ran a hand through her hair and pushed the strands away from her face. The cold made her hair staticky. "Yes, but I haven't shown it to him yet."

A variety of emotions flickered across his face. "Why don't you show me?"

Chapter Twenty

Sitting next to Abby in the car was torture. Her strawberry scent tickled his nose. All he wanted was to pull her into his arms and kiss her senseless. Pull her lip into his mouth and suck it, run his hand through her long black hair, fit her body around his. He wanted to bury himself inside of her.

It wasn't like he needed to focus on the road—he had a driver. There was plenty of room in the hired car, with large, comfortable, black leather seats. The floor was clean, there was a mini fridge with alcohol and music controls, something he cared little about. But he could set the mood, and they could enjoy the sights as they drove through the Manhattan streets. Hell, he could tell the driver to take the scenic route.

But he needed to be patient a little longer. He'd always been a patient person. Without his hearing, he learned to observe those around him, and observation led to patience. It was a positive byproduct of the short straw he'd been dealt, and he'd cultivated it to his advantage. And patience was killing him.

Case in point, he'd swear they were driving to California with the amount of time it seemed they'd spent in the car, but finally, the driver pulled in front of the hotel.

He walked into the lobby and stopped dead. If it was hard to resist her in the car, imagine how tortuous it would be in their bedroom—their single bedroom with its one gigantic bed.

"Why don't you go get your computer," he said. "We can sit in the lobby and go over your observations."

She raised an eyebrow at him, and he noticed the number of people. It would be harder to hear, but it was a challenge he was ready to tackle.

If his relationship with Abby was to work, he needed to set clear boundaries. Especially since it was a relationship he wanted, not a quick tumble. He wanted more. Therefore, sex with her while discussing business would be wrong. Know what else would be wrong? Sex with her again before they discussed their relationship.

She strode to the elevator, and he searched for a quiet spot in the lobby where they could work. Finding none, he searched for a place he could sit opposite her. That he found.

He folded his body into the small chair and watched the elevator until she returned.

"Just a minute, let me get things ready." She opened her laptop.

He read her lips, and he drummed his fingers on his lap.

"Okay, here's what I found." She spun the laptop toward him, and he watched her mouth to see if she spoke. She remained silent. He transferred his attention to the screen and found the problem she and Greg identified.

"Where's the log with who accessed the company's information?"

"Greg has it. I'm trying to develop a patch so the problem doesn't occur again."

She took her computer, typed, and turned it around to Ted. Her patch was in the rough stages, but she'd developed an elegant fix, and his opinion of her skills increased.

He texted Greg.

—What's taking so long with the log of who accessed Sentec's files?—

Dancing dots indicated Greg typed. They stopped. A minute later they started again.

—I figured it could wait until you got back.—

Ted frowned.

—No, I said we need to take care of this ASAP.—

Again, there was a pause. Finally Greg responded.

—I'll email it to you in a few.—

Abby reached across the table and touched his hand. "What's wrong?" she asked when he looked at her.

"Nothing. Greg's sending me the company log."

She resumed her work on the computer. She looked calm. If she'd caused the breach, wouldn't she look worried? In his mind, he put another check mark in the "innocent" column and continued to watch her. She had an adorable habit of biting her lower lip when she concentrated, and he couldn't help but stare. Her mouth was lush and plump, and he could still taste their sweetness from their last kiss.

He groaned. First, finish work. Second, discuss their relationship. Third, have sex. He hoped there'd be a third. When she looked at him, he blanked his expression and waited for her to go to work. He berated himself in his head. Get it together. Marshaling his thoughts and his libido, he answered emails on his phone.

Every time she moved, she distracted him. Sitting across from her was supposed to be good for him to read her lips, but all he wanted was to pull her onto his lap and bury his face in her neck. Gritting his teeth, he blocked out all sight of her. After a half hour, his inbox was empty, and his neck was stiff. Why the hell was Greg taking so long?

"How about we go upstairs and get ready for dinner?" He rubbed the nape of his neck. And have that conversation.

She shut her computer and followed him to the elevator. Inside their room, she pulled on his arm.

"What's wrong?" She pointed to his neck.

"It's stiff from bending over my phone. It's nothing; I'll be fine." He bent his head from side to side and winced.

"Sit." She pointed to the edge of the bed.

He stiffened. "It's nothing."

"Sit."

For a little thing, she sure was bossy. Maybe he should sit on the floor…she pushed him against the bed, acting out the first part of his fantasy, although with too many articles of clothing. No fantasy before conversation. The backs of his legs hit the bed, and he sat, like a reflex. She scooted around him to kneel on the bed, her hands on his shoulders. He turned toward her, but the pain restricted his movement. Instead, she leaned around so he could see her face.

"Relax, I'm just going to give you a neck massage."

There was nothing "just" about a massage from this woman. This beautiful woman with whom he'd already had sex once and hoped to have it with again, but wouldn't until they talked about the relationship he wanted them to have. This beautiful woman whose hands stroked his neck…

She pressed against the tendons at the nape of his neck, sending shivers behind his ears and around his skull. His hands jerked with a desire to reach for her, but he clenched them into fists and forced them to remain on his knees. As she applied pressure to his tight muscles, he dropped his head and froze. From this angle, he gave her a perfect view of his hearing aids. His stomach tightened…and he berated himself. This was Abby, the woman he wanted a serious relationship with. Releasing a breath, he forced his muscles to relax beneath her touch.

Her hands continued their magic across his neck and, without forethought, he rolled his shoulders under her touch. As she worked their way along the base of his skull toward his ears, he could hear the rasp of skin against skin echo, and desire crawled along his spine. She massaged the sensitive spot at the base of his skull. His breaths grew labored, and he hoped she wouldn't notice.

But when she leaned against him, her breasts against his back, he could no longer resist. Reaching for her, he grasped her wrists and brought her palm to his mouth. He kissed her hand, traced the lines with his lips, and she stiffened. He reached her wrist, the delicate skin heating beneath his kiss. Her pulse fluttered, and he smiled against her arm. He'd caused her reaction. Inhaling her scent, he paused, as much for his own sanity as for her permission to continue. She pulled her arm away.

"Is your neck better?" She scooted off the bed and

leaned against the desk facing him.

What neck? "Uh, yeah. Thanks. We should talk."

Her hands fiddled with a pen, twirled it like a baton. Any minute he expected her to toss it in the air and spin around before catching it. "I, uh, should get ready for dinner." She jumped off the bed.

She started to walk past him, but he grabbed her around the waist and pulled her against him. She squeaked.

"I'd rather talk about us."

She stood between his legs and rested her hands on his forearms. "What do you mean?" She looked away, but he grasped her chin and turned her toward him.

"Don't play dumb, Abby. You're the most intelligent woman I've ever met. You're beautiful, funny, and kind. I'm falling for you, and I want more than casual sex with you."

Her face blanched. She was going to say no.

"With me?"

"Yes." She hadn't left yet. Maybe it was a good sign.

"I don't do relationships." She bit her lip and fidgeted. Her fingers stroked his forearms, sending spikes of heat along his skin.

"I'm not asking you to do relationships plural." His stomach knotted. "I'm asking you to risk it and have one with me. I promise it won't affect your job— nothing in your off-hours will have any bearing on job performance. I'll put it in writing."

Her fingers stopped moving, and her shoulders, which were raised, lowered. She looked at him like he was an alien. Actually, like other people looked at him when he couldn't hear something. "You'd do that for me?"

What caused her to have such doubts about men? Was it all men, or him in particular? "Anything for you."

****

God, she wanted to believe him. He was everything she'd ever wanted in a man. Her feelings—not just her body—were engaged. She fantasized about the future. But he was her boss. The CEO of the company where she had her dream job. She had the most to lose. She stared at him, and he held her gaze. He'd been honest with her from the beginning. Heck, he'd confessed his fears about his hearing. He'd gone out of his way to show her she could trust him.

Her face softened, her posture loosened, and he pulled her into his arms. She wanted him. All of him. And if it meant a relationship, she'd handle the consequences. "Yes."

The worried voices in her mind quieted as her lips met his. He groaned against her open mouth, and their tongues met. Heat enveloped her, and her senses went into overdrive—his smell, taste, and touch surrounded her. Her knees weakened as he clutched her to his hard chest.

She ran her hands through his hair. The warmth of his scalp set her ablaze. She trailed kisses across his jawline, the stubble scraping her tender lips. Reaching his earlobe, she licked the soft skin where his ear met his jaw, and his breath came in harsh rasps. He gripped her waist, and his hard length pressed against her. Her hips rocked, and he lifted her. She wrapped her legs around his waist, held on, and devoured him with her lips as he carried her to the bathroom.

She pulled away. "What are you doing?"

He reached inside the shower with one hand, while holding her with the other and trailing kisses along her neck. "We need to shower before dinner."

Her gaze widened as she slid down the length of his body. With the water running behind the pebbled glass, he turned his attention to her, skimmed his hands down her sides until he reached the bottom of her sweater. As he reached beneath the soft material, her torso goose bumped, and tension pooled low in her belly.

His hands were magic, and if he kept it up, she'd come right where they stood, shower be damned. The man shouldn't be this talented. Two could play this game. She reached for his shirt and unbuttoned the middle button. She brushed against what she'd guess to be the fourth of his six-pack as she unbuttoned his shirt.

Although Ted remained silent, and Abby avoided looking at his face, from the trembling of his muscles against her hand and the way he gripped her waist, she could guess her effect on him.

Good.

When she reached the bottom of his shirt, she moved on to his pants. Her knuckles whisked against his stomach as she dipped into his waistband and unbuttoned his jeans. He hissed and sucked in his stomach. With a groan, he grabbed her and held her away from him.

"Let me handle this, woman, or I'll come before we get under the water."

She snorted. He made quick work of getting undressed, stuck his hearing aids in the pockets of his jeans, and placed his phone on the counter. When he was naked, he turned.

"Now you."

She swallowed.

He was naked. He was large. He was turned on. And he was coming for her.

He started with her hair, smoothing his palms against the sides of her head, tracing her cheekbones with his thumbs. At her mouth, he brushed her lips and her jaw, sending tingles of desire along the nape of her neck and up her scalp. He cupped her breasts through her sweater, and her nipples hardened. She stifled a moan, dying for him to take them in his hands. But he continued on his journey to her waist. He dragged her sweater off and stared at her turquoise lace bra. Her breasts ached under the heat of his gaze.

He kissed her from her collarbone to her navel. Every muscle in her upper body twitched. She reached for him, and he grasped both of her wrists in one hand, backing her against the closed bathroom door and holding them above her head.

"You tease me, I tease you."

She couldn't decide if his whispered words against her ear were a threat or a promise. Maybe it was a dare. Regardless, she wouldn't give him the upper hand, although the husky timbre of his voice melted her insides. She ignored his hold on her wrists. Instead, she took a half step forward, arched her back, and brushed her half-dressed body against his naked one. Her breasts pressed against his chest, and she shivered.

His pupils dilated, and his lips parted. His breath fanned her face. She rubbed her hips against him, and he hardened. His breath hitched, and she repeated the motion. With a growl, he captured her mouth. He was demanding and fierce, and before she ceded all thought and control to him, she silently acknowledged he'd won.

But her loss was sweet because his skills were epic. His lips devoured hers, his tongue swept the inside of her mouth, tasting, taunting, touching until she couldn't breathe. He reached around her and unclasped her bra. As it fell, he took her breasts in his hands, caressing them until she whimpered. He couldn't hear her, but he must have felt the vibration in his mouth. His lips stretched in a smile, and he squeezed. She gripped his upper arms. His taut muscles bunched beneath her palms. He unclasped her jeans and slid them over her hips. She shimmied out of them. She kept as much contact against him as possible, and her reward was his groan.

"God, I need you," he whispered against her mouth. His hands were everywhere at once, yet never where she needed them to be for long enough, leaving trails of heat and ache in their wake. Pulling her against him, he two-stepped backward until they were right outside the glass shower doors. His arm flailed behind him as he reached for the shower faucet. When he made contact, the shower jet turned on. A stream of steaming water hissed and pattered against the shower wall. The mirror steamed, and their interwoven profile—a mix of his and her limbs, curves of backs and buttocks and breasts—faded until only a café-au-lait-colored shadow in the glass betrayed any hint of their presence.

He grasped her elbows and stepped away from her. His gaze raked her body from top to bottom. Her skin heated, and the hint of a smile teased his lips. His eyes—black with desire, the pupils outlined with a rim of electric blue—worshipped her. His body reminded her of a statue of one of the gods, sculpted, fluid, radiating energy even as they stood still. His erection proved how ready he was for her, and she flared her nostrils to take in more air as the water pelted her.

She wanted him. Forget her concerns about him being her boss. They'd had sex once already, and the gates of hell hadn't opened. Forget about not wanting relationships. The thought of letting him go filled her with emptiness. Maybe it was time for her to stop thinking about imagined consequences, to stop preparing for every perceived outcome, and let lust and desire and need take over.

She jumped at the sound of a loud ring. Ted's gaze shifted to the counter. His phone shone in the pocket of his jeans. His fingers against her chin drew her to him, and he kissed her again. "Don't worry about it," he said.

But it rang again. Ted groaned.

"Let me turn my phone off." He ran his hands through her hair. "Don't move."

She stilled, enjoying the play of his muscles and the sight of his backside as he strode to the vanity. He stopped, and his body went still.

"Ted, what's wrong?"

His back was toward her. His resemblance to a statue was more pronounced. The energy he'd given off moments before evaporated, replaced by…nothing. As seconds of stillness ticked by, his muscles hardened. His neck stiffened. He turned to her, and she blanched at the icy coldness in his gaze. Once again, he looked at his phone, typing furiously.

"Ted, talk to me."

But again, he remained silent, focused on the screen. It was as if all the oxygen left the room, replaced by a void, a vacuum. She shivered.

Finally, after an endless stretch of time, he looked at her.

"What did you do?" he asked.

****

He'd never believed a heart could break. It was a muscle, not a china box. It could strain, it could atrophy, it could stop or seize, but break? Not until Greg's two texts.

—*She's guilty.*—

—*I have proof.*—

The third text was a photo of the computer security log. There were circles around IDs. All he needed was to call Greg, and he'd find out the circled IDs were Abby's. But no, it couldn't be possible. The Abby he knew would never have behaved like this. He'd trusted her. He tapped a response to Greg.

—*This doesn't prove anything.*—

Greg's fourth text was the knife to his heart. A screenshot of the ID connected to Abby's name. He shut his eyes, willing the information away. But it was still there when he opened them, and he turned. He stared at the beautiful creature who'd made him believe his difficulty hearing wasn't an obstacle, and his heart shattered. He grabbed his hearing aids, hands shaking, and put them in his ears.

"What are you talking about?"

"Don't pretend you don't know," he said. His throat hurt from trying not to yell.

"I don't." Stepping out of the shower, she wrapped her arms around her waist, then turned and pulled a towel from the heated rack and wrapped it around her body. Moments ago, it was his body wrapped around her. Now, he'd never touch her again. Remembering his own nakedness, he bent and retrieved his boxers from the floor.

"The security breach," he said. "It was you."

Her jaw dropped, her face a combination of shock and incredulity. He had to hand it to her, she played her part well.

"I told you, I found evidence of it and was creating a patch to prevent it from happening again," she said.

He handed his phone to her, loathe to be close enough to reach her. Her mouth opened, and her features froze into a mask. Without a word, she stalked past him out of the bathroom and to her computer.

"I have the proof, Abby." His heart shattered. "It was you." He followed her into the bedroom. "Don't touch it," he yelled. "The computer is company property."

She raised her hands and nodded to the screen. "Fine."

"What?"

She rose and pulled a piece of paper and a pen from her purse. After scribbling on it, she handed it to him. She was going old school?

With a look of disbelief, he read what she'd written. It wasn't a message, as he'd first thought. It was strings of letters and numbers. She nodded at the laptop. "Enter it into the computer. It will show you all my work."

"Not until we get to the office," he said. "I won't take the chance the code you gave me will destroy evidence."

"The longer you wait, the greater the chance the guilty person will get away with it."

But all he could think of was how she'd already stolen his heart. What else could she take?

Chapter Twenty-One

When their plane landed in California, Ted took Abby's arm and whisked her from the tarmac to his waiting car, which took them to the office. Once there, he led her past the rest of the employees into his office, pressed her into a seat, and sat at his desk. When she rose, he glared. When she continued to walk toward the door, he took advantage of his longer legs and met her there, blocking it with his body.

"Sit," he said.

"I need to use the bathroom." If she remained near him any longer, she would explode.

"I said sit."

"And I said I need to use the bathroom." She needed five minutes alone.

He scratched his head and expelled a breath. "Come with me." Abby marveled at how Ted managed to take her arm, yet touch her as little as possible, as he led her toward the bathrooms. Along the way, people whispered and stared. She shouldn't be surprised, but her chest ached anyway.

Ted kept hold of her even when they reached the employee restrooms.

"Are you serious?" she asked.

He opened the door, but she blocked the way.

"No way," she said. "I don't pee with an audience." The peace and quiet of the space, regardless of the type of space it was, beckoned her, and her nerves jumped with need at how close she was to being alone.

The rise of color on his cheeks gave her a small jolt of satisfaction, and she folded her arms, trying not to show her anxiety.

"Fine, but I'll be right here waiting for you."

That's what you think. She entered the ladies' room, walked into a stall, and slammed the door. The bang reverberated through the room, but her tension remained. She groaned—how could Ted think she was guilty? Her stomach roiled as reality set in, and she clenched her jaw, hoping not to throw up. Bracing her hands on either side of the sink, she rocked, eyes closed. She'd been so close to her dream. Why now? Why, why, why? Zings of electricity fizzed through her. She wanted to crawl out of her skin. She took a deep breath. No matter what, while she was in this building, she needed to remain calm. It was the only way she could hope to prove her innocence.

With a last look in the mirror, she smoothed her hair and her facial features and opened the door. As promised, Ted stood outside. Once again, he walked her to his office. She kept her focus ahead of her, and avoided eye contact with everyone else on the floor. They thought she was guilty; she owed them nothing.

Inside Ted's office, she spun around. "I want to see the security logs."

"I want you to sit and wait for Greg and my security team."

Her heartbeat quickened. Security? But she was innocent, and if they gave her computer access, she could prove it. "I'll wait for them, but I have a right to see what I'm being accused of."

"I showed you the photo earlier." He reminded her of a marble statue. How could she ever have been attracted to him?

She clenched her hands into fists. "Photos can be doctored. I want to see the originals."

"Wait for Greg."

Ten minutes later, Greg arrived and handed the file to Ted, who opened it right away. Greg turned to Abby, an unrecognizable expression in his gaze. She wrinkled her brow. It was smug, like he'd expected this of her. Seriously?

She raised her chin. "Greg, I want to see the security logs."

"You don't have a right to see anything from this company." He folded his arms.

"Of course I do," she said. "How else will I prove you wrong?"

Greg turned to his boss for guidance.

"Get her a printout." His voice was flat, his movements stiff, as if it pained him to give in. Well, screw him.

Been there, done that. Heat flooded through her. She was her mother's daughter, no matter how she tried not to be.

Turning to her, nostrils flared, Greg handed her the printout. She studied it, and her stomach knotted. There was an abundance of data, too much to have been put together in haste.

"You worked on this for a long time."

A look of triumph passed across Greg's face. "Since your meeting with Carol."

Abby's stomach dropped. Her hands went cold.

Before she and Ted got together. Before the airplane ride and the trade show. Before they'd gotten stuck in the snowstorm—in the same hotel, in the same room, in the same bed.

She turned to Ted. "Did you know about this—" She pointed to the security log. "—then?"

Silence stretched. For a moment, she wondered if he heard her question. But he rubbed the nape of his neck, his "tell" for when he was uncomfortable—she wished she didn't know him well enough to recognize it for what it was—and nodded, his face red.

If Greg wasn't next to Ted, she would have shouted questions at him, like how could he believe this of her? How could he have slept with her if he thought she might be guilty? How could he have lied? Truth be told, she'd ignored all her own warning signs as well.

Gravity pressed against her, her entire body heavy and dull. Her brain slowed. The smallest thoughts were impossible to formulate. Should she breathe or speak, for she couldn't manage both, and she couldn't determine which was more essential. Her mouth dried, and her hands became clammy.

Two security officers entered the office, and Greg nodded. Ted's expression hardened.

"Miss?"

She looked at them and glanced at Ted. Her throat dried. "This has to be a mistake. I can't believe you think I'm guilty." Ted ignored her. Raising her chin, she walked between the two officers—both tall and skinny, and wearing polos and chinos, neither of whom looked like they were capable of doing anything other than teeing off on the golf course—into the hallway and outside to a waiting car.

It was drizzling, and she ducked her head to keep her face dry. As the car pulled away from the curb, she looked at the office window. Ted stood at the glass, watching her leave.

****

Ted balled a piece of paper and hurled it at the garbage can he'd moved to the opposite end of his office. After Abby was taken away, he'd thrown other things across the room—a book, a plant, random pens and pencils. Greg handed him a ream of computer paper and suggested he'd cause less damage with it.

It took all his restraint not to throw the entire package at him.

A tree's-worth of paper was balled in a lopsided pyramid across from his desk. And he was elbow deep in work. He'd spent every minute at the office searching for more evidence of Abby's duplicity. He'd reconfigured the systems so the breach could never happen again, and discussed with his HR and marketing department how to spin this so it caused the least external damage to his company.

He was too stupid to realize what Abby had done. Just like his father said. It killed him to admit it, but he was stupid, at least when it came to women. Was he so pathetically grateful he fell for the first woman to ignore his hearing issues? What kind of a man was he?

He was the CEO of the company, a computer genius according to some, and he'd dragged his heels investigating her for the security breach. How could he put his livelihood, his one major accomplishment, in such danger?

Not to mention, he'd had sex with her. He, who excelled in gleaning information with body language and other non-verbal signs, couldn't tell she lied. He really was stupid.

Greg entered his office.

"What?" Screw his tone.

Greg held up his hands in surrender. "Checking in, Boss. Guess I have my answer. Want to get a drink later? Might be good for you."

He ignored the question. There wasn't enough whiskey in the world. "How the hell did I miss it?" Every time he looked at the log, a sharp pain sliced his heart.

Greg shrugged. "We all missed it. She was good."

"Too good. I want you to run checks on everyone else here. I don't want to be fooled again." Bile rose in his throat. Never again.

Greg saluted, spun on his heel, and left the room. Ted threw another ball of paper against the door and imagined a more satisfying thunk against the glass. His smartwatch vibrated, and he opened the calendar reminder.

CAST conference call tonight at 7 p.m. Eastern time.

He rubbed his face and searched for his notes from their last conference call. Right, establish a computer programming class for underprivileged youth.

This was his suggestion, and he was supposed to have researched opportunities for the upcoming call. He thought about the visit to the Boys and Girls Club in New York City. He could use it as a model. In fact, he should use it as a model and get in touch with the director to get information about how it was structured.

Spurred on to do something, he fished out the contact information for the club's director and composed an email, but stopped every few lines as he remembered visiting it with Abby.

"Dammit." His body thrummed thinking about her there. She'd glowed, as if from within, while talking to the kids, helping them code, and answering their questions. Her thoughtful answers gave her an added depth. Ted yearned to be closer. He felt the pull, and he sighed. For the first time, she'd let down her guard, and he'd gotten a glimpse of who she truly was.

And none of it jibed with the Abby who breached Sentec's security.

Shaking his head, he returned to the email. He listed his questions and explained what he and CAST wanted to create.

He and Abby had started to create something—a relationship, the kind he dreamed about. One based on more than his money. One where they cared about each other. One where she didn't think he was stupid for not being able to hear. At least, he thought they were. But how could he reconcile what he'd thought they built with what Abby had done?

Guilt niggled in the recesses of his mind. He'd never told her about how his father couldn't accept his son's hearing loss, or about the investigation. How could he expect a relationship to last if it wasn't based on trust?

With a groan, he forced his attention to the email once again, proofread it, and sent it off. He doubted he'd be effective on today's call, but at least he could say he tried to accumulate research, since the club director hadn't replied.

When he logged off the CAST conference call at 4:45 that afternoon, he leaned against the chair, closed his eyes, and thanked his suffering brain he hadn't made more of a fool of himself. He'd spaced out during half of the call, too busy with thoughts of Abby to pay attention to what anyone said. The club director hadn't responded yet. Ted couldn't add anything meaningful to the conversation.

He couldn't continue like this.

His watch buzzed, and he read the incoming text.

—*You okay?*—

Simon. Was he that obvious?

—*Why?*—

—*You weren't focused.*—

That answered that question.

—*Sorry. Other things on my mind.*—

—*Same woman as before?*—

—*She was arrested for breaching the cybersecurity of one of our clients.*—

—*Damn.*—

—*Tell me about it.*—

—*I guess she must have been exceptional if she was able to fool you.*—

—*She was.*—

He paced the confines of his office. She was exceptional in every way. And she'd fooled him. He frowned. Maybe he was complacent. He'd left enough of the investigation in Greg's hands. It was long past time he investigated the breach. Grabbing the security logs, he collapsed onto the couch, put up his feet, and scanned the log. Three hours later, he rubbed his face. There was something he had missed. It was so simple—

"Holy fuck."

Chapter Twenty-Two

Abby scratched her left ankle for the bazillionth time in a week. The home monitor itched like crazy and while her home was better than jail, confinement sucked. She stared with longing out the window. She'd give anything to go for a run. Turning on the TV, she flicked through stupid morning talk shows, reruns of old sitcoms, and alarmist news programs before she settled on a European football match. She couldn't care less about soccer, but she needed the noise as a distraction.

She had too much time to think.

Her phone rang, and she lunged for it. "Hello?"

"Abby, it's Peter."

Her public defender, who was too busy to talk to her during the past week, if her unanswered messages were any indication. He was cold and uncaring, but all she could afford. A frisson of anxiety ran up her spine. "Any updates?"

"I need you to come to my office now. I'll send a rideshare for you. It'll be there in twenty minutes."

"For what?" Was there evidence she was innocent? If so, why didn't he answer her multitude of messages?

"We'll discuss it when you get here."

Her stomach clenched. What now?

Twenty minutes later she was downstairs. A white sedan pulled in front of her apartment. The driver got out, showed her his ID, and held open the door. The sun was warm on her back, and she would have given anything to bask in it. Instead, she climbed into the climate-controlled car. They arrived at her lawyer's office. She took a deep breath of fresh air and memorized the blue sky before she walked into his office. The receptionist buzzed her in, and Peter met her at the door.

The other man in Peter's office piqued her curiosity. He looked like the security guards who escorted her out of the building. When he revealed his badge, her heart sank, and fear exploded in her chest.

"Abby, this is Detective Bradley."

With a swallow, she regulated her pulse. She nodded to him and sat in the chair Peter pointed to. No one spoke, and Abby tried not to jiggle her foot as her lawyer shuffled through papers on his utilitarian black metal desk. The golf-pro officer stood to the side, holding up the wall. The silence was killing her.

Demonstrating how fed up she'd been with her previous surroundings, she glanced with interest at Peter's small office. Bookshelves filled with law books at random angles filled the wall behind his desk. Framed diplomas from Duquesne Law School and the American Bar Association hung crooked on one wall. She itched to straighten them, but she was afraid any sudden moves would freak out the detective. The last thing she wanted was more false charges added to her case. The air conditioner under the windows rattled, and the hum would drive her crazy.

He cleared his throat, broke the five-second silence, and looked down his bulbous nose. "The charges have been dropped. Your record is clean, and

Detective Bradley, here, will remove the ankle monitor."

Her breath whooshed out of her like someone punched her in the stomach. She gasped and bent forward. Her chest heaved as she drew breath. Waves of dizziness overwhelmed her, and tears pricked behind her eyelids. She was free. On cue, the detective approached and knelt by her ankle.

A jumble of thoughts ping-ponged in her brain. "Why?"

The tugging on her leg distracted her, and the detective's balding, freckled pate caught her eye. He should wear a hat on the golf course. If he played golf.

"The charges have been dropped."

"But why now?" She'd cried her innocence for more than a week, and no one listened.

He held his pen like a mustache beneath his nose. "You're innocent."

No shit, Sherlock. "I've said it for a week, every time I called you. What changed?"

"According to the documents filed with the court, the log was falsified to make it look as if the culprit was you. Turns out it was—" He paused as he skimmed the document. "—Greg Stanton."

She inhaled so sharply she choked. With watery eyes, she took a shaky breath. "Greg?"

Peter shook his head. "He's not my client, you are. The judge signed off on your release. Here are copies for your files. Ms. Marlow, you're free to go."

She rose, and her knees wobbled. Once again, the detective stepped forward to help, grasped her elbow. "Thank you," she whispered. "That's it?" she asked at the door. "All of this is over?"

Peter nodded. "Congratulations. I'd suggest you hire a lawyer to sue to get your job back. Or at least a nice severance package with them."

She straightened her posture. "No, I don't want it."

As she left the public defender's office, she realized it was true. No job was worth the horror she'd gone through. As for Ted? She should have listened to her gut in the beginning and stayed far away from him.

****

"Why'd you do it?"

The words scraped from Ted's mouth as he sat in the lawyer's office across the conference room table three days after Greg's arrest. He'd been let out on bail pending trial after pleading guilty, unable to access any technology. Ted had requested this meeting, and the lawyers reluctantly agreed.

Never before had he wished for perfect hearing. He wouldn't have to look at the man he'd considered a friend. The sight of him nauseated Ted, and he wondered how he could have been duped so easily.

Greg's lawyer nodded, and his ex-friend stared at his lap. "Ever get a visceral reaction to someone?"

Ted frowned. "What do you mean?"

"Abby walked into the office, and her coding was the most elegant I'd ever seen." He ran his hand over his jaw. "I used to code like that. All of a sudden, I was looking at my successor."

Chills ran down Ted's spine. "So you decided to sabotage my company?"

"At first I was in awe of her. Then I got nervous. I figured if she was that good, she'd replace me."

Ted shook his head. "You were my friend. How could you doubt my loyalty to you?"

Greg gave a mirthless laugh. "Loyalty has no place in business, Ted."

"It does in mine." Who was this guy, and how could Ted have misjudged him? A million questions danced in his head, but he waited, trying to figure out which one to ask first.

Greg continued. "Carol approached me with a plan. At first, she presented it as a way to test the system. Internal hacking to find the stressors. But it soon became clear she was looking to take you down."

"And you let her?"

Greg shrugged. "She suggested we pin it on Abby, and I thought it was a great way to get my standing back. I planned to fix everything before word of the breach got out. The company was safe."

Ted reeled.

A week later, and he still hadn't recovered. He banged his hand against the handlebar of his bike and winced as the impact traveled up his arm. It was a small price to pay for the damage he'd inflicted on Abby. He'd spent his entire life proving himself—to his family, his friends, and himself. When he finally met someone who accepted him as he was, he blew it. Royally.

His blind loyalty to Greg caused irreparable damage. Letting the man he'd called a friend come this close to ruining his company out of what—jealousy? He'd put his faith in the wrong person. The betrayal still stung. How could he have trusted someone like Greg and not Abby? Abby was innocent, and he'd lost her.

He cringed at what he'd almost lost—the company he'd developed, his reputation…even his friendship with Greg. Was it all fake? His hands shook. He couldn't go down this road anymore.

But Abby? Abby was his everything. He needed to get her back. Needed her like the air he breathed. How could he have believed her to be capable of something like this? He took a deep breath and thought he smelled strawberries. He'd imagined her scent everywhere. He pictured the curve of her cheek, her pink lips. His hand clenched as he remembered the softness of her skin.

He sat on his bike, three doors from Abby's, and flexed and released his hands on the handlebars as he pinned his gaze to her door. What the hell was he doing?

When his mind cleared, and he'd discovered the error in the security log, he called her. Well, first he contacted the police about her innocence and Greg's guilt. Then he called her. As much as he hated using the phone, she deserved to hear his apology. But she ignored him. He expected her to answer? Heat rose in his face. Yeah. Stupid, really. What person in his right mind expected a woman falsely accused—and arrested—to want him? And when she stayed silent, he texted her a sincere and heartfelt apology. She remained unresponsive. His text log showed it was unread.

A normal person would have given up by now. He decided to approach it from a professional angle. He'd asked Human Resources to messenger over a new employment contract, which was returned with a "No thank you," written on a Post-it. Who did that?

Abby.

So against the explicit advice of his Human Resources head, he brought the battle to her.

Swinging off his bike, he locked it to the lamppost,

and walked toward her apartment. He swallowed, his throat dry. Everything hinged on his behavior. He rang the doorbell and dried his damp hands on his thighs. She would be pissed, and he understood. Motion flashed through the peephole, and the chain slid, and the door unlocked.

She opened the door, and his heart pounded hard enough he'd swear she could see his chest vibrate. Hurt and anger flashed in her gaze, and his heart stuttered. He'd destroyed her. The pain he caused her slayed him. He needed to convince her his apology was sincere. Every part of him wanted to fix what he'd damaged, but she was strong, and he doubted she'd let him. She'd refused his every advance. Still, he needed to try.

"Hi," he said. His voice rasped in his throat, and he cleared it. He'd never been so nervous in his life.

"Go away. I don't want to talk to you, and I don't want my job back."

He rubbed the nape of his neck. As expected, this wasn't going well. "I came to apologize. What I did was unforgivable, but I'd like another chance. My company was on the line, and instead of trusting you and realizing there was no way you could have been involved, I let Greg lead me astray. I could give you a list of reasons why I reacted that way, but none of them are good enough when it comes to you. I'm sorry. Please come back." He raised his head. Could he convince her?

"You already texted me an apology."

He shifted his focus to her lips. "Only because you wouldn't answer the phone." *Even for a phone call from me.* The old Abby, the one he'd fallen in love with, would have recognized the sacrifice he made to call her. This new one didn't. Not that he blamed her. Still, he'd held out hope.

"I don't work for you any longer. I'm under no obligation to take your calls." She started to close her door.

Her words punched him in the gut, and he shot out his hand to keep the door open. "I know, but there's more to us than work." Unfortunately, the two pieces were entwined, and he'd damaged both.

"You destroyed any 'us' there might have been."

Even hard of hearing, he could read the icy drip of her words. His heart froze. "I'm sorry. Is there any way I can convince you to come back?" *To me.*

"No."

His stomach clenched. "Are you concerned about what people will think? Everyone knows you're innocent. They all ask about you and want you back." *Especially me.*

"You arrested me. I'll never forget it. Neither will anyone else."

He stared at the ground and rubbed the nape of his neck. "I was wrong. I understand I put you through a terrible ordeal. I know you can never forgive me. But you loved your work, and I know how important a steady salary is to you. There's no one more qualified than you. Please, Abby, come back."

"You know nothing about me," she said.

His stomach muscles clenched.

"I wouldn't work for your stupid company if it was the last one on Earth. Not for all the money in the world."

Pressure built in his ears, like when his hearing aid batteries died, and spots appeared before his eyes. She knew how much he hated the word "stupid," yet she'd used it anyway. She'd promised never to say it again, but that was when they'd been building a relationship. Her use of the word told him better than any explanation there was no chance. He'd vowed he wouldn't jump at the use of that word, that he was beyond his father's reach. But his heart thudded in his chest. He wasn't reacting to the word, but to Abby using it. It was the clearest sign they were through. He looked past her, unable to meet her gaze.

"You're the best programmer, the best woman, I've ever known." His voice was thick.

She slammed the door. He stumbled along the walkway and returned to his bike.

It was over.

****

She slid to the floor, the wood cool through her tank top. As she landed on the floor, she started to shake. Her teeth chattered. Fumbling for her phone, she called Eden.

"He's gone," she said when her best friend answered. Her voice hitched, and her eyes welled. Sobs tore through her and made her throat raw.

"Abs? Abby, are you home?"

She couldn't answer. She whimpered.

"I'll be right over. Stay there."

Dropping the phone, Abby curled in a ball next to the door. When Eden arrived, the door pushed against Abby's hip and spun her around in slow motion.

"Oh, honey." Her friend crouched next to her and wrapped Abby in her arms. When her sobs faded to hiccups, she walked arm in arm with Eden to the living room.

All the crying exhausted her, and she curled under a light zebra-print blanket, huddled into the corner of her green sofa. It was the first piece of furniture she'd ever bought, with her first paycheck. She and her mom moved so often, they'd never owned furniture. It was another way for her not to be like her mother, and usually, it gave her comfort. Not this time. Her eyes filled again.

"Oh no," Eden said. "The Abby I know doesn't cry, and while it's okay in certain circumstances, you have to tell me what's going on first. You can cry again later."

She handed her friend a tissue, and Abby wiped her eyes and blew her nose, giving a shaky sigh when she was finished.

"What happened?"

She crumpled the tissue in her hand. "He asked me to return to work. Begged me."

"And?"

"And I told him no."

"Of course. How can you work for him?"

Abby played with the blanket, running the soft hem through her fingers. Her friend agreed with her. She should feel good about her decision.

"So what's the problem?" asked Eden.

"He apologized, but it's like he had sex with me to find out if I stole the information, and now he has his answer, I'm irrelevant."

"Abs—"

"No, it's true. CEO Ted came to my door. Ted, the guy I fell for, who acted as if I was the only woman in the world for him, was nowhere to be seen."

"Are you sure you read him right? I mean, it's been

stressful for both of you, and you said he was better at compartmentalizing your relationship than you were."

Abby shifted her position and slipped her hands inside the sleeves of her sweatshirt. "I shouldn't have gotten involved with my boss, Ede. How dumb am I to follow my mother's lead and think I can have a different outcome?"

"You're not dumb, Abby. You're the smartest person I know. And this isn't like what happened with your mom."

"No, it's worse. She never got arrested."

Eden covered her mouth. "Sorry. I shouldn't laugh."

Abby shook her head. "No, I suppose in some alternate universe it could be considered funny."

Her friend leaned over and gave Abby a hug. "You know I love you and support you, in spite of my misplaced humor."

"Yeah, I do." If Ted acknowledged their complicated relationship, she would feel better. She'd still be angry, but she'd know there was something to work toward.

"Talk to him."

She scowled. "I can't."

"Can't or won't?"

"Both." Her head throbbed.

"Abby, you're better than that. You're fearless when it comes to what you want. What have you to lose?"

She swallowed. "I loved my job, and I was good at it." She pulled in a deep breath. "He fired me because he thought I broke the law." Her face heated. "We had a relationship, and he should have trusted me, he should have come to me with his concerns about me, not just about the breach. Plus, he slept with me while he suspected I was guilty." She glared at her friend, and Eden took her hand. "And because the relationship was personal, he owed me more. I can't trust him. I can't work with him knowing how much I love him because I can't have him. I can't give myself to someone who doesn't trust me and who I can't trust."

Chapter Twenty-Three

There was a lot to be said for being a programmer in Silicon Valley, Abby thought as she watched new emails appear in her inbox. For the past week, she'd submitted her résumé to every top cybersecurity company she could think of—both those she'd seen at the conference and those she knew of on her own.

Her stomach churned the first time she'd hit send—and the second, third, and fourth time too—because of the accusation and her subsequent arrest. People talked within industries. The likelihood of other firms hearing about what happened to her was high. She hoped they'd heard of her innocence as fast, or she would never find a job.

To her surprise, responses poured in from every firm she submitted to. No one mentioned the issue—although what they'd say in an interview might be a different story. Now, a week later, and she organized the last of her interview schedule.

Pushing away from her laptop, she went into the bedroom to get ready for her first interview. Her phone rang, and she put it on speaker. From previous experience, it was better to get phone calls from her mom over with; otherwise, she'd continue to call and complain about how busy Abby was.

"Hi, Mom." *Please let this be short.*

"Hi, Baby. What are you doing?"

"Getting ready for a job interview." She sifted through her clothes.

"Oh, what are you wearing?"

She pulled out her choices. "Khaki jeans, white blouse, and flats."

"You are not. You can't show up to an interview like that."

She shimmied into the jeans. "Yes, I can, Mom. It's a programming job, not marketing."

"But haven't you heard of dressing for the position you want, rather than the one you've got?"

"I'm dressing for the job I want. Now, what else can I help you with?" She pulled her blouse off and went into the bathroom to fix her hair and makeup.

"I still don't understand why you let that man get away," her mother said. "He was perfect for you."

Abby banged her forehead against the mirror. "He had me arrested, remember?" Her throat closed, and she stopped talking. She wouldn't cry again.

"You turned out to be innocent, and trust is overrated in relationships, darling. He's loaded."

And that, right there, was why she never listened to her mother when she gave out relationship advice. "Look, Mom, I have to go. Is there something you need or can we talk later?"

"I want to come out and visit you. The snowstorm prevented me from visiting you in New York. I want to reschedule."

Oh God. "Why?"

"Is that any way to talk to me? You're my only daughter, and I want to see you."

There had to be an ulterior motive. Her mother never pulled the family strings unless there was something on the other end she wanted. "I meant I'm busy right now with job interviews. Why don't we wait until I'm more settled so I can spend more time with you."

"But you'll be busy with work. No, I think this is the perfect time. I'll be out this weekend. The airlines have a sale. It'll be great."

No, it would be awful, but she couldn't say no. "Okay, Mom. I've got to go."

****

Ted's emails poured in, as usual, and he sighed. He needed a break, and he wouldn't get one any time soon. He frowned at four emails from competitors. He opened them and pushed away from his desk.

"Hi, Ted, I'm looking at a résumé from a former employee of yours and wondered what you could tell me about her?"

All four asked the same question. Abby listed him as a reference? Seemed kind of ballsy. He knew one of the senders and shot off a response:

"She was talented. Did she list me as a reference?"

The recipient must have monitored his email. His response came in minutes.

"No, but I saw the newspaper stories, and I wanted to find out from you what the inside story was."

He should have felt better, but his chest tightened. Once again he'd suspected the worst of her. He lowered his head to his hands. God, he'd damaged her reputation badly enough that potential employers contacted him to verify her credentials. Bile rose in his throat. He stared at the screen. What could he say about the programmer he'd fired and arrested? If he praised her, he called his own judgment into question. If he criticized her, he'd be lying.

After typing and deleting numerous responses, he settled on one, hit send much harder than was necessary, and stormed out of the office. Outside, the cool air hit his face and should have refreshed him. She wasn't with him. He'd let her go. He'd been stupid. He had no idea how to fix it.

He couldn't convince her he trusted her if she wouldn't talk to him.

At the street corner, he spun around, almost knocking a woman over who was behind him—damn wind prevented him from hearing her—and raced to his office. Then he called Simon.

****

Abby tiptoed into the kitchen Sunday morning, careful not to wake her mother who was asleep on the pullout sofa in the living room. Closing the shutters over the counter that separated the two rooms, and shutting the door into the hallway, she turned on the coffeepot and opened the fridge. Her stomach rumbled and already the scent of coffee was waking her up. Grabbing a blueberry yogurt, she leaned against the counter and waited for the coffee to brew.

Her mother drove her crazy.

She'd arrived yesterday, and you'd think it wouldn't be bad, but…Abby shook her head. There was no point expecting something different from a woman who hadn't changed in years, possibly ever. Still, a small part of Abby hoped for something new—understanding, hope, a vision greater than her own survival. She licked her spoon and stared into her coffee mug.

Her thoughts drifted to the job interview. The old

Abby would have said she'd nailed it. But her confidence was shaken, and while she thought it went well, niggling doubts crept in. What if she wasn't good enough? What if no one trusted her again because of Ted's accusation? He was well respected in the industry. Though someone else was found guilty, her name was tied to the news. She squeezed the mug. She needed to stop thinking about that man. Her mother made it worse by bringing him up all the time. No matter how much she denied it, she missed him. Every bone ached like she suffered from the flu, but she couldn't show her feelings to her mother. Her mother couldn't understand why Abby wouldn't crawl back to him.

And in the middle of the night, when her body burned for him, she wondered the same thing. By the time the sun rose, she'd shored her will up again. He didn't trust her. He'd shown his distrust when he'd assumed she was after his money because Greg overheard part of her conversation with her mother, when he jumped on her use of "stupid" and assumed she referred to him, and when he'd investigated her in secret.

That's what she couldn't move past. They both carried a lot of baggage. The only way for them to succeed together was to talk and to trust each other. He couldn't manage it. *Neither can you.* Her glance flitted to the closed shutter. Regardless, they couldn't be together.

The kitchen door opened. "Dreaming about the rich lover boy again?" her mother asked.

Dammit. "Trying to wake up." Abby raised her mug. "Want some coffee?"

"I'll have it on the balcony while I smoke."

Her mother was annoyed Abby wouldn't let her smoke inside. Aside from the health hazard, the smell reminded Abby of her various temporary homes growing up, and she hated the memory. She let her mother take her coffee outside alone—a few more minutes of silence to master her resolve would be helpful.

Her phone rang, and she answered.

"Is this Abby Marlow?"

"Yes." A telemarketer on a Sunday?

"I'm Clive Perkins, and I run the community center downtown. Our computer instructor quit, and I need someone to offer a computer programming course. I...uh...saw your résumé online, and I was told you might be interested. It's part time, on Saturdays."

Her heart leaped and desire swished through her body, silencing the question she'd started to ask—who told him? "I am. Can you give me more information?"

"I hoped you could stop by today, and we could discuss it in person. I know it's last minute, but—"

"Absolutely." Her pulse thrummed as possibilities ran through her mind. This was what she loved.

She jotted down his location, and they agreed to meet in an hour.

"What was that all about?" her mother asked as she came inside.

Abby's excitement overrode her typical hesitation at telling her mother anything about her life, and she blurted out the conversation with the program director.

"You used to go to those programs when you were little." A nostalgic look passed across her mother's face before it hardened once again. "Why in the world would you want to relive something like that now?"

The question stunned Abby. "It's a chance to give back," she snapped.

"Give back? To whom? These people are nothing to you."

"You're wrong, Mom. The kids need to see what's possible so they can strive for something more. I'm giving them tools to succeed in life. If those of us who've made it don't show them, they'll never know what they can achieve."

"Made it, huh? Well, you better insist on payment. Nothing is free."

Of course her mother would say that. Given Abby's upbringing, she was always concerned with her financial security. But she had job prospects lined up—paying ones—and she'd been careful with saving for rainy days. Maybe she hadn't expected a hurricane, but she was okay for now. Sometimes doing good was more important than making money. However, it was pointless to try to explain it to her mother. "Tell you what, Mom. Why don't you come with me? You can shop nearby while I meet with the director, and we can go to lunch, my treat."

Her mom's face brightened, and Abby glimpsed the vivacious woman she used to be, before life battered her and made her the bitter woman she'd become.

"All right, I need to get ready. You never know who I might meet while we're out."

Chapter Twenty-Four

Abby sat in the vinyl and chrome seat across a scarred wooden desk and stared at Clive Perkins. After she dropped her mother at the nearby shopping center, she'd gone to the community center and arrived with five minutes to spare. Now in Clive's office, she tried not to bounce in her seat.

"I have a generous donor—a conglomerate called CAST—who will provide us with ten laptops, as well as improve our Wi-Fi, and I want to run coding lessons on weekends." Clive leaned forward. His brown skin reminded Abby of well-worn leather. "Your name was mentioned as someone I should talk to. Would you be interested?"

Who mentioned her name? She didn't recognize the conglomerate. She wanted to ask but refrained. "How many classes would you want me to teach?"

"We'd start with one class on Saturday mornings, but we might expand depending on the interest."

"I could put something together for maybe an hour for four or six weeks. We could cover basic programming concepts and, depending on what the kids are capable of, maybe run an advanced class for some of them."

Clive smiled. "I have to admit, I don't know much about computers. If you think it will work, I'm happy to let you run with it."

"Why me?"

His brown eyes twinkled. "Why not you?"

The NSA should hire this guy, he gives nothing away. "You've mentioned a few times I was suggested to you. Who suggested me?"

"Someone who asked to remain anonymous."

Abby shifted in her chair. What was the motive? Ted crossed her mind, but she dismissed him. No way.

"If you're too busy, I can look for someone else," Clive said.

Something about this man reminded her of the director of the community center where she attended classes. Like Bruce, Clive believed in possibilities. "This type of program is what got me started, and I'd love to give back."

"Great. You'd get paid, but not much."

"Keep the money for the program. I'm happy to donate my free time."

Clive rose and held out his hand. "It's generous of you." He held Abby's gaze. He was the kind of man who noticed everything, and she fought the urge to squirm. "I look forward to working with you."

Abby caught her mother a few blocks away in a clothing boutique, admiring a dress that cost more than Abby's weekly food budget. Breathing a sigh of relief when her mother replaced it on the rack, she touched her mother's shoulder.

She clenched her stomach as she realized what she'd done. She used to touch Ted's shoulder, to let him know she was there so as not to startle him. Calling across a store, no matter how upscale, was more her mother's speed. She blinked several times and refused to cry.

"So what did the delinquents want?"

"Mom."

"Sorry." Her mother rolled her eyes. "How much will they pay you?"

They left the store and walked down the street. The sun shone, and Abby enjoyed the warmth. "Nothing. I'm doing it for free."

"Are you insane?" Her mother grabbed her and spun her around. "Did I raise an idiot? Why wouldn't you insist on payment?"

She clenched her teeth. "I want—"

"—don't give me the 'I want to give something back' bullshit. You don't have a job. You can't afford 'free.' "

The start of a headache blossomed into a full-blown one, and she rubbed her temples. "You know, Mom, I'm tired of the same old argument. I love you. I'll never stop loving you. But you and I will never agree on this. Some things are more important than money."

Her mother stopped midstride and placed her hands on her hips. "Like what?"

Abby remembered the good moments of her relationship with Ted, and there were a few. "Like trust, morals, and honesty."

"None of which will put food on the table. It's why you need a ma—"

"Stop." Abby turned and looked at her mother. "I've never wanted to depend on a man for my survival, and I never will. I'm smart, like you. I'm financially responsible. My success is my own. You've taught me many things, Mom. No, I haven't liked all of them, but you've taught me the value of independence. I'll always be grateful. But I also think you and I have to agree to disagree on the importance of giving back."

Her mother opened and closed her mouth, her face coloring. "You're grateful for what I've taught you?"

The surprise in her mother's voice sliced through Abby. Had she never thanked her mother? "Yes. I am."

Her mother grabbed her in a tight hug.

Abby's eyes watered. "Let's go get lunch, Mom, my treat."

Her mother's lined face settled into planes of acceptance and pleasure. When they'd navigated the line of the café and received their order, they squashed into a corner table and ate in silence.

"I think I'll go home tonight," her mom said.

"What? Why?" Shock prevented her normal relief from flooding through. Her mother never volunteered to leave, and she never left early. Was she offended by her honesty?

"You've got interviews all this week, and now you've got to plan for your community center project. Despite our disagreement, I have taught you some things, so my work here is done." Her mother gave her a wink. "I don't want to get in the way."

"Mom, you're not in the way." *Except for taking over my living room and criticizing my every move.*

"I love you, Abby."

"I love you, too, Mom." And for once, Abby was satisfied.

****

Ted took his bike out for a ride the following weekend and pushed his muscles harder than he had in months. By the time he returned to his condo, his legs were Jell-O, his back was tight, and his hands were cramped like claws from gripping the handlebars.

And no matter how hard he'd tried, he couldn't outrun his demons.

Emails from tech CEOs poured in, thanking him for his recommendation of Abby as a candidate and raving over her credentials, abilities, and interview skills. He wasn't sure if he should be nauseated or proud—truth be told, he was a little of both, and it irked him. He already couldn't get her out of his mind, and these emails made it worse.

Clive Perkins called him and thanked him for putting him in touch with Abby, who was starting this weekend. A longing to watch her in action flared strong enough he'd had no choice but to ride in the opposite direction of the community center—up and down hills—so as not to show up unannounced.

He'd beg on his knees for her forgiveness—make a total fool of himself—if there was the slightest chance it would work. It wouldn't, and not only would he look like a fool, but he'd also look like a drooling one since her beauty made him ache.

He left his aids on the counter and climbed in the shower, let the hot water jet pulse against his stiff muscles. He braced his hands on the cool marble and willed his muscles to relax. But it was impossible. Everything reminded him of Abby, especially the shower.

He'd been an ass. First of all, he never should have pursued an attraction with an employee. But he let his dick rule his brain. When he'd first learned of the security breach, he should have hired an outside source to investigate. But he left it to Greg, who was the culprit in the first place. The man whom he'd thought was his friend was jealous of his success and plotted with Carol to take the company. He was still bitter about it, even though the two of them were under arrest and set to go to trial. And last and most important, he should have been honest with Abby. But he wasn't and...he lost her, all because he was afraid.

Wrapping an Egyptian cotton towel around his waist, he cleared off the foggy beveled mirror, and stared at his reflection. Bloodshot eyes with dark circles beneath them. Frown lines bracketed his mouth. Great, he looked like an old man.

He looked like his father.

Fuck.

At what point in his life would he stop being afraid, stop trying to prove his father wrong, and take a chance on his own happiness? He lathered on shaving cream with a brush and made quick work of a day's worth of beard. The faster he finished, the less he thought about his father.

Who might have been right about him.

When it came to Abby, he was stupid. Stupid in love.

The room rocked, and he gripped the black granite countertop.

No way.

He toweled off, threw on clothes, and texted Simon.

—The center is grateful for the computer donation, but I need to talk to you. You available?—

He drummed his fingers against his thigh as he waited for an answer. Maybe Simon was busy. Maybe he was busy with Meg. Shit, what if he interrupted...?

The dancing dots appeared, and he held his breath

as he waited for a response.

—Text or v-chat?—

Simon rarely offered a video chat because he hated people to see his face. But Meg changed him.

—Video if you don't mind.—

—Gimme 5.—

Ted did a double take when Simon appeared on screen, fully visible.

"You left the lights on," Ted said. He hoped Simon wouldn't think he reacted to his face. The man was burned in an accident years ago and was self-conscious about the scars, even with his closest friends.

"Meg threatened me."

Ted nodded. "Yeah, she can be scary."

"You have no idea."

"Well, it's good to see you, Si. I hope I didn't interrupt any—"

"You never ask for anything. If you need to talk, I'm here. What's going on?"

Ted shifted in his full-grain black leather chair. If Simon could show his face, Ted could talk about Abby. Right? "How did you know you were in love?"

"Dammit, I owe Meg a monster movie. Meg! Hold on a second, Ted."

"What?" Meg appeared on screen. "Oh, hi, Ted. How are you?"

Ted tried not to show his confusion. "How are you?"

"She's better now she's getting me to watch a stupid monster movie," Simon interrupted.

"I won? Yay! And you know you love them, Si."

Ted cleared his throat. "Is there any chance I'd understand this better if I turned on the closed captioning?"

Simon shook his head, and Meg laughed. "Sorry, Ted. I'll let Simon explain. You need to come visit soon. Please. Oh, and bring the woman."

His heart squeezed. "Doubtful. Bye, Meg."

"Sorry. Meg bet me your text for help was related to a woman. I said it was about business. The winner gets to pick the movie, and she always picks monster movies."

"I don't know how to respond, other than to repeat what I said earlier, she's scary." She was also perfect, and Ted hoped someday to find someone like her. He thought Abby was the one.

"Ha. So returning to your question..." Simon leaned against his chair and folded his hands over his midsection, his face dreamy. "Well, I couldn't stop thinking about her, I only wanted to be around her, and I showed her my face."

He ran a hand across the nape of his neck as images of Abby flickered through his memory. Every single one of Simon's criteria fit. "Fuck."

"Well, there's that, too." Simon's mouth twitched. "But lust is different than love."

"That's not what I meant."

He was in love with Abby.

"How long have you loved her?" Simon asked.

Damn good question. Was it when he'd run into her in the sporting goods store? During the conference? Sledding in New York?

"I don't know. Since I met her, I'd guess."

"Have you told her?"

"She won't speak to me."

Ted explained the last few weeks.

251

"Why don't you come for a visit?" Simon asked. "I don't know if I have a quick fix for you, but Meg might be able to help, and sometimes someplace without the memories is good. Besides, we can brainstorm our next CAST project."

"Are you sure Meg wants a houseguest?"

"She'll love having you here, and we have the guest house you can stay at—it's small, but you'll have it all to yourself. And if you let me know what tech needs you have, I can set it up before you arrive."

Ted signed off and pushed away from his desk.

He needed to get away and think. He was on his way to Gull's Point, Maine.

****

"Abby, can I see you in my office before you leave, please?"

Abby's stomach tightened, a familiar occurrence. A week into her new job, and she started to get the hang of things. But she kept up her guard. She knew how that turned out.

Following her new boss, Mackenzie, into her office, Abby shut the door behind her and sat at the worktable. Mack Inc. was a startup computer security firm, and Abby was their lead programmer. Somehow, after Ted fired her, she'd managed to land a job with a better title and more money. And a woman led the company.

Mackenzie was brilliant and egotistical—anyone who named a company after themselves was—but she possessed a great vision for the firm, and she gave Abby leeway.

Abby frowned. It was her first week here, maybe she should have asked more questions…

Mackenzie sat next to her and crossed her legs. She popped a stick of gum in her mouth. "God, I need a cigarette," she said.

Abby's surprise must have shown on her face because Mackenzie rolled her eyes. "I'm in the process of quitting, and the first week is a bitch. Anyway, I wanted to see how your first week went."

"I've started to get a feel for the place."

"I agree. You've arrived earlier and stayed later than any of us, and the amount of work you've performed in a few days is impressive. The quality, too. Now, I don't know what your experience is, but unless there's an emergency, I don't expect you to work on the weekend. However, I need to be able to reach you." They exchanged cell numbers.

"Ted Endicott was right about you," she added as Abby rose to leave.

Abby froze. "What?"

She nodded. "In his email suggesting I hire you, he talked about your talent and dedication. And if this week is any indication, I'm thrilled to have you join our team. See you Monday."

Abby spent all that evening and the following morning trying to figure out why her boss contacted Ted. When she'd put together her résumé, she'd offered references. And Mackenzie, as well as the other firms she'd interviewed with, requested three.

Ted wasn't one of them. The sooner she could forget him, the better. She'd been worried not listing her last job would be a red flag, but when she'd explained the unfortunate circumstances—which were verifiable—in her interviews, no one had a problem. And her other references glowed.

So why did Mackenzie mention Ted? Did she contact him anyway? She supposed it wasn't out of the question. Her case hit the newspapers and the trade reports. Any search of her name would bring it up. And a responsible employer would want to know the real story.

But why would Ted recommend her? Was he afraid she'd sue him? Did he feel guilty for the shitty way he'd treated her? Tough.

By the time she arrived at the community center, she still had no answer. When she entered the center, children's voices echoed down the cinder-block corridors and the odor of sweat and cleaning products greeted her, transporting her back fifteen years. She blinked a few times, focusing on where she was and how far she'd come. Then, she signed in and walked toward the new computer lab. A ball of excitement bounced in her stomach, and she pressed her hand against it, trying to remain calm. A jittery programmer made mistakes.

"Abby, it's good to see you," Clive said. "I've got four kids signed up for today, but we may get walk-ins."

"It's fine." She stowed her bag and water bottle on the table next to one of the laptops and organized the computers the kids would be using. Five minutes later, a teenaged boy hovered in the doorway.

"Anton," Clive said. "Come on in."

The gangly boy sauntered in.

"Hi, I'm Abby. Are you here to learn programming?" She held out her hand and a few seconds later, he shook it.

"Yeah."

"Come sit. Have you ever tried it?"

He shook his head.

"I hadn't either when I was your age, and I learned in a place like this."

Anton's forehead creased in a brief frown before he hid his surprise behind his teenage cool-guy façade as two girls arrived.

"Hi, I'm Abby," she said. "What are your names?"

"Tanya," said one.

"Vanessa," said the other one.

"Nice to meet you both. You know Anton, right?"

The kids looked at each other, nodded, and the three of them chatted. She was expecting one more. She decided to wait a few more minutes. Two minutes later, an older boy walked in.

"Hey, Jorge," the kids called.

He nodded to them and looked at Abby. "Our teacher's a chica?"

Across the room, Clive cleared his throat, and Jorge colored. "Sorry."

Abby shook her head. "You'd be surprised how many women are into computers."

"Cool."

She sat on the edge of the table next to them, one leg swinging. "So as I mentioned earlier, I learned computer programming in a place similar to this. It was the first time I was introduced to computers and the first time I learned there was a future for me. I thought I'd teach you what I learned and see if you're any good." The quickest way to stimulate their interest was to challenge them, and as expected, their eyes glowed.

"Today," she continued, "we'll stick to the basics."

For the next hour, she taught the kids Java and

began a demo on converting currencies. All four of the kids were quick learners and by the end of the lesson, they asked what they would learn next week.

"Okay, here's what I'll leave you with. If you have time during the week, try to write a program to convert dollars into pesos, since we converted pesos into dollars. If you finish, or if you get stuck and want to try something else, see if you can write one that prints 'Hello World' across the screen. And next Saturday, we'll write a program that asks the user for his or her name and greets the user with it."

The four kids rose and started to leave.

"Oh, and one more thing," Abby cried. "If any of your friends want to join, they're welcome to."

Clive walked over. "You were great today. The kids were engaged. Even Anton, who's kind of shy."

"Thanks. It was fun teaching them."

As she left the center, her mood was lighter than it had been in weeks.

Chapter Twenty-Five

Ted dropped his bag in the entryway of Simon's gatehouse, stretched his neck, and rolled his shoulders. Taking a quick walk through the living room, bedroom, and kitchen, and a peek into the bathroom, he nodded. The entire place could fit into his bedroom in California. It was perfect.

He wanted nothing that reminded him of home. Home reminded him of Abby. Hell, home was Abby. Although she'd never set foot in his apartment, it still reminded him of her. His bedroom and his massive king-sized bed reminded him of the bed they shared at the hotel. The marble shower in his bathroom reminded him of the "almost sex" they'd had in the hotel bathroom. The technological accommodations for his hearing—flashing lights for doorbells and alarms—reminded him of how she adapted with ease to his needs.

This tiny house—could you call it a house?—was the antithesis of it. The bedroom wasn't big enough for a king-sized bed. The bathroom, while updated and clean, was not luxurious. And there were no hearing accommodations, which could be problematic, but he'd manage.

Now all he had to manage were his memories.

He carried his bag into the bedroom, unpacked, and wandered into the kitchen. On the counter was a covered dish with a note on top.

Welcome to The Guest House. Enjoy the zucchini bread—it's one of Simon's favorites. Come over to dinner at seven.

~Meg & Simon

Pulling off the foil, he inhaled the sweet scent, grabbed a slice, and groaned when he took a bite. It was fantastic. He could understand why it was Simon's favorite. And now he looked forward to getting a good look at Simon in person rather than via a screen, especially his waistline—if Meg made all of her food this good, his friend would be fat.

Outside, he breathed in the salty air from the nearby beach, and though it was too cold to swim, Ted wanted to see it. He put his jacket on and walked outside. Behind him were trees and hills. In front of him, a little way along the gravel road was Simon's house. And behind the house was a huge expanse of sky. If he had to guess, he'd find the beach that way.

After walking a few minutes, he found steps leading to a cove. Somehow, this beach was nothing like the ones in California. It smelled different, and the texture of the sand was coarser. The beach was craggy and rock cliffs surrounded it. It was isolated and private, perfect for Simon, he suspected. Driftwood littered the sand, and the winter waves crashed onto the rocks and the shore. It was violent and awe-inspiring, and Ted was mesmerized. Icy drops of water sprayed his face as he picked his way closer to the shoreline. A dull roar filled his ears—he suspected it would be loud and overwhelming to most other people—as the waves ebbed and flowed and collided with the rocks.

It was as if the water were angry, forcing its way

where it wasn't supposed to be but wanted to go anyway, and for the first time since he lost Abby, Ted was less alone. He'd spent his life pushing his way in— showing he wasn't stupid, figuring out ways to get past his difficulty hearing, proving to everyone he was the best. He was exhausted. Abby gave him a respite, but it was over now. And somehow, he needed to figure out if he had any fight left in him. He'd gotten used to having someone special who cared about him. Until he'd blown it all. She'd never forgive him, and he couldn't blame her. But the satisfaction he'd gotten from being top in his field was hollow without her. He needed this time to figure out what direction to go—forward to maintain his place at the top or sideways onto a new path. Jamming his hands in his pockets, he watched the water along with the flotsam it churned up until the damp chilled him. He turned and walked to the house. He needed to think, and this time, he was foregoing all technology. After all, this isolated house was the perfect opportunity to go old school.

****

What the hell? Abby pushed away her laptop in frustration and paced her living room. She'd emailed Ted three days ago, asking if he'd arranged for her new job and position at the center, and he never answered.

He used to answer right away.

It took her two days to gather the nerve to send the email in the first place. During those two days, her anger simmered beneath the surface, causing her a vague discomfort. She questioned the motives behind every person she met, even her new colleagues who tried to get to know her. She was more curt than usual with her mother. And she found nothing funny when she and Eden talked.

"You need to ask him, Abs," Eden said when they met for drinks after work last week. "You'll never know what happened, much less how you feel, if you don't talk to him."

"But I don't want to talk to him." Liar. Abby wanted to talk to him more every minute they were apart.

"Bullshit." Eden could see through her faster than Abby could spot a missing line of code. "You need answers. And you won't get them complaining to me."

So that night, when she was more than a little drunk, but sober enough to string coherent sentences together, she'd sent him an email.

"Did you arrange for my new job or my position at the community center?"

Short and to the point. Of course, it took her an hour to write, since she needed to write and delete the message multiple times.

She kept trying to type, "I miss you."

She didn't miss him, though the imprint of his lips still burned her mouth. She hated him, despite how she craved the sound of his voice in her ear. How could she miss someone who distrusted her, even if she shook at his touch? How could she miss someone who lied to her, even if she'd been less than forthcoming with him?

She clicked send, and he never answered. Three. Days.

Ted was Mr. Connectivity. He always checked his email, voice mail, texts, and social media apps. Did he ignore her because he read her email or because he hadn't seen it yet? Because they'd broken up?

Texting him would be too much like when they

were together. Or when she was attracted to him. Hell, it would be like she still worked for him and texted him things so he understood her.

But she wanted an answer. With a groan, she grabbed her phone.

—*Did you arrange for my new job or my position at the community center?*—

She tapped her fingers on the table as she waited for a response, berating herself for sitting around like a lovelorn damsel. She was a strong, independent woman, dammit. She didn't need some CEO handing her a job, and she wasn't going to wait around for him to answer her.

The desire to throw or kick something overwhelmed her. And there was nothing she could throw or kick that wouldn't break. She changed into workout clothes and went for a run. Her feet pounded the pavement. The impact jarred her bones. Her teeth ached. The cool air slid over her, traffic noises faded into the background, and she headed into the hills, wanting to punish her muscles since she couldn't punish Ted. Up and up and up she went, until her legs shook, her body was boneless, and she was too exhausted to be angry. She turned around and went home.

When she made it home to her cottage, she stripped and climbed into the shower. The hot water relieved the tension in her muscles. Steam surrounded her and gave her the illusion she floated in space. When the water cooled, she wrapped a big fluffy towel around her body and lay in bed. Tears she wouldn't acknowledge slid down the sides of her face into her hair.

Why cry? Because Ted wouldn't answer her? It

shouldn't make her cry, it should anger her. She reached for her phone. Nothing.

What. The. Hell? The nerve of him! He had no excuse. He was ignoring her. Like a five-year-old. Not a grown man.

Her tears dried as her anger returned.

She was finished accommodating him. She needed to talk to him, and he would damn well listen. If the only solution was by phone, so be it.

****

Sunday was bright and clear and sunlight streamed into the windows of Ted's tiny cottage, waking him. After a quick shower, shave, and breakfast, he walked toward the beach once again. His pocket felt a little empty without his cell phone, but he was determined to take a true technology break. Being able to talk with Simon and Meg during last night's dinner without interruptions from his phone was a relief. The break was nice, and the cove was beginning to grow on him. Halfway there, Simon appeared, dressed in a hoodie.

"Hey," he said. "I was about to work in the gardens." He motioned toward the ruins of the big house in the distance. "Want to help?"

"I'm not much of a gardener."

Simon shrugged. "You'd be surprised what you can do. Meg will have lunch ready when we're finished—you can join us."

Food was a great incentive and manual labor was a good way to keep his body busy while his brain considered what he wanted to do. He walked with Simon along the gravel road toward the ruins. The house was once massive, if the cement footprint any indication. But a few blackened walls and part of a roof were all that were left of the building. Ted wondered how Simon felt seeing the destruction of his childhood home and the site of his accident day in and day out. It was one thing to live with the physical scars. In fact, in some ways, it was similar to how he lived with his hearing loss. But it was a different thing to be reminded of the horror of the fire on a daily basis. He couldn't have handled it.

But Simon appeared unaffected, walking with ease toward the back where the gardens were. Or used to be. These too were blackened and destroyed, and now overrun with weeds. Except where Simon made some inroads.

"How are you with a hammer?" Simon asked. Ted noticed that as Simon faced him so he could read his lips, his gaze often drifted, as if he still wasn't used to people, even his best friend.

"Not bad."

Simon pointed a scarred hand toward a pile of two by fours. "Care to build some garden boxes?"

When Ted nodded, Simon showed him what he wanted, and Ted got busy sawing and hammering. He'd assembled three boxes when a shadow crossed his line of vision milliseconds before something touched his shoulder, and he started.

"Sorry," Simon said when Ted looked at him.

"Didn't hear you." Admitting it to his closest friend was the same as admitting it to Abby. Longing for her filled him, and he gripped the hammer until his knuckles turned white.

"Time for a break." Simon held out a bottle of water, and Ted took it. He followed him to a large, flat boulder where they sat and faced each other.

Guess Simon wants to talk to me.

"It's great you've come for a visit, but we all know you're here for a reason. Tell me about Abby."

Ted huffed and gulped some water. "I screwed up big time."

Simon knew some of the details, but Ted filled him in on the rest. When he was finished, Simon shook his head. "Women are big on trust," he said. "Actually, we all are."

"I know. I might be able to fix the trust issue, but Si, I had her arrested. How can I atone for that?" He ran his hands across his face. "I thought we had the beginnings of something real, and I was afraid of messing it up with her. She's the one who never wanted a permanent relationship. I thought she needed baby steps. Until I took a massive leap off a cliff, and she landed in jail."

Simon tapped the water bottle against his leg. "I don't envy you. The arrest adds an entirely different dimension." He paused. "But I can tell you baby steps build to something more. And if your baby steps aren't built on trust, the foundation crumbles, and you have nothing left."

"Yeah, I know that now. What I don't know is how to fix it."

"I can't tell you what to do. I know what worked for me and Meg, and neither one of us was without our own hefty baggage."

Ted huffed. "I want her to be happy. Even if it can't be with me."

"Tell her. You know…" Simon paused and looked out at the ocean. He returned his gaze to Ted. "…I was the one with more trust issues than Meg. And she showed me, little by little, I could trust her. And now, well, I've never been happier."

Ted sighed. If only he could figure out a solution. A few minutes later, Simon rose and went to work. Taking his cue from his friend, Ted joined him and after about an hour, he built two more garden boxes and settled them into place. Wiping the sweat from his brow, he stretched his back.

Simon tapped his shoulder. "Ready for lunch?"

Nodding, he followed Simon.

Inside, they washed at the utility sink and entered the kitchen. Ted paused in the doorway, taking in the sunny kitchen, the mouthwatering aromas, and the homey feel Meg and Simon created. He watched with a lump in his throat as Simon wrapped his arms around Meg and tried not to react when she caressed his scarred face.

"Hi." Meg pulled Ted in for a tight hug. She reached his shoulder, and her auburn hair showed flecks of gold and brown in the sun's rays through the window. She pulled away from him after a moment and raised her head so he could read her lips. "Come join us for lunch. You must be starved."

"Let me help. You don't have to wait on me." Before Meg could protest, he'd lifted the plates off the counter and started to set the table, using his lack of hearing to his advantage—if he turned away from them, he could pretend he didn't hear their protests, and they'd have to let him have his way.

In minutes, they were all seated at the table, passing around plates of deli meats, bread, lettuce, tomato, and cheese. Ted always had a big appetite, but he was ravenous from working outside, and he piled his sandwich high with roast beef and turkey.

"I'm going into town this afternoon if you want to join me," Meg said to Ted. She adapted to his hearing loss with ease, speaking slowly and clearly. Like Abby. Two women who took the time to figure out what worked for him and tried their best to accommodate him.

When Meg touched his arm, he realized he hadn't answered. "Sorry, I was distracted," he said. "Yeah, I'll go with you."

He took a quick glance at Simon to see if he minded Ted spending time with his girlfriend, but Simon grasped Meg's hand and smiled. He trusted her.

Maybe Meg could give him a female perspective—and help him figure out how to fix things. He realized everything—his work, his future, his happiness—came down to one thing. Abby.

When lunch was over, Simon headed into his office while Meg and Ted climbed into her car and drove into town. The drive was silent, and Ted spent most of the time staring out the window, trying to figure out the questions he needed to ask Meg, and admiring the changing scenery—from beach to forest and finally to quaint town. She parked on the green, waved to someone entering the library and ambled along the street, Ted next to her.

"It's...have..."

Ted touched her arm, and she stopped walking. "What did you say?"

"Oh my gosh, I'm sorry. I forgot about your not being able to hear, which is weird since I remembered in the car."

He smiled. "Relax, it's fine."

This time she faced him. "It's nice to have you here. I understand Simon let you help him with the garden this morning."

"The physical labor was a good break from the navel-gazing I've been doing lately."

They passed a bakery, and his mouth watered from the cinnamon-sugar aroma. In the window were pastel-colored cakes, fluffy breads, and pies.

Meg stopped again. He thought about telling her it wasn't necessary to stop, but she was trying hard. "You know, Simon only asks people he trusts to help him."

"I'm surprised he trusts me—I have no experience with gardening, even though I'm from farm country in the Midwest."

She shook her head. "No, it's not trusting you with his plants, although it's a big thing for him too, but it's trusting you with himself. He doesn't like to admit he can't do something or to call attention to his scars. If he asked you to help him—"

"Well," Ted interrupted, "it was more like asking me to join him."

"See? For him, it's huge. He works in his garden alone. You should have seen how hard it was for me to convince him to let me help him after the storm this past fall. The point is, if he lets you in, he trusts you. He needs people around him."

Ted shoved his hands in his pockets as they crossed the street. "We all do."

They cut into a drugstore, and Meg purchased a few items she needed. When they were outside, she turned to him once again. "Who do you trust?"

His step faltered as he considered her question. "Well, I want to say Abby, but I realize I never did."

"Why?"

"I had her arrested, without questioning anything. I put the safety of my company before what I knew of her. I never let her know my concerns about the breach, never gave her a chance to help me solve the problem. I never told her how I felt or about my background."

"It's not unreasonable. You didn't know her well."

"I knew her well enough to sleep with her, even while I investigated the problem."

Meg winced. "Okay, it's pretty bad. But you don't strike me as a guy who sleeps around with just anyone."

"Not anymore. I've wanted to find someone to settle down with now for a while."

"And you thought Abby was the one?"

He nodded. "But I was afraid to tell her. I thought she'd bolt."

"Did she have an issue with your hearing loss?"

Ted frowned. "No, she saw me remove my aids at night." His mouth dropped. How could he have let Abby in yet still thought her guilty?

Meg's expression softened. "And is that a common occurrence? For you to remove your hearing aids with a woman?"

His face heated.

"So you trust her. You just didn't show her."

Ted ran a hand over the nape of his neck. "Yeah, I blew it."

She patted his arm. "You'll fix it."

"I have no idea how." His throat thickened. He'd had everything he wanted and...poof...he'd destroyed it. He'd give anything to get Abby back.

"We'll figure something out before you leave."

Chapter Twenty-Six

Later that day, Abby paced as she dialed Ted's phone and waited for him to pick it up on the other end. When a female voice answered, she hung up.

"Must have dialed the wrong number," she said out loud. Her hands shook. It was the only answer she was willing to contemplate.

With great care, she shut the phone app, reopened it, and pressed his name in her contacts. The phone rang, and this time a woman answered it right away. Abby's blood ran cold.

"Hello, Abby?"

Her mouth opened and closed. A woman answered Ted's phone and knew Abby's name. She should hang up. But something wouldn't let her.

"Who is this?" Her voice was harsh. She squeezed the phone so tight it dug into her palm.

"My name is Meg. I'm a friend of Ted's. Well, I'm Simon's girlfriend, and Simon is Ted's friend, although at this point I'm pretty sure he's my friend too. Oh my gosh, I'm babbling. I'm sorry."

Abby pulled the phone away from her ear and stared at it. Maybe some cartoon communications bubble would pop out and explain to her what was going on in ones and zeros. Or better yet, an AI voice would explain everything. But no such luck. She put the phone to her ear.

"Um, is Ted there?" Abby asked.

"He's not right here." This Meg woman's voice sounded as if she were sorry about his absence.

"But you have his phone?"

"He left it on the table, and when your name flashed, I answered. Probably shouldn't have, but…"

Whomever this woman was, she was nosy. "Can you give it to him now?"

"I can, but would you mind if we talked first?"

Who the heck is she? "About what?"

"Ted."

Abby sank onto her sofa. "Listen, I don't know who you are or why you think you should get in the middle of this, but I won't talk to some stranger. And you have a lot of nerve answering his phone."

A deep sigh came through the earpiece. "You're right. This is not how I act under normal circumstances. But something about the way Ted looks when he talks about you…he misses you. No, he needs you."

Her stomach tightened. He missed her? "I'm not interested."

"It doesn't surprise me. I'd be angry too if I were you. But I think the two of you need to talk."

Abby yanked on the ends of her hair to keep from screaming. "That's why I'm calling him."

"I think it might be better if you talk in person. Here. In Maine."

"Maine? He's in Maine?"

"Yes."

She was tired of doing all the accommodating. "I don't know if I can face him. Besides, I have work, and I don't even know if I can get a flight."

Meg sighed. "Look, no relationship can survive

without trust, and I think he's starting to understand that. But there's only so much Simon and I can do. It's up to the two of you."

Why were they involved in her relationship at all? Her pulse pounded. "You don't have any idea what he did."

"You're right. I know a small amount, and I'm sure there's a lot more I don't know. But I think you'll feel better if you can see his reactions."

The edges of her anger softened. Was it possible she had an ally? "You act as if he wants to see me." Her throat thickened. "He hasn't responded to any of my emails or texts. I called to see if maybe the shock of a phone call would get him to answer me."

"You need to come in person."

He was clear across the country. He'd had her arrested. Why should she put in so much effort? Her chest squeezed as she replayed Meg's comments. Maybe she was right. "Give me the address."

****

Ted swung the hammer. The vibration of steel against steel reverberated through the wood beneath his hand. Remembering what Meg told him about Simon, he appreciated the opportunity to help his friend. And between yesterday and today, with the number of box gardens he'd constructed, Simon could reforest the planet.

Simon tapped him on the arm.

"You ready to stop for the day?"

Ted stretched his back, wishing it were warm enough to swim. "Yeah."

They walked up the long drive.

"How's the coding program at the community

center shaping up?" Simon asked.

"Pretty well. We provided ten laptops, a variety of additional equipment, and a training budget. Classes have started, and the center director will get me an update when I get home."

"Good. I look forward to seeing the results."

"You should come visit and see it for yourself," Ted said.

Simon looked away. Ted could tell his friend wasn't ready, but maybe someday soon.

Up ahead, two figures walked toward them, and Simon paused. "Who's with Meg?" he asked.

Ted frowned. "You're asking me? I don't know your neighbors."

Simon huffed and continued to walk. "Guess we'll find out." He pulled at the collar of his sweatshirt, as if he wanted to cover his head with a nonexistent hood, and Ted admired the strength of his friend. He was trying to change.

I should do the same.

A few more feet and, this time, Ted stopped.

Simon turned toward him. "What's wrong?"

Heat radiated through his chest. His hands tingled. God, he'd missed her. She wore a light blue hat, and her hair was loose. He loved her hair and missed running his hands through it. Her cheeks were pink, and his hands curled as memories of cupping her face washed over him. The wind blew, and he inhaled the scent of strawberries. He wanted to run to her, pull her close, and never let her go. But his heart hammered in his chest. Try as he might, he couldn't move. Sweat dripped down his back.

"Abby?"

Why the hell was she here? He needed time to compose his thoughts, figure out all the things he needed to apologize for, formulate a plan to win her back. Instead, his mind went blank.

"You okay?" Simon asked, mouth tight with concern.

Ted opened and closed his hands at his sides while his nostrils flared, trying to get more air into his lungs.

"Ted?" Simon gripped his shoulder, and the contact brought him back.

Ted nodded, and Simon retreated a step. "I can tell Meg to take her to the house if you're not ready to talk."

"No."

The two women approached. Abby's mouth was drawn in a flat line, and her brow was wrinkled. He remembered that look, always loved it, even when it was directed at him. She was angry. He fought to marshal his thoughts. He had one last chance. He couldn't blow it.

When the two women reached them, Meg and Simon walked away, and Ted's vision tunneled until all but Abby faded away. His Abby.

"You're here," he said. His heart thudded. "I can't believe you're here."

She frowned. "You haven't answered me."

He must have misheard her. "What?"

"I texted and emailed you, and you ignored me. Coming here was the only way to get an answer out of you."

Like a reflex, he patted his pockets. "I needed a break from technology. I put my phone away." Had she tried to reach him? His chest expanded. Maybe he had a chance with her. "I'm sorry. What were you trying to say?"

"I want to know what the hell you did." Her cheeks were flushed. The wind whipped her hair in her face, and she pushed it away, her movements jerky.

The little bit of hope disappeared. "Did?" Too much and not enough.

"You gave my name to technology companies?" She braced her hands on her hips, and her mouth twisted in a scowl.

"I gave you references." It was the least he could do. Thanks to him, she'd lost her job and her career. He needed to help her get it back.

"Unasked-for references. Companies called me who I hadn't applied to."

"And one of those companies hired you?"

"Yes, and three others tried to recruit me."

His chest expanded in relief. "Good."

"Good?" Her voice reminded him of the audio feedback he got when he pressed against his hearing aids by mistake—high and shrieky.

"You have a new job," he said. "So yeah, it's good."

"I never asked for help."

"So?"

"So you had no right to interfere."

He rubbed his eyes in an attempt to relieve the pressure behind his eyeballs. "But I helped you."

"You turned me into what my mother was—what she wanted me to be."

"What are you talking about?" He'd heard her words, but he'd be damned if he understood them. For once, it wasn't his ears.

"You used your money and your influence to get me a job."

He took a step toward her. "Abby, I tried to fix the damage I caused."

"I don't want your help. I never asked for it, even when my mother thought I should."

He frowned. "I don't understand."

"My mother uses men for what they can give her. I always vowed I'd never be like her. When she nagged me to take advantage of your wealth and position, I always said no. And your helping me turned me into exactly who I refused to be." Tears streaked her face.

"Sweetheart, I never meant to belittle you." The glimpses into her past he'd seen fit into place, and his heart sank. He thought about how he'd accused her of being interested in his money.

She flared her nostrils. "Don't 'sweetheart' me. Once again, you didn't trust me. You doubted my ability to be independent. And the community center?"

"I wanted to make up for destroying your life."

"You interfered with everything after getting me arrested and not trusting me. I don't want anything from you."

The strength of her fury hit him like a punch in the gut. While he'd spent the time away trying to figure out how to get together with her, she'd grown angrier.

He shoved his hands in his pockets. "I'm sorry. God, I'm sorry. I never...it was unforgivable, and all I wanted was to somehow find a way to make it up to you. I knew how happy you were at the community center, and I wanted to give you back some happiness."

Her body vibrated with anger, and nothing he said helped. The air closed in around him. He couldn't breathe. After a few days here, he'd started to hope he might be able to find a path back to Abby, to salvage their relationship. But her words and her body language showed him he was wrong. It was over. He should say something, but there was nothing he could say. He couldn't convince her he trusted her when he hadn't shown her.

Silence stretched between them. Movement drew his attention away from Abby. Simon and Meg approached.

"Why don't we all go to the house and talk," Simon said.

Abby wrapped her arms around her middle. "I can't right now." She turned and started to walk away.

Meg gave Ted a sympathetic look and ran after Abby. Their heads were bent together, and he couldn't hear them. He cursed and stalked away. Simon's hand on his arm stopped him.

"Give her time," he said. "Let Meg talk to her."

"She's had plenty of time. She hates me," Ted said.

Simon grasped his upper arm. "If she's worth your feelings, you've got to show her you trust her."

He clenched his jaw, nodded once to Simon, and strode to his house. He needed this to work.

****

"Abby, wait," Meg called, and Abby paused. She wasn't friends with this woman, but she couldn't be rude.

"Don't leave yet," Meg said. "Stay with us."

Abby shook her head. "Not with Ted—"

"He's across the street. You can stay with us in one of the guest bedrooms. Please. There has to be a way to work this out."

She walked with Meg. "Why are you involved with this? With us?"

"Ted is Simon's best friend. Simon cares about Ted, and Ted cares about you."

Abby snorted. "He's got a funny way of showing it."

Meg stopped. "Maybe I don't know everything, and I know there are issues, but he got you a new job, a project you loved, a project he and his business associates—Simon included—financed."

Abby twisted her hair around her hand. She'd yank it out if she could, but she balked at the pain and the bald look. Meg had a point. "Yes, he got me two positions and enabled me to get others if I'd wanted them. But it's symptomatic of a bigger problem. He sees a problem that involves me, and rather than talk to me about it to see what I need, he jumps to conclusions."

Meg smiled. "Yeah, it drives me crazy when men do that."

Abby paused in surprise. Her attention focused on Meg for the first time, instead of her own troubles. "Does Simon?"

"Simon solved a problem of mine when we first started dating, so yes. He kept me in the dark for much of the plan, but ultimately he told me what he wanted beforehand."

"See?"

"There's a difference though, Abby."

"What?"

"Simon did everything so I could be free to be with him. Ted doesn't think he's good enough for you. He knows he destroyed you. He's giving you the means to take back your independence. Without him."

Abby froze. "What do you mean he doesn't think he's good enough for me?"

Meg shrugged. "You'll have to dig it out of him. He won't confess his vulnerabilities, and it will take time. I'm not saying you don't have cause to be angry. But you need to get the information from him."

Abby shivered from the cold.

"Please come inside," Meg said.

With a nod, Abby followed Meg into their house. Meg made hot chocolate and a few minutes later, Simon walked into the kitchen.

Abby put down her cup of cocoa and approached him. "Hi, we haven't met." She held out her hand. "I'm Abby. I appreciate your opening your home to me. I hope you're not uncomfortable having me here."

He frowned, a look of confusion crossing his features, and he shifted his gaze between Abby and Meg. "What do you mean?"

"Ted's your best friend. With me here, you're kind of hosting the enemy…"

"We'll be fine," Simon said. "I hope you two can work things out. I'm pretty sure you're the best thing that's ever happened to him."

All the air left her lungs, and she stared into her mug of chocolate. How could he possibly know? What did Ted tell him? What was she missing?

And is he the best thing that's ever happened to me?

Chapter Twenty-Seven

Ted stood at the shore and watched the pull of the tide. Hands jammed in his pockets to keep them warm, hunched to block the wind, he let the ebb and flow of the ocean soothe him.

Abby had avoided him for a day and a half. Every time he went over to Simon's house, she was out. At least, it's what Meg told him. She skipped dinner last night. He'd blown it.

Disappointment was bitter in his throat. He should leave and go home. Bury his thoughts in work. The solace he'd found here was ruined now that Abby was here and avoiding him.

Turning around, he pulled up short.

She stood twenty feet away, silent, staring. His stomach flipped, and his heart stuttered at the sudden opportunity to talk to her. He fisted his hands in his pockets as he figured out what to say.

"Abby."

She opened her mouth, and reality crashed into him. He couldn't hear what she said. The noise of the wind and the waves drowned out her voice. It wouldn't matter if he were twenty feet or twenty millimeters away from her. Talking here was impossible, and he pointed to his ears.

The small flame of hope died. The one time he had a chance to talk to her, and he was here.

She walked closer and stopped in front of him. When she reached for her phone, he pointed to his bare wrist—no phone, no smartwatch.

Looking around, he held up a finger, jogged away, and returned with two sticks. He handed one to her, leaned over, and drew in the sand.

"Please let me talk to you."

"Why?"

"Give me one last chance."

She bit her lip, and he waited, gripping his stick until it cracked in two.

"Follow me?"

He read it, stared into her face, and nodded. He wasn't about to say no.

He followed her across the beach, watched her hair sway like a pendulum across her back, remembered the silky feel of it between his hands. As they mounted the cliff stairs, he admired the shape of her bottom filling out her jeans, remembered the warmth of their bodies at rest together. Sadness squelched his desire, knowing he might never touch her again.

When she paused in front of Simon and Meg's house, he pointed to his own. If he were to bare his soul, he needed privacy. This time, she followed him as he led her to his tiny house, opened the door, and pointed to the couch. The silence that greeted him was a welcome relief.

"Coffee?" he asked, jingling his keys in his hand. Now that they were here, he was loath to start. When she nodded, he left her where she sat and made two cups. Handing her one, he took his and sat across from her, gripping the cup to warm his hands. He'd tried to talk to her earlier, and he'd been unsuccessful. This time he needed to get it right.

"Simon thinks I'm the best thing that's ever happened to you," she said.

He huffed and tried not to break the ceramic mug as his hands tightened further around it. "I was an idiot not to recognize it sooner."

"I can't make sense of what happened." Her knee bounced.

He focused on her lips, not wanting to miss anything.

"It's like code that doesn't add up to anything. No matter which way I look at things between us, nothing works."

He swallowed.

"But Meg says I don't understand everything. She says there's something you've struggled to tell me."

She sat on the sofa and waited. "I'm here."

It was now or never.

"I'm sorry—"

She shook her head. "I don't want to hear an apology. I want to understand why you acted that way."

"—for not explaining things to you sooner," he finished. He waited for her to interrupt him. When she remained silent, he took a deep breath.

His chest constricted, and he fought for air. Beads of sweat popped out on his forehead and the nape of his neck, and he closed his eyes.

I am the CEO of a company. I've won awards for innovation. I am a millionaire several times over. I am not stupid.

He looked at Abby and focused over her right shoulder at the white molding surrounding the picture window.

"My father spent my entire childhood telling me I was stupid because I couldn't hear. It showed in his gaze whenever I misunderstood anything, whenever he looked at me. No matter what I've done, no matter how successful I am, I've always pictured his disappointment in my mind, and it overshadowed my every accomplishment. Until you, nothing convinced me otherwise."

Abby leaned forward. "I never once thought you were stupid. No matter how angry you made me, no matter how much you hurt me, I've always admired your intelligence. You notice things about people no one else does, precisely because you can't hear."

Except she would never do the things he'd accused her of, the things he'd had her arrested for. He rose, walked to the doorway, and returned to the sofa. He hated looking down at Abby, so he sat.

"I've dated many women in my life and none of them have treated me as anything other than odd because of my hearing. When they found out about my financial success, it became their motivation to be with me. They were fun and beautiful, and I let it go. Until the behavior got old, and I wanted more. But I let it continue far longer than I should have."

He rubbed his hands over his knees to keep from fiddling with his ears.

"I never wanted to be attracted to you because of money. Your wealth is one of the things that made me resist you."

"I know." He blew out a breath. "When I met you, you ignored my hearing aids, other than the first day." He smiled at the memory. For the first time, he found it sweet. "And you didn't care about my money. In fact, you didn't seem to care about me at all." He snuck a brief glance at Abby. "While not great for the ego, at least to you, I wasn't stupid." His chest expanded at the thought.

"You're not stupid." Her gaze was fierce, and he swallowed. "You. Are. Not. Stupid."

He frowned. "But I messed up—"

"Yeah. Big time. But it doesn't mean you're stupid. It means you're human."

Human. A ray of hope wormed its way into his chest. He wanted to be hers.

"I wanted you," he said. "Your intelligence, wit, and drive fascinated me, and your beauty stopped me in my tracks. But I respected you more for not wanting to jeopardize your career. And I should have paid more attention."

Abby sighed, and an array of emotions flitted across her face. "My mother went through men faster than anyone I knew. She was always desperate to please them and relied on them for everything. I never wanted to be that way. I wanted financial security, but I wanted to be the one to provide it for myself."

"I know. And I took it away from you." He stood again and paced. "Greg came to me about the breach, and at first, I wasn't willing to believe him. I talked to you, and what you said made sense. I was sure he was wrong. But he showed me the logs, and I couldn't ignore the facts presented to me. My fear of losing my company, of all my work being destroyed, of losing the opportunity to prove to myself and the world I'm not stupid, overruled everything. Including my common sense."

She blinked away tears, and his chest tightened.

He hated making her cry.

"When I first met you," she said, "you were everything I admired, everything I wanted. But I couldn't let myself fall for you. I never wanted to be like my mother. I resisted. I couldn't risk losing my job. But I couldn't keep away from you. You were the first man I could imagine a future with, not because you're richer than God, but because I thought you trusted me."

His heart rate increased, and he cursed under his breath. "I know. Somehow, all those threads—proving to myself how wrong my father was, wanting you, needing to find out how the breach happened—got tangled in my mind. I was afraid of losing you, but I was also afraid somehow, my feelings for you blinded me, and I missed the signs Greg showed me. Instead of talking to you, I believed him. And I lost you."

She shook her head. "I would have helped you find the breach." She huffed. "I would have done anything for you. But you believed everything Greg told you, while you claimed to care about me. You became someone I couldn't count on."

His hands grew cold. "I know. Once everything fell apart, I realized I was wrong. It was obvious. Anyone could see—I should have seen it. But I didn't trust you or myself. And you might not care about my aids or about my money, but you're too intelligent and amazing to want to saddle yourself with someone who's too stupid to trust you. I tried to give you opportunities to rebuild the life I'd destroyed."

He was finished. He'd swear he'd run a marathon, but there was no adrenaline rush at the finish line. All he wanted was to get away, but he couldn't. Abby was here. He waited for her verdict, head bowed. His hands were seized in a warm grasp.

Her grasp.

He raised his head, and she was there, inches away from him. He looked at her fingers wrapped around his, trying to figure out what she was doing.

The scent of her shampoo wafted around him, and he wanted to inhale, but he was afraid if he took too deep a breath, he'd either scare her away or worse, fall apart right here. Her solemn gaze pinned him. His breath hitched.

"Can you ever forgive me?"

She brushed her hand through the hair at his temple, and he closed his eyes, letting her touch wash over him. When he opened them, her lip was between her teeth.

"I'm working on it."

His voice grated against his throat. "Please give me—give us—a second chance. I love you."

Abby stopped touching him, and he was bereft, until she leaned into him and wrapped her arms around him. She rested against his chest, her face tilted so he could see her lips. "I love you, too. I hate what you did, but I love you."

He curved his body around hers and rocked. "I know. I hate what I did, too. Nothing I have, nothing I am or have achieved matters if you're not with me. And I will spend the rest of my life proving it to you if only you'll stay with me."

She nodded. A tear escaped and trailed down her cheek. He caught it with his finger, vowing it would be the last time she cried over him. And for the first time in weeks, peace washed over him.

****

Three weeks later, she stood in the community center between Clive and Ted. She squeezed Ted's hand. Since their reconciliation, he had barely left her side, and he never stopped praising her work to everyone. It was a little embarrassing, but in a good way. When they'd arrived a half hour ago, he'd spent a good deal of their time admiring her work here, shrugging off any thanks Clive offered him. All around her were kids and their parents, and at the back of the room were Ted's other CAST partners—Caleb, Simon, and Alexander. In the corner were a few employees from Ted's company, and she looked their way and smiled.

She tugged Ted's arm, and when he looked at her, she pointed to the corner. "They came."

"Of course they came," he said. "They admire you."

She squeezed his forearm. "They admire you, too."

His quiet smile reflected a new confidence in this man she loved. Before she could say anything else, Clive stepped forward.

"I'd like to welcome everyone to our ribbon-cutting ceremony of the Endicott & Marlow Computer Coding Center. Ted Endicott's company donated all of the computers you see in this room, Abby Marlow created our training programs, and we offer our sincerest thanks to both of them." Everyone applauded, and Clive waited for people to settle. "Ted, would you honor us with a few words?"

Ted stepped forward. "My partners and I may have provided the technology to get this project off the ground, but none of it would have been possible without Abby's love of coding and her desire to instill that love in the next generation." He motioned her forward.

Her cheeks heated at the shouts from the kids she'd already begun training. Ted's hand on the small of her back warmed her.

Clearing her throat, she spoke. "Growing up, my community center was my refuge, its single computer, my magic carpet into another world where I was the key to my own future. While I would like to thank Ted and Clive and everyone else for making this dream a reality, I'd like to thank the kids and parents who are here today. Without you, there would be no one to teach. And the one piece of advice I'd like to share with everyone is the reminder that you are the key to unlocking your future."

Everyone clapped.

Caleb approached. "Nice job." He shook her hand, his large body dwarfing her, his expression stoic. Only when he glanced at Ted did she see a hint of emotion— of satisfaction—glint in his eyes. He banked it immediately. Out of all of Ted's friends, Caleb was the one Abby understood the least, but Ted assured her the man was pleased with CAST's investment and impressed by her talent. He'd also mentioned something about a heart of gold, but Abby didn't know him well enough to recognize it.

Simon walked over and gave her a hug, shook Ted's hand, and faded into the background. Alexander nodded to them and remained in his corner of the room. With the ceremony complete, parents and kids milled around, the kids eager to show off their new skills.

Ted pulled Abby into an embrace and finally, she relaxed. He was warm and solid and steady. She'd begun to trust him again. His constant presence by her side helped rather than stifled her, a new experience for her. They were taking things slowly, but she was filled with hope. In his arms was the one place she wanted to be, and she couldn't wait to leave to show him how much she loved him. He leaned toward her.

"Good speech," he said. "But just so you know, you are key to unlocking my heart," he whispered. "I love you." His attempt to whisper failed, and the people around them turned and smiled at them. But Abby didn't care.

He was hers.

A word about the author…

Jennifer started telling herself stories as a little girl when she couldn't fall asleep at night. Pretty soon, her head was filled with these stories and the characters that populated them. Even as an adult, she thinks about the characters and stories at night before she falls asleep or when walking the dog. Eventually, she started writing them down. Her favorite stories to write are those with smart, sassy, independent heroines; handsome, strong, and slightly vulnerable heroes; and her stories always end with happily ever after.

In the real world, she's the mother of two amazing daughters and wife of one of the smartest men she knows. She believes humor is the only way to get through the day and does not believe in sharing her chocolate.

She writes contemporary romances, many of which feature Jewish characters in non-religious settings (#ownvoices). She's published with The Wild Rose Press and all her books are available where books are sold.

Website: http://www.jenniferwilck.com

Facebook: https://www.facebook.com/Jennifer-Wilck-201342863240160/

Newsletter: https://www.jenniferwilck.com/contact.html#newsletter

Twitter: https://twitter.com/JWilck

Instagram: https://www.instagram.com/authorjenniferwilck/

BookBub: https://www.bookbub.com/profile/jennifer-wilck

Thank you for purchasing
this publication of The Wild Rose Press, Inc.

For questions or more information
contact us at
info@thewildrosepress.com.

The Wild Rose Press, Inc.
www.thewildrosepress.com

CPSIA information can be obtained
at www.ICGtesting.com
Printed in the USA
LVHW020032120222
710698LV00013BA/372

9 781509 239641